so close

NEAR MISS BOOK #2: AN INDIGO KING ROCK STAR ROMANCE

NEAR MISS
BOOK 2

AMY BOOKER

So Close

NEAR MISS, BOOK #2

by

AMY BOOKER

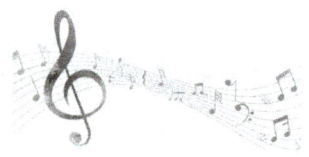

ISBN: 979-8-9859875-1-5

Published by Renaissan Publishing Limited, Cuyahoga Falls, Ohio

www.amybookerauthor.com

author's note

If you've read any of my books, you'll know that the chapter names are all song titles. Music has been an integral part of my life, and it always sets the mood. Whether it's the overall energy of a song, the lyrics, or even just the title, that tone carries through into my written words on the page. The playlist and a link can be found at the back of each book, or you can find them on my website: www.amybooker author.com.

dedication

*Don't get so close to your demons
that you think they are your friends.
They are beguiling.*

When my college friend Sarah Lawrence asked me to film her music videos for her a few months ago, I never thought it would lead to me filming a documentary film about the hottest band on the planet, yet here we are. That band is Indigo King, whose lead singer happens to be Sarah's boyfriend, Ryan Crawford. What a coinkydink, as my grandmother used to say.

After filming Sarah's music videos, I got several inquiries from Blackmore Records, her record label, to start this new documentary project. I tried to tell them I really didn't have experience in this kind of thing, but they seemed to think my music history degree, with a minor in filmmaking, qualified me for the job. I'm not arguing their life choices with what they offered to pay me. And it's not like there are tons of employment opportunities for someone with a music history degree in the first place, so when this kind of thing drops in your lap, you grab it. I'm not going to lie; to witness and experience the rise of a band like Indigo King will be something special for me. I hope to bring something interesting to the medium, not be a cheesy 'Behind the Music' type of circus, or worse, a Spinal Tap remake.

I was so happy for Sarah when she got her record deal after the videos we produced together took off online. The recognition is well deserved since she's so talented, and I was lucky to hitch a ride on her star to get here. I still don't know if she directly had anything to do with me getting this gig, but once I find out who is responsible, they are getting a huge kiss, a fruit basket, or something from me. I don't know the proper gift-giving etiquette for something like this.

Luckily, I'm in a position where I can drop every-thing and jump on the road with the band as soon as possible. I recently broke up with my boyfriend, Nick, and we were living together in his house, so to be able to throw my things in storage and hit the tour right away is a godsend. We didn't have a contentious split or anything, but it was quick. We became too comfortable. We were complacent about everything, and when I pointed that out to him, he didn't want to change or take any steps to improve the situation. He was perfectly happy with how things were, so now he can go ahead and be perfectly happy alone with those thoughts and without me.

The day I don't care what someone is thinking is the day I need to leave. And I didn't care what Nick thought anymore because he never thought anything new. He's happy with his life where he is and has zero ambition for any further growth.

Everything about our relationship had gotten stale, even the sex, and I do *not* like boring sex. I am all about being confident; in myself and my partner. Not that I crave adrenaline rushes or stress or chaos, or even swinging from the chandeliers, but a relationship needs to keep me curious about the other person. I need passion. Enthusiasm. Desire, and not just sexual. I want to be interested in everything about the other person. I want the dream.

I wonder what Nick is doing right now. Is he missing me at all? Regretting anything? Ugh. I need to stop that loop right now. I can't care what Nick is doing. He obviously didn't care about me. Well, not enough to try to change or work with me. Damn, nowhere near wanting to actually fight for me in any way. He was so god-damned apathetic about the whole thing. There's nothing I hate more than apathy. It's worse than him disliking me or being angry at me; at least those are visceral, tangible; something you can feel. Indifference is so empty and absent of any emotional worth. It makes me think I don't even rate any emotion. I'm that forgettable to him. Two years were wasted with him. Two of my best years, since these are supposed to be my 'prime' years if the magazines are to be believed. I'm not sure I buy into the whole thing, but if the theory is correct, it pisses me off if I think about it too much that I wasted years on Nick. He doesn't deserve my seconds or minutes, let alone years.

Now that I'm out of Nick's house, I'm a bit of a homeless gypsy on my way to join a traveling band for the summer. Sounds like a premise for a 1960s Jack Kerouac novel. And that puts me here, on a flight from Cleveland to Salt Lake City for the beginning of the summer shed tour for Incendiary Ink, the headlining band. Indigo King opens up for them all summer, and Sarah opens for them.

Flying is not my favorite thing to do, and I'm looking forward to the more freeing bus life. Not just because the dude sitting next to me, now known from this day forward as Cookie Guy, is a complete and utter slob with his complimentary cookies, either. Which he is. But because on a plane, you can't stop to see something. You can't turn around to take a picture of a weird cactus you just passed because it looks like Ozzy Osbourne from the cover of his Diary of a Madman album. *Which I may or may not have done...* On a plane, you're held captive for as long as you travel, and I don't know if that counts as being claustrophobic or not, but I don't like not having freedom of movement. I like knowing I can up and leave to go somewhere else if I want to. Hopefully, the bus isn't simply a different kind of captivity.

With all of these life changes, maybe I should focus on myself. And my career. This documentary could lead to bigger things if it goes well. I refuse to waste any more years. I owe myself to spend my time on things that matter to me and will benefit me in the long run. Regardless of what it leads to, this job is a chance for me to expand my mind and my active experiences. Someday I'll be able to tell my grandchildren I once toured with a rock band and got to document them becoming common household names.

Grandchildren...that's rich. I don't even have a freaking boyfriend anymore.

The seat belt light comes on, and the pilot tells us to expect turbulence soon. Lovely. I sure hope this isn't an omen of things to come.

two

BLEED AMERICA
MATT

A documentary. *Fuck me.* This is the last thing I need. What I need is to go for a run. Get rid of this excess energy making my skin crawl. But I can't go for a run because I'm stuck on this fucking bus for another two hours on our way to Salt Lake City. When the label told us we'd have a documentarian touring with us this summer, both Ryan and Jude, the rest of my band Indigo King, thought it was a fanfuckingtastic idea. I was outnumbered. Unfortunately, we only require a majority to make decisions, not a unanimous vote. This sucks for me because now I'm going to be followed all summer by some chick with a camera getting up in my business, and asking questions I don't want to answer. I signed the obligatory contract for it but told everyone not to expect me to participate willingly. If they want a truthful documentary, there is nothing more honest than me not wanting to go along with it.

Vanessa, our manager, isn't happy with my attitude, but she'll need to get over it. I've been more than accommodating on this tour for months. I go along with most things that are asked of me without complaint, and I don't ask for much in return. To want some semblance of privacy when we have a rare second to ourselves shouldn't be too much to ask for. But apparently, privacy is a thing of the past when it comes to Indigo King. Our shiny and new rising star is more important than anything else.

I am more than thankful and grateful for all the success we're experiencing at the moment, and I absolutely know how fleeting this can be. But fame shouldn't cost each of us our souls. That price is too damn high, and I don't want to pay. I can sense myself losing who I am, my entire identity. I'm no longer Matt Sturridge. No, I'm Matt, the drummer of Indigo King. A face, a name, and a little of my talent peeking through. Who I am as a person doesn't even factor into the equation anymore. We all knew there would be sacrifices as we and our music got more popular; they are part and parcel of the whole rock n' roll gig and initially part of the attraction. You *want* to be famous. You *want* everyone to know your name. Until they *do*. Then you don't want that anymore. If there were a way to be paid attention to without being noticed, that would be great. It would probably break the physics of the universe, but I would be okay with that, so long as I didn't have to give another fucking interview.

I agreed to participate in the group activities for the documentary, but I told them in no uncertain terms that I wanted nothing about myself individually in the film. I think they understand, but we'll see what happens when this chick shows up.

The person doing the film is a friend of our fellow tour mate, Sarah Lawrence, so she does have a positive reference coming into this. Typically, anyone who is cool with her should be cool with us, but I still don't have the warm fuzzies. I don't feel good about it, and I can't shake the sense that her touring with us will upset everything we're used to. Like a significant change is coming on like a tidal wave, and I should be using this time to prepare somehow. But I don't know what the fuck to prepare for. It's beyond unsettling.

Usually, when I start to feel claustrophobic like this, I can throw on my earbuds and listen to some lo-fi music to chill out and relax. That isn't working today, and I'm simply frustrated by the slow beats. This is new too. I open my eyes and bang the back of my head on the couch behind me, wishing I could jump out and run the rest of the way to Salt Lake City.

"Dude," Jude says, eyeing me suspiciously over his book from the couch across from me. Finding

Jude with his reading glasses on and a book in hand is always surprising since he's not your typical bookworm, with his tattoos and constant sarcastic attitude. He's currently reading one of the Lord of the Rings books for the millionth time. "What's up with you? You're bouncing your knees like you're the drummer for Slayer."

I stop my bouncing legs. I don't notice when it happens, but the guys sure let me know about it. The movement is just a habit that I'm not always aware I'm doing.

"Shit, if I was with Slayer, they wouldn't care." My words come out like I'm an annoying child. *Wow, Matt, mature.*

Jude raises an eyebrow at me. "Go do some sit-ups or something if you've got the energy to burn. Ryan does."

I glance towards the back of the bus where our bunks are and then back to Jude. "Do you see Ryan up here?"

He looks around, then back to his book. "Never mind. Forget I said anything. Bounce away."

Ryan is in the back bunk area with Sarah, doing god knows what. Whatever they're doing could be completely innocent, but I don't particularly want to find out. This is when I'm the most caged, when none of my usual distractions distract me anymore.

I look out the window at the nothingness we're passing by. The late May day is lovely, but everything appears colorless to me. Nothing has any vibrance. I don't know what's going on with me today, but as soon as we pull up to our hotel, I'm going for the longest run my body can handle.

Vanessa calls me over to the booth area to talk to her. She must recognize that I'm bouncing off the walls.

"So, Matt," she starts, glancing over her laptop at me, her bright eyes unreadable. "About the documentary..."

I run my hands down my face, rubbing at the stubble, itching for a shave. "Seriously, Van? Now?" I can't believe she sees me in this state and thinks the best idea is to bring up the stupid documentary. The last thing I would want to talk about is the damned film.

"Hear me out." She sighs heavily, shuts her computer, and folds her hands together on top. Her jaw sets into a hard line, and her eyes narrow, so I know she's trying to reign in emotions of some kind. *Is she pissed at me?*

"What is it now?" I might vault right off this bus while we're moving if there's some new hoop I need to jump through for this damned documentary.

"Nothing new. I only want to make sure we're on the same page."

"I already agreed to the group stuff." I didn't even want to do that, but I needed to give something or never catch the end of it. "That was our compromise, remember?"

"I know you did, and I appreciate it. I don't want to see you just sitting in on the group stuff. I want you to participate."

"I participate."

"True... but you don't always appear to be happy doing it..."

"Because I'm not always happy doing it. I can't be fake like Ryan and Jude can. You know that."

"Hey, I resemble that remark." Jude pipes in, not looking up from his book. "And fake it till you make it, man."

Vanessa lets out a deep, calming breath. "That's the thing, Matt. Why would you need to fake smiles? What are you unhappy about? You've been like this for a few weeks now."

I glance out the window to scan the passing landscape again, trying to find something to focus on while I collect my thoughts. "Van, I'm not unhappy..."

"But you're not happy. Right?" She reaches over and puts a hand on my arm. I look down at it, wondering what the hell she's talking about.

"I didn't say that." I pat her hand but move my arm away. I don't need coddling, sympathy, or whatever the fuck this is. "I'm in between somewhere, I guess."

"He's just got resting dick face," Jude says,

chuckling to himself. "If resting dick face isn't a thing, it should be. Am I right?"

Vanessa rolls her eyes but doesn't give Jude the satisfaction of responding. "You know you can talk to me, right? About anything."

I nod but avoid looking at her. I don't know where all this is coming from. Nobody's ever cared about how I felt about anything until this stupid documentary came up. And since then, I've become some sort of problem child because I'm not gung-ho with it like everyone else is.

"C'mon, Vanessa. I'm fine. You don't need to worry about me. I'll do what I'm told like I always do." She flinches at my words. "Sorry. You know what I mean."

"I don't know that I do." The worried expression on her face deepens, but she doesn't press me. Hopefully, she notices that this conversation is only agitating me even more. "Okay. I'll drop it for now. Please talk to me if you need to. Alright?"

"Will do," I say, forcing a smile for her. One of my few fake smiles. "How much longer until we get to the hotel?" I *really* need to run now.

She checks her watch. "About an hour, maybe less."

Good. The sooner, the better. This could be a long three months. I don't want to imagine a whole summer of this horrible vibe.

three

WHERE IS MY MIND?
SAMANTHA

"**A**re you sure there isn't a reservation for Samantha Fisher? In the block of rooms with Indigo King?"

"I've checked, and I'm sorry, we don't have anything for that name."

I've been traveling for nearly ten hours, and my nerves won't be able to take much more. There is no reservation for me here at the hotel, and they don't have a room available to give me if I want to pay for it myself either. I can't believe how unhelpful this hotel clerk is being.

"Can you please check one more time?" I'm trying so hard to keep my voice on the right side of polite, but even I could sense the edge to my tone this time. I don't blame her for the nasty glare she gives me. But she nods and is double-checking.

I scan my emails, trying to find a confirmation number, but I can't find anything. All my calls to Vanessa and Sarah for help go to their voicemail. I did note the tour buses in the back parking lot as I arrived, but they didn't look like anyone was around them.

"I'm sorry, ma'am, but I'm not finding anything for you."

I stare at her for a long minute, unsure what I'm supposed to do in this situation. I glance down at my bags. One for personal items and clothes, and one for my equipment. That one is too heavy to be lugging around for much longer.

"Can you hold my bags while I figure this out?" The edge in my voice is even sharper, and I think I just did in any chance of this woman helping me. The eyebrow she raises is beyond suspicious.

"No. I'm sorry, ma'am. We can only hold bags for registered guests."

Well, that shut that shit right down.

"Fine," I say. I hope the panic in my voice isn't too apparent. I don't know what to do now. If I could reach someone, I could at least have confirmation I'm at the right place and I am really supposed to be here. I feel like I imagined the whole job offer, and I just showed up to surprise everyone. "I'll be back." It sounds more like a threat than anything else, and the clerk shrinks back as I say it. *I'm really not a bitch, I swear.*

I head out to the parking lot, dragging my luggage behind me. One of the wheels now chooses to go wonky and make rolling it smoothly impossible. *Of course. Why not?* I decide to go to the back lot to check if anyone is in the tour buses I saw. There are no lights on in any of them, but I knock anyway and start calling out names.

"What are you doing?" A deep and breathy male voice startles me. I turn around and find one of the most beautiful specimens of a male human being I've ever seen. He's tall, he's tanned, he's muscled, he's absolutely chiseled, and he's sweating so sexily I can't take my eyes off his chest. His shaggy brown hair looks to be pasted to his neck. I almost swoon in the parking lot right here but somehow compose myself. I've never had that visceral kind of reaction to a man before, and I don't know where that came from, especially in the middle of this chaos.

"Oh," I gasp, a reflexive hand coming to my throat. "You startled me." My mind has gone blank of all coherent thoughts or words.

The man doesn't apologize or react to the fact he scared me. This concerns me some; as he takes a step closer to me, his face is slightly shadowed. I'm starting to wonder if I should be afraid and glance around the parking lot, looking for anyone else that might be out there. I don't spot anyone, but I don't step back or away from him. I don't want to show how scared I am. *Don't show weakness.*

"What are you doing?" he repeats. "Who are you?" His tone is almost angry now. I don't like this at all.

"Who are *you*?" I ask, straightening my shoulders. I at least know *I'm* supposed to be here. Who knows who this guy is, hanging around the band's bus. He could be a crazy person or a murderer, for all I know.

"I asked you first." His voice *is* angry, and I take a small step away from him. Regardless of how hot this guy is, and damn, he is so hot, it doesn't give him a right to scare me like this.

"Well, I'm not telling you anything. I belong here. You don't need to know any more information. Thank you. You can go on about your business." I'm trying to sound authoritative, like I know what the fuck I'm doing when I'm sure it shows that I don't. I don't know that I'm in the right place since I haven't gotten confirmation from anyone, but I'm scared and feeling very, very alone.

"I can assure you, I definitely belong here. This is my bus." He steps toward me again, and I back into the bus behind me, stumbling and almost falling. He reaches a hand out to catch me by the elbow to stop me from diving headfirst into the parking lot's asphalt. The firmness of his grasp and the warmth of his hand on my bare arm makes my skin tingle. His touch lingers for a moment as we stand there silently.

Once I get my senses back, it dawns on me to be scared. He's standing too close. I don't care if it was hot a second ago; I don't know who the fuck this guy is or what his intentions are. *What did he mean, this is his bus?* I shake free of his hold.

"Don't touch me," I say forcefully, stepping sideways and out of his reach. "I will scream."

He acts confused like he doesn't understand my reaction to him. Doesn't he know you don't approach a woman in a parking lot like this?

"What the fuck?" he asks. "You were falling. I caught you..."

"I wouldn't have been falling if you weren't scaring me."

"I...what? How..."

"Sam, is that you?" I hear Sarah's voice call from behind me. I can't take my eyes off this man, though. I have such a mixed reaction to him. Part fear, part attraction. It's crazy.

"Sarah?" I finally say, turning to see my friend approaching with her arms spread for a welcoming hug. I release all the tension built up in my shoulders and run to hug her. I'm relieved to have other people around, at least. Then I notice her boyfriend, Ryan, go and talk to the man I was confronting. "Do you guys know him?" I ask her.

"Um, yeah. That's Matt..."

"Matt?" I ask, confused. "The drummer of Indigo King?" *How the hell did I not recognize him?* Now that I

19

know who he is, of course, Matt Sturridge is obviously in front of me. But I don't remember him being this hot in any of the pictures I've seen of him. He looks different somehow. Maybe I was too stressed about being potentially stranded to think straight. "Oh my god. I thought he was some strange stalker or something..." I chuckle to myself, relieved he's not some crazy killer.

"Let me introduce you." She takes me over to the two and introduces me. Ryan is polite and seems very kind. Matt has his angry face back and barely nods at me once he's told who I am. *Did I really piss him off that badly? It was just a tiny misunderstanding.*

"So, the hotel doesn't have a room for me..." I tell Sarah about the botched reservation. "I came out here to see if anyone was with the buses. And I ran into Matt..." I avoid his eyes, but it's for nothing because he's literally running away. *What the hell?* "Did I do something...?"

Sarah and Ryan give each other a knowing look. "Don't mind him. He's been in a mood lately. And hey, you can have my room," Sarah says, grabbing Ryan's hand and heading back into the hotel. "I stay with Ryan, so my room is empty. Here take the key." She hands me her key card.

"Thanks..." I say. Watching the silhouette of Matt get smaller and smaller in the distance, I can't help but wonder what life is going to be like for the next three months. I have to be in such close quarters with Matt, who apparently already hates me. Three months of the cold shoulder could get old; no matter how hot the guy is that shoulder is attached to.

four

THE RED
MATT

Well, that went like shit. I can't believe that was Samantha, the woman filming our fucking documentary. She was not what I was expecting. Those bright blue eyes seemed to pierce right through me to my soul behind those sexy glasses. And her blonde hair caught almost every color of the sunset in the strands. *Fuck, I'm waxing poetic about her?* This is not going to fly.

I pick up my pace and push again through another sprint. I had finished my run and was headed back to my room when I saw her knocking on the bus door. I couldn't help but be drawn to her to find out what she was doing. And now I need to run again. I'm going to regret pushing myself this much tomorrow, but after meeting Samantha, being so close to her, and seeing those lips...*fuck!* I need to get my head straight and not allow myself to be caught up with her.

I need to remember she's here to turn our worlds upside down and try to pry into our private lives to put them on full display for everyone to gawk at. Something I do not want to do. I'm going to need to resist her in more ways than one. *Great.*

I turn around and head back to the hotel. Once I shower, I go down to the restaurant to grab dinner with the rest of the group. The guys from Incendiary Ink, the band we're opening for all summer, are in their own corner, trying to hide from prying fan eyes. I don't think they have to worry too much, though. Other than Samantha, it didn't look like there were too many people milling about without rooms that would raise any concerns.

Toward the end of our own headlining tour, we had to be more careful about stragglers and hangers-on. As we become more and more popular, our circle of trust gets smaller, and anyone outside of the circle is automatically under suspicion. I feel bad that I treated Samantha so shitty, but she didn't give me any other choice when she wouldn't tell me who she was. *What else was I supposed to think?* A pretty woman hanging around our bus, unfortunately, it isn't the first time I've seen that. I shiver at what could have happened if Jude had come across her instead of me. Jude would have made his moves on her, I'm sure. I have a feeling she would have put him in his place, though. The thought makes me smile to myself. She's a spitfire.

"What's so funny?" Jude asks, sitting down at my table.

"You, actually." And I'm not lying. I *was* just thinking about him. Weird how that happens.

"Oh, really? What makes me so funny?" He looks around and waves down a server.

"Have you seen yourself?" I don't want to dive into my honest thoughts about Samantha and him. Even now, the idea of Jude with her is making me uncomfortable. *What the hell do I have to be jealous about? Jesus.* I just met the woman and barely at that.

"Dude, what's your problem?" Jude's brow is furrowed with concern. It seems genuine. "Now you look like you want to punch someone."

"Are you offering?" I shake my head, trying to clear out all these new and intrusive thoughts of Samantha. This is getting out of hand.

He puts his hands up in surrender. "I was only making an observation. No need to bite my head off."

"Sorry," I say, focusing on the menu. The need for food is finally taking the forefront of my thoughts. After my run, I'm starving. "I'm just hungry. You know how I am." I hope I sound convincing. I don't want to get into anything about Samantha with Jude or give him any reason to think about her. *And I'm jealous again. Jesus Christ.*

The server arrives, and we order our dinners. The sound of laughing female voices carries in from the lobby, and when I look up, I see Samantha and Vanessa arm in arm. I didn't think they knew each other, but maybe they do.

"Does Vanessa know Samantha?" I ask Jude.

"Not that I know of." Jude shakes his head, and I catch when his eyes land on her. His pupils dilate, and a muscle in his jaw twitches. *I don't like it. I don't like it one bit.* "Damn. She is fucking hot."

I pretend to be disinterested and change the subject. Trying to distract Jude from Samantha. "What was that chick's name in LA you liked? Ren? Or Wren with a 'W'?"

"Who?" Jude shifts his attention back to me clumsily.

"The redhead with the record store you were hooking up with. What was her name? And what's up with her?" Maybe if he remembers her, he'll stop looking at and thinking about Samantha, who walked past our table with a gorgeous smile and smelled like a god-damned field full of lilac bushes. I'm not going to be able to handle three months of this.

"Oh, yeah. Ren." He shrugs, but something in the tension settling in his shoulders at the thought makes me think there *is* more to it.

I raise an eyebrow at him. "Okay. Ren. What's up with her?" He definitely looks uncomfortable.

"Nothing. Why?" He's deflecting. Something is there for sure. "We're just friends. Nothing more. And we never hooked up."

"Okay, okay." I decide to let it go. My work is done in getting his mind off Samantha. "Don't twist your panties in a bunch."

"Shit. She's starting already." Jude nods his head in Samantha's direction.

I glance around to see what he's talking about and when I find Samantha, she has a camera pointed directly at us from her table. Not being surreptitious or anything. Out in the open like people film other people in restaurants all the time. Everybody does it.

"Fucking hell." I stand up and storm out of the restaurant, almost upending a server carrying a tray loaded with food along the way. I make it all the way to my room without looking back. Once inside, I throw my earbuds in and try not to think about what hell this tour is going to be.

About an hour later, there's a knock on my door. When I look through the peephole, I spy a pretty blonde with glasses. Samantha. I let out a deep breath and open the door a few inches, peeking out in case she's fucking filming me answering the fucking door.

"Hey." Her voice is almost kind. *Almost.* She has an edge to her tone that borders on sarcastic. I'm not sure what to make of that. "You left the restaurant without eating your dinner. Here." She holds out a white container to me that ostensibly has my dinner in it. I catch a whiff of the food inside, and my stomach growls.

I open the door, barely enough to take the box from her. "Thanks." I want to say something else, but I can't think of words. *Any* words. They don't exist anymore.

"Sure thing." She waits for a beat but turns and heads down the hall. "Good talk."

I step back into my room and shut the door. *What the actual fuck, Matt?* I guess I should be lucky I thanked her for bringing my food. But then, I'm not supposed to be happy she's here. Like, *what was she doing in the restaurant? Filming us eating our dinner? Is that what this documentary is about? Our meals? It's bullshit.* I hope she got a good angle of me leaving because that's all she'll be getting from me.

Bringing me dinner isn't going to win me over to her documentary. Even if it is delicious.

five

HOW TO FIGHT LONELINESS
SAMANTHA

Well, that was an exciting introduction to the band. What a weird evening. Between initially not having a place to stay, the confrontation with Matt in the parking lot, his storming out of the restaurant, and now his strange behavior at his door when I delivered his dinner, I don't know what to make of any of it. *Is it normal for him to act like this to people? Or just to me?* Sarah did say he's been in a bad mood lately, and I'm gathering the reason is the documentary I'm filming. I thought everyone gave their okay for me to film them, but I could be wrong. Maybe the label only told me that, so I'd accept the job.

Even if he didn't want to go along with the filming, he doesn't have to be such an asshole to me personally. I'm just doing my job. I don't want to intrude on their personal lives, but there will be behind-the-scenes things I'll want to include. Especially dull things, like eating in a restaurant, to show the monotonous cycle of being a band on the road. I did take a good shot of Matt's ass as he left. But I'll most likely keep that out of the final film and save it for myself.

During dinner, I had a nice chat with Vanessa about the schedule and arrangements for the bus rides between cities. She wouldn't stop apologizing for the mix-up about my hotel room. I told her it was okay since I was in Sarah's room. I gave her a quick rundown of my ideas for the documentary too, including the different things I'd like to capture if they happen naturally. I don't want anything in the film to be staged except for interviews, and I want to start those right away. I want a travel diary with each band member as the tour progresses. I think it will be a cool way to track the tour's progress and their fame.

She did mention Matt wasn't too keen on the idea of the documentary but said to give him time, and he will come around. I hope she's right. I want everyone in the band to have equal time on screen since they have insisted in the past they are an actual trio and not a lead singer with a band. I like the idea they consider themselves peers, and not one individual deserves more credit than another. That says a lot about who they are and what their character is made of.

My phone buzzes, and I see my mother is calling. It's got to be late for her in Ohio. "Hey, mom, what are you still doing up?"

"Hey, honey." She does sound tired. "I wanted to make sure you made it okay. I didn't hear from you saying you landed."

I can't help but roll my eyes a little. I'm almost twenty-seven, but my mother still wants me to check in when I travel. "Sorry about that. Things were a little crazy when I got here."

"Oh?" She sounds worried now, so I quickly catch her up on the hotel room fiasco and the strange meeting with Matt. My mother and I are very close. There isn't a whole lot I don't tell her. "He sounds handsome," she says about Matt after I describe him to her.

"Handsome, yes. But he doesn't have much else going for him." I lean back against the headboard of my bed and pull my legs up to stretch them out. "He's pretty rude otherwise, to be honest."

"Well, touring can't be all fun and games. They've been touring all year, right?"

"Yeah, I think so. And they still have to go to Europe after this summer tour."

"He's probably tired. I mean, when was the last time he saw his home? Or family? Does he have any family?"

"I'm not sure," I say, yawning loudly. "I was able to find stuff like that on the other guys when I was doing research, but for Matt, there was almost nothing online. E*verything* outside of his involvement with Indigo King was scrubbed clean off the internet. It's kind of strange. I've never seen so little about someone online. He's like the Invisible Man."

"That is weird." My mom yawns in an echo of my own.

"You should go to bed, mom. Isn't it late there?"

"I won't argue with you. I'm glad you made it safely. Call me soon and keep me updated on your hot mystery man." There's definite mischief in her voice. My mom, a long-distance matchmaker.

"Okay, mom. Love you." I distinctly avoid mentioning the hot mystery man again as we hang up. I refuse to play along with that one this time.

My mother and father have been married for nearly thirty years, and they're still as in love today as they were when they first met in high school. It's almost nauseating how cute they are together, and I can't help but compare any of my own relationships with theirs. It's natural to want what they have. But as time goes on, I realize how rare their love is. I'm starting to think I'll never find that kind of partner. It's almost not fair. Actually, no - not almost; it *is* unfair. I shouldn't want to compare anything to something so incomparable.

When I broke up with Nick, my mother understood and encouraged it since I was unhappy. I still couldn't help but feel like I disappointed her with the failure of our relationship, though I know it's a feeling I imposed on myself. I know she doesn't judge me or my decisions, so I don't know why I put that kind of pressure on myself to be perfect. Especially when it comes to love. My track record in that department is less than stellar. I think my parent's relationship may have my expectations set too high for any mortal man to meet. But I don't want to lower my standard, regardless of how hard it will make finding someone. I'm still holding out for the happily-ever-after.

Thinking about Nick, I realize I don't miss him at all. I am completely unaffected by our now being apart. I think that's proof I did the right thing by breaking things off. I've already moved on if I don't even have a slight pang of regret, remorse, or residual thoughts or emotions. My heart moved on a long time ago; my head just caught up after trying to convince myself otherwise. And I'm okay with that. I'm okay that we're over. He was obviously okay with it, so there is no reason I shouldn't be too.

Tomorrow begins the three days of planning and gathering of everyone involved with the tour before the first show and hitting the road in earnest. There will be meetings of the crews for setup planning and others for coordination and logistics for equipment and personnel. I'm expecting a buzz of activity once I wake up, and I'm excited to put some of it on film.

Getting the behind-the-scenes footage people don't usually see will set this film apart from the others.

Before I head to bed, I start preparing questions for my one-on-one interviews with the band and some for when I sit them all together as a group. I can only hope Matt is in a better mood tomorrow. Not sure what I'll do if he's not. I don't like stalemates.

six

RUN
MATT

T he following day I force myself to go for another run before breakfast, despite the screaming of my legs from overdoing it last night. We don't have much to do for the next three days except for soundchecks at the amphitheater, where our first show will be here in Salt Lake City. The crews will be practicing their setup and knock-down processes, and we'll mostly try to stay out of their way. The only thing I have planned is to avoid Samantha as much as possible.

Unfortunately, I think that's going to be what I do every day for the rest of the tour. Not my idea of a fun way to spend the summer, to say the least. I don't know how to pull off keeping my private life private when I have a camera shoved in my face twenty-four-seven. I think this will be an impos- sible situation and will keep me pissed off and distracted. I didn't sign up for this shit. I signed up to play drums in a rock band, not be a fucking movie star.

I'm turning the corner around the back of the hotel when I crash into someone running in the opposite direction. A blur of blonde hair flashes in front of me, and a female yells, "Hey!" as I bounce off them and perform some sort of stunt roll to the side. I avoid hitting the pavement face first, thank god, but my shoulder gets scraped up as I spiral over the ground. It takes me a minute to regain my bearings. Then I hear that voice again, but this time she's whimpering. I find Samantha curled up on the ground a few yards away with her back to me. I jump up and run over to her. She's holding her right wrist, and the right side of her face is covered in blood.

"Oh my god. Are you okay?" I am now in full-blown panic mode. *What the fuck did I do?* "I am so sorry. I didn't see you, I swear."

"My wrist." Her voice is barely a whisper and is threaded with pain. "I think I broke it." Her tears are now mixing with the blood on her cheek and won't seem to stop flowing. *Fuck. This is not good.*

"Is it just your wrist?" I examine the rest of her head to toe, trying to spot any other apparent injuries, but I don't find any.

She glares up at me. "*Just* my wrist?" Now the pain in her voice is accompanied by fury. "This isn't *just* anything, asshole." She starts to try to stand up but can't without using her hands.

"Shit. I know. I'm sorry. I meant, is anything else injured?" I can't catch a break with this woman. "I don't think you should move until we're sure nothing else is hurt."

"I think I'd know if something else was hurt." And now she's indignant. *For fuck's sake.* "I'm not having an out-of-body experience."

"You're bleeding," I say, pulling my shirt over my head and folding it to wipe the blood off her cheek. She pulls away with a hiss when the fabric comes in contact with the cut. "Sorry." And she must sense that I am sorry because she lets me finish cleaning off her face and holding the shirt to staunch the bleeding. It gives me a second to note how blue her eyes are. I knew they were blue but didn't realize they were *that* blue. They were hidden behind her glasses... "Were you wearing your glasses?"

"Really?" The anger is back. "You ran into me, dipshit. I had no chance of seeing you, even with my glasses on."

"I know, Jesus. I meant..." I glance around the ground and spot her glasses near the curb by a flower bed next to the building. It doesn't appear they survived either. I grab them, and sure enough, one of the lenses is cracked. *Fuck.* I meet her eyes again, as apologetic as I can be. "I am so, so sorry. I'll pay for all of this."

Her face goes through several emotions, but she swallows hard and kind of nods and shrugs at the same time. I don't know what that means, but she moves to stand up again, so I rush back to help her. This time she lets me when I put a hand under her elbow and a supportive arm around her to lift her up.

"Fuuuuuuuuck, this hurts," she whimpers again. The agony in her voice cuts right through me.

"I am so, so sorry," I repeat. "I swear I didn't see you. I wasn't paying attention..."

"I need to get to an ER... we can dish out blame later."

"Of course. Fuck, I don't have a car. Let's head inside. I'll call Vanessa." I pull my phone out of my running armband and call our manager. She'll know what to do. She answers on the first ring.

"Matt? What's the matter? You never call me." At least she knows that this is important then.

"Samantha needs to get to the hospital right away. She may have a broken wrist and a possible head injury."

"My head is fine." Samantha glares at me as I walk her through the hotel's front doors.

"Totally something someone with a head injury would say."

"Matt. What happened? Where are you? I'm on my way." Vanessa is on the verge of shrieking.

"We're in the lobby now. I ran into her behind the hotel."

"Like, literally ran into her?"

"Yes. Literally." I maneuver Samantha into one of the lobby chairs and detect blood streaking her cheek again. "Shit. Your face is bleeding again. Where's my shirt?" I must have dropped the shirt outside. *Dammit.*

"I'm hanging up and calling 911. I'll be there in a minute." And she disconnects before I can say anything else.

I let Samantha know what's happening. Then I rush to the front desk, searching for tissue to stop her bleeding again. A gasp sounds behind me, and I turn to check what's wrong.

She points at me with her good hand, pure horror on her face. I instinctively look down at myself but don't notice anything wrong. I glance back up at her, not understanding what she sees.

"What is it? What's wrong?"

"Your back. You're bleeding...a lot."

What the fuck? I try to search over my shoulder, and sure enough, my back is ripped up pretty bad. Strange that I didn't feel it. I still don't. I need to find something for Samantha's face, though. She's my priority. My shoulder can wait.

"I'll be fine. Don't worry about me." I turn back to the front desk, grab a tissue box, and take it back to her. I rip it open and wad up a bunch to press against her cheek. She doesn't pull away this time, but I can't read her emotions. I'm sure she's hurting. I'm caught up in her blue eyes again, trying to express to her my regret. There are green flecks in them I didn't spot before. *Emerald green.* After a moment, she looks away.

I can't believe I did all this. I can't believe I did this to her. *What the fuck is wrong with me? How did I not see her? What if her wrist is broken? How is she supposed to do her job without a hand?* While sure, I don't want the fucking documentary, this is not how I wanted it to go away. Not with her hurt.

Vanessa enters the lobby at the same time the ambulance arrives. "Matt! You didn't tell me you were hurt too!"

I shrug it off. "Just some road rash. I'll be fine. Samantha's the one hurt."

"I'll be okay," she squeaks weakly. She's gotten extremely pale since we came inside.

"Are you alright? You don't look so hot." Vanessa leans over to touch her forehead, which now has a light sheen of sweat.

"His blood is handsome too..." she whispers and passes out.

Luckily, I'm already right by her and catch her easily. I put an arm under her legs and scoop her up, taking her outside to meet the ambulance.

"Oh my god. Oh my god." Vanessa is freaking

out, following me outside. "Is she going to be okay? I should come along."

"No," I say, facing her as the paramedics approach us. "Go to her room and check her purse or phone. Check if you can find any health information. If she's allergic to anything or if she's on any medication. Stuff like that a doctor might want to know. I don't know. Text me if you find anything."

"Wow," Vanessa says, impressed. "You're sure calm under pressure." I don't respond to that, hoping she'll hurry up and do what I said.

The paramedics eye me curiously and ask, "Should we bring the gurney?"

I shake my head. "No. I've got her."

seven

IN THE CLEAR
SAMANTHA

I come to in an ambulance with an oxygen mask on my face and my wrist now splinted in an air cast of some kind, but it still hurts like a bitch. The big surprise is Matt sitting next to me, holding my good hand with a worried expression on his face.

"There you are." The tension in his shoulders releases a little. "Welcome back." His hair is still sticking to his neck from his run, and it's starting to curl up at the ends. I want to reach up and touch it.

I glance down at his hands, holding on to mine so tightly it almost hurts. I'm not sure what to think about him holding my hand after he basically put me in this ambulance. Well, no, he *literally did* put me in this ambulance. I slide my hand out of his, so I can think about it more before letting him do that again. Our interactions the past day have been too volatile to suddenly let him be amorous. He sits up and rubs his hands on his thighs now that they're free.

"Where...?" I can't make a complete question or sentence. Hopefully, I appear as confused as I am to push my point across.

"We're about five minutes away from the hospital," Matt says, confirming with a nod to the paramedic on the other side of me I just noticed.

"Oh, hey," I mumble to the paramedic. He gives me an odd look, a curt nod, and a hesitant smile. The morning events come back to me in a rush, and I remember Matt is also hurt. "Hey, he's hurt too. Make sure you check out his shoulder."

The paramedic glares briefly at Matt. "We checked his shoulder, and he's refused treatment."

"I said to focus on her." Matt's tone is harsh enough to shut him up, but he's not happy.

"Yes, sir. But once we're at the hospital..." A second paramedic attempts to chime in.

"Once we're at the hospital, we'll deal with it."

I don't understand why he's being so rude. They're just doing their jobs.

"Whoa, easy, Killer. I'm fine," I say, putting a hand on Matt's knee, trying to calm him down. He's startled but covers my hand with his. "I'm much better. Really."

"Well, you look like shit." He instantly regrets his words.

I chuckle. "You do flatter me."

"I didn't mean like that." He's getting flustered and starting to blush a little. Through my pain, he could be adorable if I let him. Never mind that he still isn't wearing a shirt, which is distracting me. "I meant you still look like you're in pain."

"Oh, well, yeah. There's that." And I am. Besides my wrist throbbing and stabbing pain up my arm, my head is starting to ache something fierce. I feel like my head's been hit with an anvil, like the old cartoons I used to consume every Saturday morning. "My head is killing me now too."

Matt stares pointedly at the paramedic next to me, who looks back at him blankly. "Did you get that? She's got new symptoms. Have you checked her for concussion?" The poor guy is scared to death but starts peppering me with a million questions I assume are part of some test for a concussion. I don't know if I pass or not, but he writes furiously on his clipboard. I glance back at Matt, whose worried expression now has a steely edge. I'm not following why he's so intense about all this. It was a crazy accident.

Things move swiftly once we arrive at the hospital, and I'm whisked away to take x-rays. Matt, too, gets x-rays taken of his shoulder, though he's not happy about it. We're placed side by side in the triage unit and talk to each other through the curtain dividing us. I can see his feet dangling on the side of his bed under the curtain. It's kind of cute watching them sway.

"Do you still have my glasses?" I'm curious about what happened to them. I'm going to have a hell of a time seeing without them, and I don't carry a spare pair.

"I gave them to Vanessa to hold." He sounds so remorseful. I can't take much more.

"I don't blame you, you know. It was an accident."

Silence. And his feet stop swinging. "It was my fault." He's ghostly quiet. "I wasn't watching where I was going, and I cut that back corner. It was bad running form."

"I'm not going to argue with you, but know I don't blame you." He will be hellbent on taking the blame for everything, regardless of what I say. I bet if I push him, we'll be back at each other's throats.

I hear him sigh heavily but spot another set of shoes that appears under the curtain. "Mr. Sturridge?" The faceless voice asks. "I've taken a gander at your x-rays, and it doesn't show any current fracture. But...it was a little tricky to read the films with all the previously healed fractures in that arm. Were you in an accident or something?"

"Or something." Matt mumbles. "So, is that it?"

"Well, we still need to clean and dress the area on your shoulder to prevent infection." The doctor sounds like he was taken aback by his response. I don't blame him. I'm surprised by everything too. *What's that about? Previous fractures? Plural? Was he in an accident?* My curiosity is stoked, and I can't help but wonder about Matt's life. With my internet search results yielding nothing, this news adds to the mystery surrounding him.

The doctor comes through the curtain to my side once he's done with Matt and studies my chart. "Miss Fisher, you certainly broke your wrist, but luckily your cheekbone suffered only a laceration and not a fracture."

"Okay, that's not so bad." We've only been here like an hour, but I'm dying to go back to the hotel. I do not like hospitals. Or blood. Or hospitals. Or blood.

"No, you were pretty lucky. We'll get your wrist in a cast you'll need to wear for about six weeks, but you should be right as rain."

"What about concussion?" Matt's voice, now strong, carries over to us. The doctor and I both stare at the apparently possessed curtain and then at each other.

I raise an eyebrow at him in a 'yeah, what about a concussion, like that haunted curtain asked?' look.

The doctor takes a last wary glare at the divider, then turns to me. "No obvious signs of concussion. We'll give you a list of symptoms to watch out for back at home. If any of them pop up, you should definitely head back here to be checked out."

"I will. Thank you." I say it loud enough, so Matt gets I'm thanking both of them.

When he leaves, the curtain billows again, and Matt peeks in. "All clear?" I nod, and he steps through. I don't know why, but I'm surprised he's still shirtless, flaunting his perfectly chiseled and smooth chest. I don't know where I expected him to find a shirt since the last time I saw him, but it isn't fair for him to be walking around all hot like that when I'm sure I could be captain of a zombie team in an apocalypse. That is even more reason for me to want to jet out of here and back to the hotel. "Casts don't take long. We'll be out of here soon." He's some sort of mind reader, I swear.

I try to arrange my face into some semblance of being brave and push my shoulders back a little. "I'm fine. Seriously. I'm fine." *Wow*. I'm sure that was totally convincing. I need to move my gaze away from him. I'm already unsettled, and his being in only running shorts isn't helping matters. But then, I'm caught remembering what he just said: "Casts don't take long." Pair that with the question from the doctor about his arm, and I can't help but look back at him with a different eye. I may have a different prism to analyze him through, but he doesn't seem different. He doesn't give anything away. His face is a stone mask of neutrality. I do sense a lot of practice at that mask, though. He's almost perfected it, but I can spy the beginning of cracks. *Would he ever let me in? What an odd thought.*

He catches me looking at him, and something in him seems to know I see through the facade. His face shifts, and now he appears scared. *What on earth could he possibly be afraid of?*

eight

ROOM TO BREATHE

MATT

*S*hit. *Why is she looking at me like that?* I don't like it. I'm too exposed. But then, I can't stop looking at her either. I don't know what it is about this woman that has me so fucking riled up all the time. Ever since I looked into those deep blue eyes, I've been off. My quick reactions are still on point, at least. I haven't lost that part of my training.

"Mr. Sturridge?"

I break my gaze away from Samantha and find a nurse leaning in with her hands full of supplies I can only assume are for my shoulder.

"I'll be back," I say and pat her feet under her hospital blanket before entering my side of the curtain. *Patting her feet? What the fuck was I thinking? Who pats someone else's feet?* I really am losing it. I don't like this response. I'm starting to lose control, and that can't happen. That can never happen.

I sit through the nurse cleaning and dressing the wounds on my back without complaint, though it stings like a bitch. I'm sure this is nothing compared to what Samantha is going through. She's trying to be brave, but I saw the pain in her eyes. She can't hide her emotions, and I can read her like a book.

I eavesdrop through the curtain when her nurse appears with a shot of a pain killer for her. She proceeds to pass out again at the sight of the needle too. I've never seen someone as squeamish as she is. Luckily, she was already lying down this time. When she comes around, she's feeling no pain, and I discover her sharp sense of humor as she jokes with her nurse. I stay on my side, even when my nurse finishes with me, so I can listen to her joke around. She'll clam up if I go over to her side, and I enjoy hearing her laugh. There's a quirkiness to her laughter so distinctive and unique from anything else. Now I know if I ever hear a laugh like it again, it belongs to only her. *What a weird thing to think.*

Once they're done with her cast, and we're both discharged, I order a car to take us back to the hotel. Vanessa meets us in the lobby as though she had waited for us the whole time we were gone. She swarms around Samantha and takes over for me with her care. Once she's out of my hands and out of sight, I feel a little lost. A little empty. I couldn't explain it if I tried. I sense her absence in a way I've never felt before from anyone else. An ache in my bones rises to be back in her presence. I shake it off as much as possible and head back to my room to clean up.

It's mid-afternoon, and the rest of the band has done the day's soundcheck without me. The drum technician handled my part in the whole thing, which is a relief. I'd hate for anything else to go wrong because of my stupidity this morning. I've caused enough damage for one day.

I'm starving and figure Samantha probably hasn't eaten either because of everything happening today. *Everything I caused.* I decide to do the nice thing and grab us some lunch to take to her room. When she opens the door, it appears as though I've woken her up. *Shit.*

"Sorry, I didn't mean to wake you up." She doesn't say anything but leaves the door open and walks back into her room. I assume I'm meant to follow her, so I do, shutting the door behind me. She flops back onto her bed, keeping her cast raised in the air to avoid being jostled. She seems to have adapted to the cast pretty easily. "I thought you might be as hungry as I am, so I got us some food." I hold up the bags of food I've brought, full of different kinds of sandwiches, bags of chips, and various types of soda.

"I see you've finally decided to put some clothes on." She's smiling to herself, but her eyes are now closed. I can't tell if she's making fun of me or joking with me.

"Well, I didn't want to add heart attack to the list of injuries I've given you today." I'm being purposely cheeky to try to match her mood. I put the bags down on the table and start pulling out the food.

She starts fanning herself with her good hand, "Ooh! You got that right. I almost got the vapors earlier. You had me swooning in my petticoats." She laughs that laugh of hers, and I can't help but join in, even if it is at my expense.

"Yeah, yeah, Vapor Girl. I was shirtless because I was administering aid to a damsel in distress."

"Oh, I am no damsel, I assure you." She sits up and points her cast at me.

I put my hands up, "I'm just saying. I provided a service."

She laughs louder, and my face reddens as I read her thoughts. Her dirty thoughts. Then my thoughts go to ideas of servicing her too. *Jesus Christ.* I turn back to the table and back to the food before my mind runs away with me.

"But seriously, thanks for bringing me food. I am ravenous." She comes up behind me and places a hand on my back so casually as she assesses the food choices like it's something she does every day. Typically, I would have stiffened at the uninvited contact, but I don't. My body is so weirdly in tune with hers and is used to her. I'm not sure what to make of it. My head wants me to pull away, but the rest of me doesn't. The rest of me wants *more*.

"You're welcome." I want to be sure she knows how sorry I am for this morning's accident. "It is the least I could do."

She looks up at me with those eyes whose depths I could drown in, and though they say she forgives me, she quips, "No. The least you can do is open the wrapper of this sandwich, this bag of chips, and this pop for me." She grabs each one and shoves them at me to take care of for her. I immediately comply and hand them back.

"Are you going to be able to function with that cast on?"

She sits down at the table, and I take the chair across from her, grabbing my own food.

"That is TBD." She tosses a chip into her mouth, chewing loudly, and I love she's being so comfortable with me. "I've never had a cast before." A shadow crosses her face, and I wonder what she is thinking about. Though she's so easy to read, that one eluded me. "What about you? Are you going to be able to play with your shoulder all jacked up? You're the important one here. I'm just a camera jockey."

"Don't say that." I don't like it when women put themselves down. "You're not 'just' anything."

She gives me another unreadable look, and I

think my ability to read her is now gone for good. "You didn't want me to do the documentary. Why would you care if I can go forward with it or not?"

"Because I would never want to be the reason someone couldn't do their job. And I especially don't want the reason to be because I hurt them. Regardless of whether you are filming a documentary, serving beers, or scanning tickets. It makes me sick I'd be why you can't do your job."

She raises a beautiful eyebrow at me. "Oh, I'll still do my job. This won't stop me from filming the documentary. When I said my functioning was TBD, I meant changing clothes or washing my hair. I can do the documentary without those." She scrunches up her face after she thinks about what she said. "Eww. Forget I said that."

I chuckle. "Totally forgotten. And my apologies. I didn't mean to insinuate you were incapable of doing your job." Man, I am sticking my foot in it left and right.

"No worries. And *I* apologize. This has been a crazy day, and I *do* need to figure out how I'm going to do my job. I'm trying to be overconfident in the off chance it manifests into working out." She drags her hair behind her ear clumsily with her casted hand. I instinctively lean across the table and help, my fingers tingling when they touch her hair. I'm careful to avoid her bandaged cheekbone, and her eyes meet mine and hold for a long minute before I bring my hand back. I don't know what happened between us, but something just did. *Wow. This can't happen.*

I jump up, crumpling up my food wrappers, and throw them into one of the bags. "Well, I... need to get out of here." I exit quickly and retreat to my room, not looking back to see how she reacted or anything, just needing to get away as soon as possible. I stay in my room the rest of the day, trying to figure out what had happened and what to do about it. Samantha Fisher has needled her way through my exterior barriers, and I can't let that happen. I can't allow myself to let my guard down for a minute.

nine

MISTAKEN FOR STRANGERS

SAMANTHA

After Matt basically runs out of my room, I'm left to wonder what the hell just happened. I replay our conversation and don't think I said or did anything that would have made him go so hastily, but I don't know him well yet. Right before he left, he had helped me push my hair back, and something passed between us. I swear I can still sense the tips of his fingers on my cheek. And then he "had to get out of here?" *What the hell is up with that?* Everything happened so quickly, I hardly knew what was happening, and poof, he was gone. And damn if I don't feel hurt.

The more I know Matt, the less I know him. Every interaction between us is like opening a Russian doll, only to find another figurine inside. It's both frustrating and intriguing at the same time. I want to know what makes him tick because I have the sense he is hiding so much of himself behind a carefully constructed wall. I got a glimpse today of him being so caring and attentive when I was injured. The entire time I felt like I was taken care of and safe, something vital to me in situations like that, knowing how my body reacts to blood and needles. I've been in the position to be even more hurt from my reactions than from accidents before, but today I was completely safe with Matt.

It's pretty obvious he wants nothing to do with me, though. He was in such a hurry to run out of here after bringing me food; I'm surprised he had enough time to eat. He apparently harbors a ton of guilt from the accident and needed to do something nice for me to make him feel better about himself. And that's fine. I can't be thinking about him in any way other than a subject of interest in the film. No matter how bright the sparks are between us, it wouldn't be wise of me to want or try to be anything more. *No. He can have his way. Nothing from me.*

A knock on the door draws me back to the present. When I open the door, Sarah looks like she's going to jump out of her skin.

"Oh my gosh, Sam, are you okay?" She rushes in and throws her arms around my neck. "I couldn't come back here until now. I'm so sorry."

"It's fine. I'm fine." I laugh, hugging her back. "I'll be okay."

"The way I heard, Matt almost killed you."

"Well, as you can observe for yourself, I'm very much alive."

"Yeah, but wow." She runs a hand gingerly along my face where the bandage covers my cheekbone and lifts my cast to examine it. "All this just from running into someone."

"'Running into' is putting it lightly. I got plowed into." The look on Sarah's face changes, and I am officially the biggest idiot in the universe. Her brother was in a bad accident this past Christmas with a snowplow and barely survived. "Oh my god, I'm so sorry. That was thoughtless of me to say."

"No, no. Not at all." She assures me. "I know it's a figure of speech. Don't worry."

"Do you want a sandwich? Chips? or a pop?" I try to change the subject immediately to cover my faux pas.

"What's with all the food? Were your eyes bigger than your stomach at the sandwich counter or what?"

"Actually, Matt brought all this over for me."

"He must be feeling guilty about hurting you."

"Yeah, I think you're right. I keep telling him I don't blame him. It was an accident. But he's hell-bent on making amends." I picture him rushing out of the room not too long ago, and a pang of hurt runs through me since he was in such a hurry to get away from me.

"What's wrong, Sam? Are you okay?" She sits

where Matt sat not long ago, and I take the seat across from her.

I take a second before answering. The thoughts I've had about Matt for the last twenty-four hours are confusing to me. On the one hand, he was a total asshole last night by the buses when I arrived. And this morning, after the accident, he was so caring and protective. This makes how he acted a little while ago more confusing as he ran away from me as soon as possible.

"How well do you know Matt?" I ask, considering her more closely for her reaction to him.

She looks a little surprised at the question. "How well?" She has to think for a minute, which tells me a lot. "Hard to say. I don't think any of us know Matt super well, you know?"

I nod. Knowing exactly what she means since it's what I suspected. "I do know, which is why I asked you. I thought maybe since you've been touring with him for a couple of months now, you might have gotten a chance to get to know him better."

"I mean, he's super nice and has a great sense of humor. But he doesn't talk about his personal life, like, at all." A crease deepens between her eyes as she considers further. "Now that I think about it, I don't know anything about him outside of the band."

"He seems pretty good at deflecting."

"Yeah, I guess he is." She still looks concerned. "Weird, I never saw that before."

"Well, I didn't mean to make things weird. I wanted to gain some insight into him since he's so shut off and cold at times."

She gives me a look. "Cold? Really?"

I tell her about him leaving so abruptly not too long ago. "I mean, it's fine. I'm not looking to be buddies or anything, but it seemed a bit harsh."

"Yeah, none of what you describe from today sounds like the Matt I know." She laughs, and she's probably not wrong. Matt's actions today are far from what little I know about him. "I wouldn't read too much into things, though. I'm sure he'll come around the more you know him."

"Like I said, I'm not worried about it. Or him."

She eyes me warily, "Are you sure you're not crushing on Matt? You've got a look..."

"What? No..." I hedge. "I mean, he *is* hot, but he's also an asshole. But he is *so fucking hot*, Sarah." I can't deny that part. Even if I hated his guts, the man is physical perfection in my eyes. Just the thought of him, shirtless as he almost always is, gets my pulse quickening. "It's not fair that hot guys tend to be dicks."

"I don't think Matt's a dick," she chuckles. "Maybe you intimidate him?"

I think about that. It could be intimidation. It wouldn't be the first time my openness came across as too strong. I nod. "Maybe. Still, message received that he's not interested in me, so it's a moot point anyway."

"Give him some time. He'll come around." Sarah can be such an optimist. "So, do you think you'll have any trouble with the documentary since you're down a hand?"

I glare down at the cast on my wrist and shrug. "To be honest, I don't know. I haven't even tried to pick up a camera yet to see if I can." I rub my temples, trying to stave off another headache I can tell is coming on. "And speaking of seeing, my glasses broke in the accident too, so I can't see for shit."

"Oh no, I didn't realize that. Can you have another pair sent to you?"

"Vanessa is working on it since we will be a moving target soon. I swear that woman knows witchcraft the way she gets things done."

"True. But in the meantime..."

"In the meantime... I make do." I shrug. "You know me. I'll make it work. I always find a way." Not like I ever have a choice.

ten

THE LOST ART OF KEEPING A SECRET

MATT

The following day I skip my run altogether to avoid anything like yesterday happening again, and I catch a ride with the first group that heads to the amphitheater. I try to help with the equipment set up but am summarily yelled at for screwing up their practice with their personnel only, so I'm left on the sidelines doing nothing until soundcheck. I hate feeling useless like this. Especially about my own fucking equipment. I don't think letting other people set my stuff up is going to be easy for me to adjust to.

My phone buzzes in my pocket, and it's Vanessa. "Hey Van, what's up?"

"Matthew?" *Uh oh.* I know if she uses my full name, I'm in trouble, but I can't think what the hell I did wrong today. It's too early to fuck up anything yet. "Where are you?"

"Um... the amphitheater? Why?" What a weird question. *Where would she expect me to be?*

"Didn't you read today's itinerary?" She sounds agitated.

"No. What itinerary?" I didn't receive anything, and no one told me I needed to be anywhere but here today.

"The one that got slid under your door this morning."

"When? I haven't been in my room since 6 AM. I came over with the first crew. I didn't know I was supposed to be anywhere else."

"Well, shit." She sighs with a loud exhalation. "We've got press here waiting to do interviews, and only a duo, not a trio, to meet with them."

Damn. "I'm sorry, Van. I didn't know that was on the schedule today." I'm not sorry that I'm missing the interviews, but I am sorry for causing problems for Vanessa. I know Ryan and Jude won't care that I'm not there. They answer all the questions when we're in a group. I usually smile and nod like a good boy. "Can't Ryan and Jude handle it today?"

Vanessa swears under her breath again, resigned to the situation. "I guess they'll need to."

"I am sorry."

"I know. From now on, there will be itineraries under your door each morning, so please wait until you get it before you go gallivanting around town."

"But gallivanting is kinda my thing." I try to insert some levity into the situation. Vanessa is starting to become wound a little too tight.

"Hilarious, Matthew." I find it hysterical that she acts like such a den mother when she's only a few years older than us, but I keep my laughter on the inside.

We hang up after she makes me swear on the grave of John Bonham to wait for the schedule from now on before I leave my room. And the vice tightens around my neck that little bit more.

I head out to the seating area of the pavilion to wait for Ryan and Jude to arrive for soundcheck, which could be a while. After finding a seat, I put in my earbuds and turn my playlist on shuffle to pass the time. Samantha's attempting to set up a tripod and other equipment out of the corner of my eye, but she's struggling with the cast on her wrist. I watch her, not wanting to assume she needs help, and offend her in offering assistance. After watching for a few minutes, I can't take it anymore and jump up to help her attach the camera to the tripod.

"Here, let me help," I say, taking the camera from her and snapping it onto her tripod.

Instead of being grateful for the help as I expected her to be, she's glaring at me with her jaw set in a hard line. She clears her throat. "Thanks, but I don't need your help." Her neck and cheeks are starting to redden, and I can't tell if it's from embarrassment, anger, or both. And now, I don't know what I did to cause either.

"Sorry. You looked like you could use some help."

"Well, I don't. I've got this handled." She moves to turn her back to me and leans down to peer through the camera, pointing at the stage.

I have to take a step back to move out of her way, and I don't understand where this attitude is coming from all of a sudden. I thought we kind of shared a moment last night. It wasn't a moment I wanted, but it happened nonetheless. I know I felt it. I would swear she did too. I did not imagine it.

"Is everything okay?" Now I'm concerned that maybe that moment yesterday crossed a line I didn't know about. It's entirely possible. I don't know anything about her, her love life, or anything else. I just don't know her. Parts of me that I can't control want to get to know her intimately, but I know I can't act on that.

"Just peachy keen." Her voice is emotionless, and she doesn't turn away from the viewfinder. I can't win with her. I try to be helpful and am shot down. I try to be friendly and am shot down. I don't know why I'm even trying. I don't want anything to do with this damn documentary. And yesterday morning's incident was an accident. I can't apologize any more than I already have.

Fuck it. I walk through the seats out to the lawn

area and find a sunny spot to sit and wait, putting my playlist back on at full volume. I shut my eyes and force myself not to glance in Samantha's direction. If she doesn't want my help, fine. She can't say I didn't offer, though. I also have to admit that I don't want her to struggle either. When I first saw her having trouble, something in my chest was yanked out and sent me into action. I don't think I could've stopped myself, honestly. Like I couldn't prevent myself from touching her hair yesterday. The thought of the silky strands in my fingers sends something electric skittering across my skin.

I twitch and smooth the hair on my arms standing on end. I glance up in her direction, curiosity getting the better of me, and find her leaning over her camera again, but now it's pointed directly at me. She's too far away to tell if it is actually me she's filming or only my general direction, but I'm not an idiot. She caught me with my eyes closed, so I couldn't protest.

Fucking hell. What the hell kind of game is she playing? I stand slowly and head in the opposite direction from her to put as much distance between us as possible. Not running; not in a hurry. I don't want to give her the satisfaction of knowing how she's affecting me.

This summer's going to be one long game of cat and mouse, and the cat has a fucking camera and a license to use it. I don't handle being hunted well at all.

As I reach the top of the lawn area, my phone rings, and the screen displays an unknown number, so I send it to voicemail. As I study the number more closely, it's a 512 area code; my hometown of Wimberly, Texas. I quickly open my voicemail, noticing my fingers shake as I press play.

JAX: "Hey, Matty. Long time no see... And I do mean *see*. I see that you're doing pretty well for yourself, huh? Top ten album. World tour. I can only imagine what else... Impressive. *Very* impressive. You've done your family proud. Anyway, I just wanted to say hello since it's been such a long time since we last spoke. What's it been eight years now? I think it's high time for a little Holloway brothers' reunion, don't you? Salt Lake's not my thing, but Denver should make for a nice family get together. I'll be in touch."

The sound of that voice makes my blood run ice-cold. I instinctively look around the lawn and pavilion for any sign of him, even though I know the idea is impossible. My pulse is starting to race uncontrollably, and the phone in my hand feels woefully inadequate compared to what I need to be holding.

There's no way my brother could be here. Right? How the fuck did he get my number? Nothing good is going to come of this. Nothing at all.

eleven

SAMANTHA
WHO WE ARE

Did I really look like a damsel in distress? God, I hope not. I'd be mortified. No, I *am* mortified because Matt even said I looked like I needed help. I *hate* being helpless, and this stupid cast hinders everything I want to be doing. And after last night, if I'm going to accept anyone's help, it won't be from Matt Sturridge. I've had enough of his mixed messages. He was damned loud and clear yesterday when he basically ran out of my room. *I can take a hint.*

I did sneak a nice shot of him sitting on the lawn with his eyes closed as he relaxed for a few minutes. That is until he noticed I was filming him. *Whoops. My bad.* I also make sure I take a close-up of him walking away up the hill. The back is almost as good of a view as the front, but not quite. I almost stop filming once he gets on his phone, but the expression on his face is one I've not seen on him before. He's downright frightened and then paranoid as he glances around nervously. I stop filming and watch him, trying to see what he'll do next since he's obviously upset by the call, but he pockets his phone as he composes himself and heads to the backstage area and out of sight.

What was all that about? I don't know him very well, but I've never seen him so freaked out. He's usually so in control of his emotions. To think something's gotten him so riled up makes me wonder what could upset that balance. I rewind the recording to examine his reaction again, and sure enough, he looks scared to death. For a brief second, sheer terror flashes on his face. Something inside me tightens, wanting to protect him for some reason I don't understand. It makes me feel like a total bitch at how I acted toward him minutes ago. Of course, I didn't know any of this before.

This brings me back to how I don't really know him. I thought I had glimpses yesterday, but he is more and more intriguing and mysterious with every new view of him. This is going to make getting to know him almost impossible. Never mind that he doesn't want me to get to know him either.

Something tugs at me, and though I try to ignore it so I can work, whatever it is has persistence for days. I stop filming and glance around to find Matt, but no luck. It takes me a minute, but I finally pack up my equipment and roll it back toward where I last saw Matt go. I leave my case near others and head out to search for him. It takes around twenty minutes, and asking four different people, but I find him lying on the grass behind a food truck. He sure did not want to be found.

I sit down beside him, being quiet in case he's sleeping and not wanting to wake him. It takes him a second, but when he realizes someone is next to him, he jumps straight to his feet and reaches to his side as if grabbing for a phantom weapon.

Stunned, I stare at him. Afraid if I move, he'll freak the fuck out even more than he has. I don't raise my hands in surrender or self-defense. Honestly, I'm so shocked at his overreaction; I don't know what to do with myself other than blink at him and prepare myself mentally to run if I need to. I think I may be more freaked out than him at this point.

He relaxes once he realizes the situation but glares daggers at me. "What the fuck, Samantha?"

I still can't move or say anything. I can't tell if he was so offended I sat next to him; he had to get away as soon as humanly possible, or if I surprised or scared him. It could be either. And either way, I can't help but be hurt, especially since he just yelled and swore at me. Tears are pricking behind my eyes, but I'm willing them to stay put. I don't want him to catch me crying. Not two days in a row.

My emotions must be on my face, whether I want them there or not because Matt is instantly regretful. "Shit. I'm sorry." He runs a hand through his hair and paces for a second, gathering himself.

I still haven't moved a muscle, keeping perfectly still. He glances up at me again and lunges towards me, kneeling down and reaching out his hands. He moves so fast, though, I don't know what he's doing, and I jerk away from him, flinching. It's an instinctive reaction to his quick movements.

He pulls his hands back and drops his face into them. "Shit. Sorry again." He turns his head up to the sky and scrubs his hands down his face in frustration. His shoulders slump as his eyes meet mine, and the regret is there again. I still see a twinge of that fear I spotted earlier when he was on the phone.

"Are you okay?" My voice is so low I almost don't recognize it as my own.

"Yeah," he forces a small laugh. "Outstanding. You just surprised me."

My eyebrows go up. That reaction was more than surprise. *Way more*. "That's you surprised? What the fuck, Matt?" I scoot back a little, then get up and step away from him. I'm still not comfortable with all that just happened.

"I know. I know. I'm sorry. I must have fallen asleep, and it was discombobulating when I discovered you next to me. I just freaked out a little. Sorry about that." He's still kneeling in front of me with an almost defeated expression. This whole situation isn't making any sense to me.

All at once, the environment makes itself real again. The mid-day sun beats down on my shoulders, the smell of food from the service truck in front of us drifts over, and the music pumping through the speaker system is almost too loud. They had all disappeared in the last minute while I watched Matt go through his Rolodex of emotions.

Part of me still feels a tugging sensation and wants to go hug him because I think he could use a hug. Something about him screams, "Hug me!". But there's a stronger side of him screaming louder, "Don't fucking touch me!" which is the side I'm going to listen to for now. I don't want to piss him off more than he is.

"Well, I'm sorry I woke you up. I didn't realize you were sleeping." I start to walk past him to head to the front of the food truck to grab some lunch and leave him be. I didn't mean to wake him up or interrupt him or whatever I did. My tone was probably a bit snarkier than I intended, but I can't help that now.

He grabs my hand as I walk past him to stop me. I don't jerk away this time, but I slowly slide my hand out of his. The jolt of electricity shooting through me at his touch is too much. And knowing what it does to me, and doesn't do for him, makes me need to pull away.

He stands and now towers over me, blocking out the sun, whose rays prism around his outline, casting his face in shadow. "I really am sorry for how I reacted there."

"I'm fine. Forget about it." His face is hidden with the sun in my eyes, but I try to flash a smile as I walk away. This time he lets me leave.

I don't know what I was thinking, seeking him out like this. I thought I was concerned for him after how distraught he looked after his phone call, but apparently, he was fine. Fine enough to fall asleep even, so I went through all that for no reason whatsoever. The day has barely hit noon, and we've already been assholes to each other for no apparent reason. I don't know why we keep butting heads like this, but if it continues the rest of the tour, this will be the longest summer known to mankind.

twelve

MATT
EASILY

Samantha walks away from me, and I feel like absolute shit. I wish I hadn't reacted like that to her sitting next to me. But fuck, I had dozed off, and I do not like being startled awake at all, especially in unfamiliar surroundings. It was reckless of me to put myself in that situation to begin with. Ryan and Jude at least know to make themselves known, even if they don't know why. They just think I startle easily, but they don't know the half of it. However, the voicemail from my brother could mean I'll need to put even more effort into keeping it that way.

Eight years is not enough distance between my brother and me. The enormous steps I've taken to ensure he'd never find me have been useless with the band's success, and my face plastered all over the place. I don't know what I was thinking. I don't think I ever expected the band to be this popular. I was happy being a band with underground popularity. I did not expect to have top ten records and be on a massive tour with the biggest band on the planet. That does shit for my anonymity. So now I have to deal with my asshole brother. And asshole is the understatement of the century when it comes to him.

What the fuck could he possibly want from me? I've already given him my soul and several years of my life on top of everything else. He shouldn't need anything else from me. *Changing my name hasn't done any good since my face is now everywhere, but how the fuck did he get my phone number?* I can count on two hands who has my number, so someone in my circle of trust can't be trusted anymore. *But who? Who could know Jax? And know him enough to give him my number?*

Regardless of my number, voicemail, or any of that, I treated Samantha like shit, and I did not mean to. But it seems like every time I try to do the right thing with her, she throws it back in my face. I don't understand. *Was I so wrong to offer to help her earlier?* She was having a hard time, and I thought I was doing the right thing. The nice thing. Something an average person would want. But she is far from average. I can tell she's way too independent to accept help if she's determined to do something on her own. Perhaps I'm approaching this all wrong. I don't have many independent women role models from which to glean this type of behavioral response. I guess I have Vanessa and Sarah; they're both independent women. *What would they want in this situation? Should I ask them? Fuck no, idiot. You are not asking for advice on this.*

I rake my hands through my hair again. I want to pound the shit out of my drums for an hour. Two. Okay, three. Checking my phone, I've still got an hour or so before Ryan and Jude show up for soundcheck. I should have gone back for the press stuff, but the thought of it makes me shudder. I am in the wrong fucking business.

The smell of food from the truck behind me is enough to pull me out of my thoughts, so I head that way. I notice Samantha trying to juggle her food and drink to carry to a table as I approach. I rush over, but before I help, I ask, "Can I give you a hand?" I learned my lesson earlier when I helped uninvited.

She stares up at me, those blue eyes prying into mine, trying to read me. I don't know what she sees, but she nods, and I grab her drink and follow her to a table. She sits and deftly unwraps her burger with her good hand.

"You're getting expert at that part." I try to give her a smile but know it's weak. I don't know why I keep trying to talk with her; she wants nothing to do with me. *But why was she sitting next to me behind the truck?*

She smiles back. The corners of her eyes crinkle the way people who smile a lot do. "I practice at home." The words are sarcastic, but her tone is light.

"Can I grab some food and join you, Samantha?" *What the fuck am I doing right now?*

The surprised expression she gives me reflects my inner thoughts. "Really?"

Something inside me shrinks as she asks that. I have been so confused around her I don't know what the hell I'm doing most of the time. The way I've acted the last two days is so unlike me; I don't blame her for being wary.

"Yeah, really. That is if it's okay with you..." I find myself holding my breath, waiting for her to respond. There has got to be a reason I'm determined to be near her, and I want to find out what it is.

Her eyes narrow slightly as she studies me for a second. "Sure. If you want to."

I hurry to the food truck and back to her table, not sure why I'm feeling almost giddy about being able to spend time with her again. When I sit across from her, she assesses me with an inquisitive sparkle in her bright eyes, like I've amused her somehow, but I have no clue how.

"What?" I wipe at my chin with a napkin, thinking I've made a mess of myself, which is not entirely out of the realm of possibilities.

"Why do you call me that?"

"What? Samantha?" I'm not following her question at all. "Isn't that your name?"

She laughs, and the sound feels like a warm hug. "It is, but you're the only one that calls me by my full name. Most people call me Sam."

"Would you rather I called you Sam?"

She considers me and the question before answering, tapping a finger on her chin, drawing my eyes to her full lips, and I'm instantly distracted. My thoughts are racing around how those lips would fit against mine, how they would taste. "No. I like that you call me by my full name." Her lips curve into a seductive smile, and she bites on a fingernail, unaware of how sexy that is to me. *Or is she aware? Could she be flirting with me?*

A muscle in my jaw twitches as I stare at her mouth. "Well then, Samantha it is." I move my eyes to meet hers, and sparks ignite between us. The mental foreplay in just that gaze is insane. I've never felt such a concrete physical attraction with another person. And I know she feels it too. She's as unsettled as I am. She doesn't know what to do with what just happened between us. It was only an exchange of looks, but god damn, if it wasn't a hell of a lot more than that. And we both know it.

"What's your deal, Matt?" She's recovered from whatever the fuck that was and is leaning in, examining me more closely. I love how open she is. So confident. So carefree with her questions. Most of the time. Right now, she's throwing me off my game. Like I have a game. *Should I have a game?*

"What do you mean?" I swallow hard. Not sure what she's getting at, and not sure what all I want to reveal to her.

"Well, you're kind of giving me whiplash over here." She giggles but with an edge of exasperation. "One minute you're avoiding me like the plague, then you're holding my hand, running out of my room like your pants are on fire, trying to help me set up my equipment, and jumping away at the very sight of me. And now, you're sitting and eating lunch with me, looking as though you want to rip my clothes off. You tell me if any of that's normal."

"I never claimed to be normal." I shrug, grinning. She's right, though, I have been all over the place the last few days, and she's witnessed almost everything. The clothes ripping thing is relatively new, however. *And sounds amazing.*

She crosses her arms over her chest and raises an eyebrow, and I know I'm not going to be able to get away with that answer. *How is she able to read me so well?* She can read me like a fucking open book, in large print.

I shift my eyes away from her piercing gaze and sigh. I can't lie to her; I can tell. Even if I tried, she'd see right through me, so I may as well be as honest as possible. Not entirely, but enough to pass this inquisition. "The last few days have been weird, so no, this isn't normal for me."

"What's been so different for you?" The exasperation is now gone and replaced with concern. She truly cares about what's going on with me.

"You," I say before realizing what's coming out of my mouth. I want to reach into the air between us and grab the word back before it hits her ears, but I can't. I check her reaction and find my response shocked her almost as much as me.

"Me? What did I do?"

"You didn't have to do anything. Being around you makes me act like an idiot for some reason."

"Well, how do I do that, exactly?" Her cheeks are growing a little pink, which is cute, but she's not one to back down when she wants something. I like that about her, but I wish she wasn't so forthright right now.

"Like I said, you don't have to do anything. Something about you... makes me crazy." Now the heat rises in my face. *For fuck's sake.* I didn't want to say any of this, but she's somehow dragged it out of me that being around her drives me insane.

"I thought you hated me..." She still seems stunned.

"Hated you? Au contraire. Quite the opposite." May as well dump it all on the floor while we're at it. *I'm going to regret all of this.*

"Ah bon?" Her eyebrow arches as she speaks

French to me. At least, I think it was French. I don't know what the fuck she just said, but damn, she looked and sounded stellar while she said it. I want to hear more of it.

"Suuuuure?" I can't help but agree with whatever she says from now on.

"Well, for the record, you make me crazy too." Her intense gaze shoots straight to my core, making my jeans suddenly too restrictive. A heat shimmers behind her eyes, a smoldering fire matching my own that I've been trying to ignore.

"Oh yeah?" Thinking she reciprocated these feelings isn't something I ever envisioned as a possibility. But now that they apparently are, options are becoming interesting. *Very* interesting.

"Yeah." She's chewing on her bottom lip. "Maybe we should be crazy together... and see where that leads us." This is seriously becoming interesting if she's suggesting what I think she's suggesting.

"Maybe we should." Jesus. Am I just going to repeat everything she says back to her? Is this now the breadth of my vocabulary? Considering I'm not thinking with my brain now, I should cut myself some slack.

"I should be back at the hotel by seven... If you want to stop by..." She's looking up at me from under her lashes, and god damn, if she isn't the hottest woman I've ever seen. Disregard my previous complaint about her forthrightness. I now absolutely *love* it.

"I'm not sure what time I'll be back, but I think seven should work." I have no clue what else is on the itinerary I didn't get this morning. Hopefully, I'm totally free for the evening.

She holds a hand out to me, palm up. "Give me your phone."

I raise a brow quizzically but open my phone and give it to her. She takes it and enters her contact information, then hands it back. Thoughts of my earlier call from my brother cross my mind briefly, but I chase those away.

"In case you're running late. Just let me know."

On my phone, I see she's entered her full name. Not Sam. "Okay, Samantha. I look forward to seeing you tonight."

"Ditto." She gets up, tosses her trash, then gives me the most wicked smile as she walks away.

I watch her go, and the pleasure is all mine. The afternoon sun pulls out the honey color of her hair that flows down her back as it sways while she walks. Thoughts of my hands in that hair carry me the rest of the day until Ryan and Jude show up for our soundcheck.

thirteen

PERFUME
SAMANTHA

Lunch with Matt sure turned a corner I wasn't expecting, but one I'm looking forward to. I've never been one to mince words, but I think I took Matt by surprise with how bold I was with him. I kind of like that. Being the unexpected. *Why be boring?* It always surprises me when I come across guys that aren't used to straightforward women like me.

I'm not looking to be swept off my feet by him. On the contrary, I don't think he could. I'm supposed to be in rebound mode from Nick. Plus, we haven't connected on that level yet. However, the level we *are* clicking on is very enticing. Something is definitely sparking between us, and I don't think I want it to stop.

I spend the afternoon filming their soundcheck and getting behind-the-scenes footage of the crew setting up and tearing equipment down. I try very hard not to be preferential to Matt in my filming, though the camera does love him. He's so intense when he plays, with his longish shaggy hair flying around as the different colored spotlights shine on him; it's enthralling to watch. Watching his muscles flex and strain as he plays is something I see in a different light now, and I can't help but be drawn to him.

Tomorrow we're supposed to have a group interview. One of many I hope to have throughout the tour. I think this one will capture the hopes and expectations of the tour ahead, which will be an interesting contrast to how they'll find themselves at the end. Plus, they're starting this tour being more popular than Incendiary Ink, who they're opening up for, which should make for interesting interviews. I hope to talk to them as well but will need to craft my questions carefully.

I make it back to the hotel with enough time to take a quick shower before Matt shows up, but not much else. A little left-handed makeup application is all that I dare for fear of squiggly eyeliner or botched mascara. It'll have to do. I've got on jean shorts and an Indigo King tank top, taking advantage of the merch discount. I hope the shirt's not too cheeky for Matt, but I want him to know I support his band... *yeah, that's it.*

At seven o'clock precisely, he knocks on the door.

Through the peephole, he looks nervous, but he's carrying bags full of something.

I open the door, and he's already raking a hand through his ash brown locks, making me want to reach out and run my fingers through them too. Somehow, I restrain myself and just step back for him to come in.

"I brought food." He passes, and I can smell his soap mixed with a cologne that makes the most intriguing combination. My senses are all of a sudden heightened, and my skin tingles.

"Okay...?" I laugh a little. That was unexpected. I hadn't even considered dinner. My mind was on more carnal things than food.

I shut the door and watch as he unpacks the bags of food. He fills out his jeans so perfectly, and I find it hard not to take a minute to admire him. Realizing I'm objectifying him, I head over to the table. I instinctively put a hand to his lower back as I come up behind him like I did last night. This time he stiffens slightly. Not enough to be completely obvious, but enough for me to notice. He might be intimidated like Sarah suggested after all.

"So, what hotel delicacies have you brought me today?" I try not to glance at the bag of sandwiches still left over from yesterday on top of my dresser, but he catches me looking.

"Oh shit, I did bring too many options yesterday, didn't I?" He laughs with a sheepish smile. Damn, that smile undoes me every time I see it. I try to deny the fact, but I can't.

"Well, today we have actual entrées. But wait, there's more."

And as if timed to what he's just said another knock sounds. I give him a quizzical glance, but his smile hasn't faltered. In fact, the devious grin deepens, which intrigues me more.

When I open the door this time, a hotel staffer greets me with an ice bucket and a bottle of wine. I step aside to let her in and gape in awe as she uncorks the wine and presents it to Matt, who nods his approval before she pours it into wine glasses. *Real* wine glasses, not plastic ones. I do believe we've upgraded.

Once she leaves, I turn to Matt, my smile growing as I move closer to him, and his is mirroring mine with each step. He knows I'm impressed, and he's proud of himself, which endears me to him even more than I already was.

He holds a glass to me, a confident gleam in his eye that wasn't there when he got here. I like that he's found it.

"To happy accidents." His eyes glitter with a little bit of mischief as he refers to our unconventional meeting yesterday.

"Clever boy." I grin as I clink his glass and sit across from him, letting him dish out our dinners.

He's picked the food and wine well, and I realize how hungry I am as the food gets presented to me.

We devour our dinners with comfortable small talk, and towards the end, the silence sits heavily between us. The air is charged with electricity, and neither of us can figure out what to do with it. I still can't believe he's here right now after thinking he hated me just yesterday. I'm curious where this might go now that he seems open to it.

I get up, take my wine, move to my bed, and lie across the top, propped on my elbow. Not shut off, but not inviting either. I want him to interpret all of this how he wants. I want him to make the next move. The ball is in his court. I think my intentions have been pretty straightforward, so I need to know what he thinks when it comes to the next steps. I'm just getting comfortable.

He turns in his chair to study me, his eyes taking their time as he takes in every inch of me, slowly and with a purpose clearly written on his face. I appreciate the candor of his salacious stare and reciprocate with my own, taking all of him in. I can feel my pulse thrumming harder through my veins as I focus on him. The heat in just his eyes is enough to make me squirm a little.

"Can I join you?" He motions to the bed but doesn't wait for me to answer and lies across from me. He takes my wine glass out of my hand and sets it on the nightstand before coming back to face me.

I look at him expectantly, and he doesn't disappoint, leaning over and kissing me with a purpose and intention that is unmistakable. I kiss him back, meeting his passion with my own. The want exchanged between us by our mouths at that moment is undeniable. When we come up for air, we stare at each other, and I discover his eyes are verdant green, and their gold flecks sparkle in the low lamplight. I've never seen a color like it before.

I don't get to think about his eyes too much because he reaches his hand behind my waist, pulling me against him. His fingers run through my hair, and he grabs the strands in a fist to tilt my face as he slants his mouth to mine. Commanding it. Taking what he wants from me. His tongue seeks mine and promises so much more to come.

His body is against mine now, and he's so hard for me, making my own body rock into him. I can't stop myself from moving in concert with his movements. The taste of the wine on his lips, the strength of his arms, and the heat of his body against me are almost too much.

Our legs are tangled, our arms are tangled, and our tongues tangle in the sweetest way. As we move closer together, my bad wrist gets pushed the wrong way, and I flinch and make a pained noise. I can't help it, but everything stops. *Fuck. Everything stops. I do not want this to stop right now.*

"Sorry," I whisper, my voice barely a rasp.

"No, I'm sorry." He adjusts himself to ensure he's not hurting me, but our eyes catch, and we're both bare for a second. Our souls are open and vulnerable. I can see something in him that I don't think he's shown anyone else. There is so much pain behind his eyes, so much unhealed hurt that seems ancient. I don't know what to do with that. To think that pain is informing how he sees me is unsettling.

I pull away from him, though the absolute last thing I want to do is separate from him. "Hey... Are you okay?"

He gazes at me, his intense eyes hooded with desire and a glimmer of surprise at my seeing behind it. He studies me for a long time; considering my question, the weight was heavier than I intended. I didn't know my question would be so sobering, but apparently, it is.

"No." Something in him twists. He groans, and as he speaks, he pulls me into the deepest and most ardent kiss of my life.

fourteen

I'LL BE YOUR MIRROR

MATT

I cannot get enough of her. I want to touch and taste every inch of her, and she seems to want the same thing. Our bodies move in response to each other's touch like we're helpless not to. The next thing I know, we're down to our underwear, and when our skin meets for the first time, a switch goes off between us and ramps up our desire even more.

We're getting close to the point of no return, so I pull back and try to read her face. She's gasping for air like me, and as our eyes meet, I know she's in this as much as I am. That look and the fact she reaches into my boxers, wrapping a hand along my length with exquisite long strokes. I repay the favor, sliding my fingers into her panties, meeting her as she rocks into my hand, our rhythm smooth and perfect.

Our skin is damp and slippery with sweat as we

slide against each other. I trace a line of kisses down her neck, across her shoulder, and down to a perfect breast. The scent of her perfume mixing with the salty essence of her soft flesh is intoxicating. She arches into me, and it feels so natural between us, like we've done this a hundred times and know each other's wants and needs without asking.

"Matt..." Her voice is husky with an undeniable urgency as she says my name. She's close, and I can sense her muscles tighten as she gives in. Her body begins to shudder as she climaxes around my fingers. She pulls in her breath through her teeth, and the sound is so hot I almost join her in finishing right then and there. But then, the look of pure ecstasy growing on her face as she rides her orgasm does me in. She must be able to tell I'm about to lose it because she tightens her grip around me and speeds up her rhythm until I let go and release into her hand.

I fall back beside her, both of us panting and trying to catch our breath. *Holy shit. That just happened.* Once I've recovered somewhat, I reach over to the nightstand and grab the box of tissues for us to clean up with. As I lean over Samantha to return the box, she wraps her hand around the back of my neck and pulls me down into a deep kiss. The perfect way to cap off what transpired between us.

We pull apart, and I press my forehead to hers, content for the first time in what could be years.

This was not what I was expecting when I came here tonight. I thought things would be intense but didn't think we would go this far. Not that I'm complaining. It's a nice surprise. Shit, not *nice*. *Stupendous*.

She grins as our eyes meet. "Hey there."

I can't help but smile back. "Hey yourself, gorgeous."

"That was a surprising turn of events, huh?"

I cock my head at her. "Surprising? I thought I was lured here to be seduced."

"Oh yeah. My diabolical mutual hand job plan. I totally forgot." She laughs, and the sound rings right through me. "I have so many sexy plans that I sometimes lose track of them."

I quirk an eyebrow at her. "Oh really? So, when can I learn the rest of these sexy plans?" I'm intrigued. Her sense of humor, accompanying her security in her sexuality, is tantalizing and refreshing.

She reaches up and pushes the hair falling across my eyes away. Seriousness has taken her over as she studies me, running a finger along my cheekbone, then along my jaw, and down my neck. I close my eyes and have to physically suppress a shiver from her touch.

"I see you, Matt Sturridge," she says.

I gaze back into her eyes, wondering what she's referring to. *What does she think she sees in me?* I'm locked down. People only see what I want them to see, and I've not shown myself to her. At least, I don't *think* I have. *Could she somehow see through my mask?* It would be a first. Maybe I've gotten too comfortable and complacent. Probably how my brother found me after all these years...

"Matt? Are you okay?"

"Yeah. I'm great." I refocus on her face and force a smile. I don't have to try too hard since laying here with her fills me with the closest thing to happiness I've felt in a long time. "So, what do you think you see when you say you 'see me?'" I'm curious what her answer is going to be. Kind of a presumptuous thing to say to someone, but then she isn't one to mince words.

"I don't know what it is." A crease forms between her brows, her fingers running through my hair; the gentleness of her touch is mesmerizing. "A combination of things, I think. There's a lot of pain there. I do know that. And for some reason...fear. But I don't know why you'd be afraid of anything."

I lower the blinds on my emotions. Shut myself right the fuck down. She is way too insightful, and I don't understand how she could observe all that. She's nailed it but fuck if I'm going to let her know. Somewhere in the last couple of days, I've let my guard down and didn't even fucking know. That was all she needed to access inside my head, though.

"Everyone has something painful in their past,

don't they?" I deflect, ignoring the fear portion of her mind-reading. "Nobody's life is perfect. Some people hide their pain better than others." I instinctively pull away from her and grab my jeans off the floor and start to get dressed. Not in an obvious rush, but a signal the conversation should stop there.

"I didn't say anyone was perfect or didn't have pain." She sits up and kneels on the bed, grabbing her tank top and pulling it over her head, her frown deepening. "I just said you're trying to hide yours, but I see it. You don't have to hide with me." Frustration grows in her tone and kind of starts to piss me off. *Who the fuck does she think she is? My therapist?* Thinking she knows the real me after only a few days... *bullshit.*

I pull my shirt over my head and slide into my shoes, ready to make my escape. This evening has taken a turn, and not in a good direction. "I don't have to hide anything because I have nothing to hide," I lie. My voice is clipped as I try to contain my growing anger. I don't know how to dodge this, especially after what just happened between us. *How rude will it be for me to jet out of here as if nothing happened?* Extremely rude, that's how much. *But what the fuck am I supposed to do?* She's crossing lines in the sand I drew around myself years ago. I can't let her any closer than she now is.

"Why are you getting so upset?" She's flustered

and fumbling with the button of her shorts. Part of me wants to reach out and help her, but I also want to take the opportunity to run the fuck out of here while she's busy. *What a dick move that would be.*

"You're presuming to know me in a couple of days. You're playing the oldest trick in the book, Samantha." *Here comes the asshole.* "Trying to move in close to a musician by planting a fake connection with them. '*You see me.*' Give me a fucking break." The demons inside of me cheer at my cruelty. And it *is* cruel. And I *know* it but say it anyway.

Boom. Hit the target. The hurt that overtakes her is visceral, and it takes everything in my being not to grab her and apologize. I can't believe how much this night got twisted and how quickly it happened.

"Get out."

I don't move. Even though this is precisely what I now want to happen, I can't bring myself to leave. My mind races, trying to piece everything together. *I am doing the right thing, aren't I?* It would be too dangerous for her to be too close to me. This is for her, not because I'm actually an asshole. *Right.*

"Samantha..." *I don't know why I'm speaking. I want to leave as much as she wants me to, don't I? Then why did you just do what you did with her?*

"I am not your fucking groupie, Matt Sturridge. Mr. Big Shot Drummer of Indigo King. Leave my room and never come near me again unless I have to be around you for my film. But that will be *my* choice. *Not* yours."

I stare at her for a minute, taking everything in; everything she's saying, everything she's doing. I know I'm going to regret this because I already do. I nod at her, my eyes dead, and turn and leave the room without a single glance back.

I'm making this bed, and I'll need to lie in it. I've probably ruined the best thing to ever happen to me, but I can't risk it. I don't know why I thought I could come here and be with her but not get close to her. That's on me. I thought I had better control than this.

I don't know what the fuck my brother is up to, but knowing him, it's not going to be good. It will likely be downright evil, just like his soul. And I need to face that alone. *Completely* alone.

fifteen

INSENSITIVE

SAMANTHA

I should have known better than to think starting something with Matt was a good idea. To begin with, our relationship was volatile and unpredictable, so I don't understand why I pursued him. I thought I saw some sort of vulnerability in him calling to something inside me. Something that wanted to care about him and protect him from whatever haunts him. *Why would I feel so protective of him?* It's so not like me. I'm a very independent person and have never been considered anything resembling nurturing. Not that I'm a bitch, I'm actually very affectionate. Something about Matt Sturridge makes me want to hold and console him. And maybe while I'm holding him, strangle him... It's the strangest sensation.

It's also a completely moot point now. Anything having to do with him is now past tense. For him to insinuate I'm some sort of groupie is the most offensive thing anyone has ever said to me. And I've had some mean things said to me throughout my life. Okay, maybe it wasn't the worst, but the timing felt like it. We had spent a special time together, and I thought we connected more than physically. *How could I be so wrong?* I've never been so wrong about someone before. He didn't give off the vibes of being a stereotypical rock star, so for him to act like one threw me.

All I did was try to connect with him, let him know he was safe with me, and everything blew up in my face. *Did I touch a nerve somehow?* I can't imagine what I said that would make him react so severely. Maybe I don't know him like I thought I did. It's entirely possible. Perhaps he *is* an asshole.

My phone buzzes as I'm ruminating on the disaster that just unfolded. I'm tempted to ignore the alert in case Matt is suddenly remorseful for what happened, but I figure I should see who it is. It's a text from Sarah. Apparently, Indigo King called an emergency band meeting, and she wants to get together for a drink in the hotel bar since she's free. Considering I'm probably the subject of their urgent meeting, a drink sounds exactly like what the doctor ordered. *And I also just started calling myself doctor.*

I freshen up, change clothes, and throw my hair into a messy bun. I was going for a real bun, but it turned out messy, so it's staying that way. I can still only do so much with this fucking cast on my wrist. As I look at myself in the vanity mirror, all I can do is sigh. The emotions wrung out of me today have left their prints on my face. Sarah will know something is wrong as soon as she sees me. She's as intuitive as I am, but I don't know what I'm going to tell her. I barely know what happened myself.

When I get there, Sarah's at the bar, looking calm, tanned, and not like a musician about to start on her first huge summer tour. She catches me coming in and stands to give me a hug.

"So, how's life with that bum wrist of yours? Are you able to function okay?" Leave it to her to be concerned about me first and foremost.

I glance down at my cast and glare, something I do a lot. It reminds me of Matt. "I'm getting by, I guess."

She frowns, her features shifting from calm to concerned. "You sound angry. Did something happen?"

I didn't mean my words to come across as so heated, but I can't help it either. I glance around to make sure we're not in earshot of anyone. It's still early, so the bar hasn't filled up yet. Most of the crew are still either at the amphitheater or coming back from there now.

"Remember how I was asking you about Matt the other day?" I need to decide how to frame this discussion, and it's not going to be easy.

"Sure. We basically figured out nobody knows him that well." Sarah chuckles.

"Well, I thought I was getting to know him...then we *really* got to know each other this evening, but now I'm back to not knowing him at all. And he's an asshole. I have a bad feeling the 'emergency' band meeting is about me, and the documentary too."

"Wow. *Really* got to know each other, huh?" She pulls a sly grin but turns serious. "That's so unlike him. At least, the him I know, which we've established, isn't much at all. Shit. So, what happened between you two that you think the meeting is about you?"

I order a drink and give her a rundown of the evening's events, skipping over details best not shared, even with friends. She gets the gist of what happened. "I have interviews scheduled with them tomorrow, and now I don't know if he will participate at all. It won't be a complete story without him. I don't know what to do."

"Well, that would be too dickish, even for Matt. I can't picture him being that rude."

"He's already been rude..." I can still picture how

blank his eyes were before he left. He was so cold. "So I wouldn't put it past him to take things to the next level."

"Yeah, but that would impact your ability to do your job. No way Matt would do that to anyone. That much I do know." She reaches over and puts a warm hand on my arm. "I don't think you need to worry. Truly. As much as he is an asshole now, he isn't a monster."

I search her eyes, trying to find the truth in what she says. I want so badly to believe her. I want to think Matt would be a better person than he showed himself to be earlier this evening, but I don't know if I can. The whole situation feels wrong somehow. Like the frame of the picture is there but out of focus. I have to trust Sarah believes what she's saying. She has been on the road with them for a couple of months now, so she has been near him but admitted she doesn't know him. This is all becoming such a headache. I need to forget about pursuing any relationship with him and focus on my damn job. *If* I still have one.

"I hope you're right. Matt issues aside, I'm excited about this job, and I'd hate for what happened to fuck that up somehow. Pretty unprofessional of me to be in this situation."

"Oh, whatever. That's bullshit, and you know it. Sparks have been bouncing off you guys since you met. Something was bound to happen." Her mischievous smile is back. "Who knew it would go so far, so fast?"

"Ha. Ha. You're so funny." I glower at her, not amused.

"We should ask Ryan what the meeting was about." A sparkle takes over her eyes as she looks over my shoulder.

"What do you-"

I don't finish what I was saying because Ryan comes up and pulls Sarah into a hug and deep kiss. Like they haven't seen each other in years. *Ugh.* Nothing like sitting next to PDA when you're the third wheel.

"Sorry," Ryan says to me, finally releasing Sarah and noticing me. Impressive, he sees anyone else in the world, let alone the room with how in love he obviously is with her. It's both gross and fucking adorable.

I shrug in response. I don't trust myself to say anything; I'm so nervous to find out what their meeting was about. It didn't last long. *But how long would Matt need to blow up the world? He only took a minute to blow up mine.*

"So, how did the meeting go?" Sarah asks, waiving down the bartender.

Ryan orders a club soda, then turns and narrows his eyes at me, but a grin grows. "What did you do to Matt?"

"What?" I can't believe this. *Does he think I did*

something to Matt? More like the other way around. "*I* didn't do anything! He's the one being an asshole here."

Ryan puts his hands up, not wanting to be the object of my anger. "I'm just saying, I've never seen him so riled up before. It was almost funny."

"Well, it's not funny, Ryan," she scolds, giving me a sympathetic glance. "He hurt Sam's feelings tonight. That's not cool. What did he say?"

"Oh shit, I'm sorry. Jude and I just thought this was a lighthearted spat or something. We didn't take him seriously." The remorse on his face is genuine. He didn't realize the gravity of the situation. "He went on a rant about how he wouldn't do the documentary, and nobody could force him. Blah, blah, blah. We told him we could force him since we signed contracts to participate, and he stormed off, swearing. The shortest band meeting in the entire history of the music industry. It could have been a text."

I sigh inwardly with relief that nothing bad will come of the meeting. Still, it hurts again that Matt would go to such lengths to have nothing to do with me.

"So he'll be at the interviews tomorrow?" They may be contracted to participate, but that doesn't mean Matt will cooperate. Even if he does show up, who knows what he'll be like.

"He will definitely be there," Ryan nods to me. "I will make sure of it myself. You have my word."

"Thanks, Ryan." Now I don't know if I want Matt there. If he's going to be forced to deal with me and the documentary now, it'll be shitty content. I can't worry about the content yet. I need him to show up first. I'll deal with emotions later.

sixteen

ONE STEP CLOSER

MATT

As if last night wasn't bad enough, now I need to face Samantha with a fucking audience. And not just face her, but answer questions. *That won't be awkward at all.* My run this morning did absolutely nothing to calm me down. Something, unfortunately, becoming the norm, and I do not like the new trend. If I don't have outlets for my anxiety outside of smacking the shit out of my drums, I don't know what that will look like. That could turn out very badly for me and the people around me.

After my useless run, I shower and head out to the buses where the interview is supposed to take place. All of our group interviews will be by the buses, and their individual ones will be inside the current venue or on the bus traveling. That's the plan anyway. I hope they don't expect me to do the

111

individual interview because that is not happening. I'll repeat myself to Vanessa as many times as I have to. *However, now that my asshole brother Jax has somehow tracked me down, do I need to bother with the secrecy shit anymore?* I guess I'll find out in Denver in two days.

When I arrive at the bus parking area, everyone is already there, waiting for me apparently. *Fanfuck-ingtastic.* I'm fucking late too.

"Thanks for joining us, Matt." Ryan smiles, arms wide open in greeting as he and Jude lounge in their lawn chairs. I don't miss the sarcasm in his voice.

"Whatever," I mutter as I reach into the bus's cargo area for my own chair. I unfold it and sit next to Jude, who gives me a wicked side-eye. We must be recording, or he would have chimed in with his own snarky remark.

Samantha and Vanessa have their heads together, looking at a laptop screen. Samantha looks amazing; her hair is pulled up in some kind of twist, and her ripped t-shirt slides off a shoulder, exposing perfect skin. Her exposed collarbone reminds me of what her skin tasted like last night. *And my mind has gone completely off the rails. Fuck.*

The women stop their conversation, and Samantha glances at me. Her poker face is fucking terrible. She's obviously still hurt from last night, and the invisible icepick in my chest twists a little deeper.

"Matt, you need to be miked up." She deftly avoids meeting my eyes as she reaches into her equipment case for the microphone and transmitter I'm supposed to wear. Vanessa slinks off back to the hotel without a word. I'm tempted to slink off after her.

I glance around at the other two, and Jude smiles as he clips and unclips the mic attached to his t-shirt collar. He also throws in an eyebrow waggle for good measure. I pull myself out of my chair and over to Samantha, eager to finish this.

"Do you have any adhesive or latex allergies?" She still won't meet my eyes, and she's as uncomfortable about this as I am.

"No."

"Lift your shirt up."

I hesitate, and I don't know why. She fucking saw me basically naked last night, and I can't lift a shirt for her now?

Her eyes reluctantly travel up to meet mine, and her jaw is clenched. She gives me a '*just fucking do it*' look, and I comply, lifting my shirt up for her to tape the mic down. Her hands shake slightly as she clumsily tapes the wires to my skin, clips the mic to my t-shirt collar, and checks the receiver. "Say something."

"What would you like me to say?"

"Good enough." She sets some levels on the transmitter and then shoves it into the back pocket of my jeans, not being gentle at all. I can see Ryan and Jude's eyebrows go up from the corner of my eye as she manhandles me. She's not being unprofessional, but she's not being particularly careful either.

Being near her and smelling her shampoo, her touching my chest throws me into a tailspin. I do my best to keep my face blank of any emotion, but it's so fucking hard. *How can one woman I barely know have such an effect on me? If 'barely' meant 'naked,' we'd be closer to the truth...*

"You can take your seat."

I realize I was just watching her, for God only knows how long. Jude and Ryan snicker behind me, but I ignore them and take my seat without a word. If I want this to be over, I need to stop standing around ogling the damned director.

Samantha adjusts the camera, takes her own seat, and pulls her laptop back open. She leans into the screen, squinting her eyes, and I'm reminded that I broke her glasses the other day when I ran into her. I shift in my chair, nauseous all of a sudden. Guilt is not something I handle well. While I may be a closed-off person, I'm honest and try to do the right thing if I can. The number of things I have guilt for when it comes to Samantha compounds every day. I can't do anything right when it comes to her.

"Okay, so to start, how about you guys tell me a little bit about what you're looking forward to on this summer tour with Incendiary Ink. Any expectations? Goals?"

"To have a fucking great time," Jude says, not waiting for anyone to take turns. Leave it to him to jump headfirst into the shallow end with a cliché rock 'n roll answer. Ryan and I both furrow our brows and shake our heads at him. "What?" he asks us both. "That is the point of a concert, right? To have a fucking blast?"

I glare at him, but Ryan speaks up. "Of course, having a good time is a goal, but speaking for myself," he puts a hand to his chest, "I want our music out to more people. The new album fucking rocks and I want everybody to hear it."

"Yeah, yeah," Jude laughs. "But we can have a fucking blast while we do that, right?" Ryan rolls his eyes. "Fucking hell, Jude. You're impossible."

"How about you, Matt? What are you looking forward to?" Samantha's eyes are doing that thing where they bore straight into my soul, seeing everything I don't want her to see.

I can sense Ryan and Jude staring at me, and my palms begin to sweat, and the nausea increases, my stomach churning and bitter. *What the fuck dude? Chill out.* "Same as them," I finally sputter out, my voice sounding strange to my ears. Now I'm lightheaded. I've felt like this before. It's been years, but this is all too familiar.

"Dude, you're turning green." Jude sounds concerned for a change.

"Yeah, are you okay?" Samantha sits up, looking around for something. She puts her laptop down, goes over to a cooler with bottles of water in it that I hadn't noticed, and grabs one to give me. "Here. Drink some of this."

I take the bottle from her, our fingers brushing, and I'm not going to make it. I grab the water but run around to the other side of the bus and dry heave since I haven't eaten anything yet today. I came here straight after my run, so all I've had is water. "Fuck." I'm leaning with one hand on the bus to keep me steady. My vision is starting to tunnel, so I sit on the ground, leaning back against the bus, trying to take some solace in its shade.

I glance up and see all three of them standing at the front of the bus with worry taking them over. Samantha's the only one that comes near me, placing the back of her cool hand on my forehead and then her palm on my cheek.

"You don't have a fever, but you're sweating. Have you eaten today? Could it be food poisoning?" There's a crease between her brows, but her palm hasn't left my face. I want to lean into it and let her take this all away, but I know I can't. I also know how I've treated her is causing this. Not food.

"It's not food poisoning." The absoluteness of my words surprises her. *And why wouldn't it?*

"Well, what is it then?" She withdraws her hand, and the absence of her cool touch immediately hits me. It makes my entire body shiver.

"I'll be fine. I need a minute." My tone is harsh, but I don't care. I turn away and open the water bottle, taking a small sip, then a longer one, and continuing until I'm chugging it. Nobody's moved. "I said give me a fucking minute!"

Samantha flinches at my shouting but backs up and joins Ryan and Jude as they walk away without saying anything. Nausea begins to crest all over again, but I focus on my breathing like I've trained myself to do in this situation. This is fucking stress manifesting itself physically in my body since I don't deal with it fucking mentally. A full-blown panic attack. I've been here before, but all of my previous coping methods aren't working, and I don't know what's different this time. That fact is stressing me out even more and throwing me into a fucking vicious circle. *Shit, I'm on a god-damned spinning circus carousel full of clowns that won't stop at this point.*

After several long minutes of deep breathing, and with my shit temporarily together, I head back to the other side of the bus. My goal now is to just get this interview over with, so I can get away from Samantha. Seeing her hurt by my actions is giving me too much guilt. I can't handle it. I take my seat as everyone eyes me warily.

"If you're gonna spew, spew into this," Jude

holds an imaginary cup out to me. His pop culture references are so fucking random. I don't understand him sometimes.

I swat at his hand, forcing myself to smile. "Get the fuck outta here with that," I say, in my best Soprano's voice. If anything lightens the mood and deflects from seriousness, its impersonation swaps with Jude.

"Seriously, though," Samantha's voice is small but cuts through. "Are you going to be okay?" She's trying to smile along with us but is still hesitant to join in. Again, she sees right through me.

"I'll be fine." I wave her off like nothing ever happened, but my stomach clenches.

"So, I'd like to change my earlier answer." Jude is raising his hand like he's in class or something. She nods at him to go on. "My goal this tour is to finish an interview without Matt dry-heaving next to the bus." He reaches over and pats the top of my head lightly. "Can we do that, buddy?"

I give him the dirtiest scowl I can, which probably isn't very menacing. "Fuck you."

"Are you volunteering?" he smirks. It's become a running joke with the three of us to say that in response to a 'fuck you.' It definitely takes the fun out of saying it but does take the edge off if said in genuine anger. I flip him off and turn my attention back to Samantha, who is watching us like she wishes she had a bowl of popcorn to watch the show. I can't help but smile at her; she's so entertained.

She catches my smile, and her mood darkens. Her smile falters and fades as she turns away. I deserve that. I've earned every bit of hatred she has for me. Just because I have guilt about how I've treated her doesn't make anything I've done okay. *It's not. It's far from okay.*

seventeen

32 FLAVORS

SAMANTHA

Thank goodness we make it through the rest of the group chat without anybody being sick. I conduct Ryan and Jude's first individual interviews before wrapping for the day. They sure are fun to hang around, and I think I took some fantastic footage of them joking around. Jude's impressions alone should make the documentary a winner.

Vanessa tries her best to make Matt participate via text, but I don't press the issue. He didn't look well today, and I told her I'd do his interview another time, so he could rest. He was so adamant that it wasn't food poisoning despite looking seriously ill, and he bounced back so fast for the group interview like nothing happened. His behavior's been so strange, I don't know what to make of him. I honestly don't. Nothing he does makes sense to me anymore. When I think I'm finally getting a handle on him, he pivots and slips away. I need to forget him and move on. *It was a terrific hookup and nothing more.* I know that's a total lie, but maybe if I keep saying it, I'll believe it.

When I'm done for the day, I decide to go for my first run since the accident. I have time to kill and nothing else to do. I don't want to stay holed up in my room staring at the walls, so I throw on some shorts and head outside to warm up.

I'm retying a shoe on a concrete bench along the side of the hotel when Matt comes out of the entrance, looking like he has the same idea I do. *Shit.* I was hoping to do this while avoiding him. I attempt to hurry my shoelace tying but end up making a mess. As I'm hurriedly trying to untie the knots I made, he approaches me. *Damn. Why does he have to be so hot in those running shorts?* It's not fair that he's such a fucking asshole.

"Going for a run?" he asks.

"Captain Obvious, you're not in uniform today." If he's going to ask a stupid question, I will give him the most sarcastic answer I can come up with. I fight fair.

"Casual Fridays are spreading through the weekend now." He quirks his lips into a smile, but it's totally forced.

I smirk at him and finish with my shoelace, getting one last stretch in. *What is with him?* He's so hot and cold with me, which leaves me lukewarm with him. I don't know why he's even talking to me, and I don't want to deal with him now. Not only that, I know he went for a run this morning before our interview, *so what is he doing, going for another run?* No wonder he's sick. He's running himself ragged.

"See ya," I say over my shoulder as I put my earbuds in and run in the opposite direction. I notice that he looked a little stunned that I ran away from him. As if he expected me to stay and hold a conversation with him or something. How arrogant. I'm not into whatever game he's playing. He is going through something; I can tell that much. But if he won't let anyone help him, there isn't much I can do. I already made myself vulnerable with him and got my ass burned because of it. I'm not dumb enough to do it again. Fool me once...

How many times has he fooled me now? I'm losing count. Something still tugs at my chest when I think about him, though, no matter how much he hurt me. And I don't know if I want to be the one to fix him. *Shit, I need to fix myself first before I can do that for someone else.*

I throw myself into my run and try to clear my head of Matt Sturridge, forcing my muscles to push their limits as I go. My playlist of running songs accompanies my mood perfectly with lots of heavy guitars and driving beats. By the time I get back to the hotel, the sun is starting to set, and I've worked up a thorough sweat.

I'm invigorated instead of tired, however, and after a shower, I head down to the restaurant to meet Vanessa for a quick dinner. Only a few women on the tour aren't paired up with someone else, so we tend to gravitate toward each other for things like meals. Vanessa is fun company too, and she has an excellent knowledge of the music industry. I learn a lot every time we get together.

Spotting her at a table, I give her a quick wave and head over. She looks sharp, even in jeans; she is always so put together, it makes me feel like a degenerate sitting across from her. She pulls it off by exchanging sneakers like mine with high heels, and a pretty blouse for my band t-shirt. If I cared what people thought of me or my appearance, I'd be in trouble around her.

After we order and make small talk as we wait, Matt comes into the restaurant and talks to the cashier. He must be here to pick up food. Vanessa follows my stare and sees who's caught my attention.

"What's up with you two?"

"Absolutely nothing." My voice comes out flatter than I intended, and she cocks her head at me curiously.

"Do you want there to be something?"

I consider evading her question with a deflection

but decide to be honest. "I thought I did. But he's too difficult to get to know."

"That is true. Matt is an enigma."

I shift my gaze back to studying him as he waits for his food. He hasn't noticed us yet. Or, if he did, he's ignoring us, which is fine with me. I do like looking at him; he's a fine-looking man. In that, there is no doubt.

"Do you know anything about his past?" Surely Vanessa must know Matt as well as, if not better, than most.

"How do you mean?" She takes a sip of her wine and her brows crease.

"I don't know. What's his story? Does he even have a story? Family? Things like that."

"I'm sure that man holds several anthologies in his head full of stories, but he's not telling them to anyone. As for family, no. I don't think he has any family. At least none that he's ever mentioned. I think he'd have said something about someone by now."

I examine Matt while he scrolls on his phone. He's tall and muscular, but not too much so. Just enough to let you know he's strong. He's funny, damned good in bed, and usually a good guy. But the secrets he's harboring are eating him alive from the inside out. Without those secrets, he would be almost perfect. Almost, because there is no such thing.

"I don't know. Matt's an expert at keeping things to himself. For all we know, he could be hiding a husband and kids in Des Moines."

"True of anyone, really. If someone is determined to keep things from you, there isn't a lot you can do about it." She gives me a knowing smile and nods.

Matt's food arrives, and he grabs the bag, turning to the exit. He catches me watching him and halts for a second, our eyes meeting. Electricity jolts through me from the once-over he gives me, and I have to shift my eyes away. Out of the corner of my eye, I can see he stays still for a little longer but then leaves. I glance up as he exits without looking back.

"You have it in for him, don't you?" Vanessa smiles to herself.

"What? No." I'm sure the truth of it is all over my face, but I need to try to stop feeling anything for him.

"That flush traveling up your neck and into your cheeks tells me otherwise, Missy."

I cover my face with my hands, hiding my shame with a laugh. "There's a reason I don't play poker."

"I think that's refreshing, especially in this business. I talk to so many fake people daily; it's nice to talk to someone who can be nothing but honest, let me tell you."

"Well, lately, my honesty has only gotten me in

trouble." I finish off my wine and slump back in my chair, dejected.

"Yeah, but you're a fun kind of trouble." She flashes a big grin. She's so fucking optimistic about life; it's annoyingly endearing. "Don't let it drag you down." She checks her watch and gives me a mysterious look. "Let's go hit the bar for a few. It's still early, and this is our last night before we start this crazy rodeo."

"Let's do it." After the last few days, I could use a stiff drink.

eighteen

NOT STRONG ENOUGH

MATT

I take my time eating my dinner, so I can sit alone with my thoughts for a minute. Everything's been *go, go, go* for months now, and I haven't had time to seriously reflect on the last few years that have led me to this point. Joining a famous rock band was never in my plans. I was perfectly happy playing LA dives, cycling through bands that went nowhere like clockwork. I joined Indigo King because moving around the country was idyllic for me. If you're someone who doesn't want to be found, not having a home address is perfect. I keep a P.O. box and share Jude's apartment. Even though the lease is under his name, I have the run of the house since he's always at some chick's place. Being in my situation, the arrangement is ideal.

My situation. Fuck. Today's panic attack makes

me face shit I don't want to face. Shit I thought I buried years ago. Jax threatening a reunion is causing all this. That isn't entirely true, though. This has been coming on for months. The Jax thing is a new wrinkle. Well, an old wrinkle bent on resurfacing.

I had a flash of a thought of talking to Samantha about it but dismissed it just as quickly as it came. Maybe I should revisit that thought. Jax found me, and I'm in a no-win situation. I can't quit the band now. I thought I could outrun the past, but that fucker is quick. Samantha said she saw my pain and fear, and that alone scared the shit out of me. I'm smart enough to at least admit that much to myself. She's too intuitive for her own fucking good.

But did she actually see it? What I hide from everyone, even sometimes myself? As my sergeant used to say, "Ignoring the problem doesn't make it go away. No matter how strong your ignorance."

And now, thoughts of my time in the military flood in. Shit. The Marines were initially a means to an end, a way for me to run away from Jax, but it turned into so much more. It is where I learned how to be a person, be strong both physically and mentally, and what loyalty really means. Something Jax would know nothing about.

Jax. Jax. Jax. Everything keeps coming back to him and his impending threats, whatever the fuck they are. Whenever I think about what he could be planning for Denver, I break out in a cold sweat. *Does he want money?* Everything is always about money with him. *Or is it now something more than that?* I already gave him my soul when I was a kid; I don't have much left to give him.

A deep sigh pulls its way in and out of my chest but doesn't calm me. I have a feeling I'm going to be wound up tight the rest of the night unless I can somehow chill myself out. I clean up the trash from my dinner and try watching some TV, but nothing worth watching is on. I need activity. I need atmospheric noise of some kind.

I grab my phone and take the elevator down to the hotel lobby. As I exit and start heading toward the bar, two teenage girls sitting on a couple of the lobby couches jump up and run directly at me.

"Oh my god! Matt Sturridge!!!" One of them shrieks, waving an Indigo King record and marker at me.

Fuck.

"Go next to him. I'll take your picture," the other one instructs, flapping her hands around and bouncing on her tip-toes.

I stand frozen, not sure what the fuck is happening. I search the area for our security detail, and not a single person from security is in sight. *What the fuck?*

The shrieker comes up to me, thrusting the record and marker at my chest. "Oh my god, oh my god, oh my god. I love you. Can you sign this for me? I love you. Pleeeeeease? I love you. Oh my god."

I grab the items thrust at me before I drop them, still glancing around for security. Still, nobody. *Fuck. What if this were Jax...*

"Put your arm around him, and I'll take a picture." The one with the phone says. Neither of these girls can be old enough to drink. I feel like they're breaking a curfew or something, or maybe I should call their parents.

The one next to me puts her arm around me and squeezes way too tightly. I think I smiled, but fuck if I know. I'm signing the album when someone from security finally comes by. I make friendly with the fans for a second but indicate for the security guy to wait nearby.

"Thanks a lot, ladies. Have fun at the show tomorrow night." I slide away from them as smoothly as possible and glare daggers at security to follow me.

When we find a reasonably quiet corner, he clears his throat roughly, "Mr. Sturridge, I am so sorry about that. We were in the middle of a shift change, and those two somehow slipped in..."

"A fucking shift change? I hired you guys to be discreet, not completely fucking invisible." After Jax's voicemail, I thought it would be wise to hire additional security. Only the tour's main security detail was told about it, so they could coordinate.

Even the rest of the band and Vanessa don't know. They'd only ask questions I don't want to answer. Then more questions about how I know a security company and why I hired them would come up, and I don't want to answer that shit right now either.

"Believe me, Mr. Sturridge, no one is more upset about this than I am." And I'll give it to him; he *does* look pretty pissed. It doesn't ease my mind that he's upset, though.

"Awesome. I'm glad you're pissed. But I highly doubt you're more pissed than I am. Now, what are you going to do about it?"

"Make sure it doesn't happen again, sir." He swallows hard, and I can tell he's almost sweating. Something about how he just answered makes me think he must be ex-military too. Taylor, my Marine buddy whose security company I hired, did say he was going to try to hire ex-military when he could.

"Let's break this down, Barney style." I have not said those words in years, but this guy knows what the fuck I'm talking about. We're going over this slowly and in baby steps, in a way that a child could understand, so this fuckwad gets the importance of this. He nods at me, definitely sweating now. I'm not being an asshole. He needs to know this isn't a game. "I don't care who doesn't get to go home, or who needs a cup of coffee, or who needs to take a fucking piss; access points are never, *ever*, left unattended. Understood?"

"Yes, sir." He straightens, never breaking my gaze. "This was completely *unsat*. It won't happen again."

I draw a slow circle in the air, indicating the hotel building. "This is a sanctuary. Wherever we are is Sanctum Sanctorum. Zero breach policy from now on. Got it?"

"Yes, sir." His gaze shifts to the front doors, where a guard intercepts another group of people trying to get in.

Fuck. I guess the word must have leaked that all of us are here. I sigh inwardly and nod my head for him to go and help at the door. *Jesus Christ.* I send a quick text to Taylor to ensure this doesn't happen again.

I make my way to the bar, trying to shake off the last few intense minutes. When I arrive, I discover that just about everyone on the fucking crew has the same idea I do. This is our last night before the tour starts in earnest, and people are obviously anxious to let loose one last time. I spot Ryan and Sarah at the bar, a small group surrounding them as always, and Jude against the wall, talking to his flavor of the week. That'll be interesting if she's one of the crew. He won't be able to escape her when we leave town like he usually does. I wonder if he's considered that yet. Well, that's his problem. I've got my own.

Incendiary Ink's music blasts through the music system at a volume bordering on uncomfortably loud for the relatively small space. Anyone speaking is either yelling over the music or bending their heads together to be heard.

I get the bartender's attention and order a beer. While I wait, I scan the crowd for anyone else I might know. My eyes land on Vanessa's booth, where she's in an intense animated conversation with Incendiary Ink's manager, Josh something-or-other. Next to him is Samantha, as beautiful as ever, sandwiched between Josh and a guy from their crew I vaguely recognize. She's bored to tears by whatever Crew Guy is saying. He's got his arm draped over the back of the booth, and while he doesn't touch her, something about the proximity of his hand to her back makes a muscle in my jaw twitch. I grab my beer, tip the bartender, and can't stop my feet from directing me toward their table.

Vanessa breaks from her conversation with Josh and yells, "Matt, you're out and about in the land of the living! How are you?"

My jaw is still clenched, and I can't unhinge it. I also can't help but give Crew Guy a nasty glare, making sure I include his arm so close to Samantha, so he notices. He does and slides his arm back to his side. Where it'll be safe.

"Yeah, I figured it's the last night of freedom, may as well take advantage of it," I yell back, still not breaking my gaze from Crew Guy, though he's now shifted away from Samantha in the booth. He almost looks like he's going to bolt out of his seat any second, so I keep my gaze steady, challenging him to stay where he is at his own peril.

"I… think I see my…," he stutters and doesn't finish his sentence as he slides out of the booth. "I'll catch you later."

"See you, dude," I say, patting him on the back more heavily than necessary and taking his seat. When I glance around, Vanessa and Josh resume their conversation, and Samantha is shooting fire at me with her eyes.

She leans in as if to kiss me but then turns her head to speak into my ear. "Can I talk to you?" Her polite tone does not match her expression, but her breath on my skin sends shivers through me.

"Suuuuure." My lips brush her ear, and the shivers intensify.

"Somewhere… else, maybe?"

nineteen

SOMEONE YOU LOVED

SAMANTHA

"What the fuck was that?" I can't believe him. I can't believe he could be so rude.

"What are you talking about?" The guilt sinking into his face lets me know that he's fully aware of what he just did and what I'm talking about, but he's still going to make me spell it out for him.

We're in the darkened, empty hallway by the bar restrooms, where it's a little quieter than the main bar, but not much more. We have to stand close to each other to hear ourselves. He's leaning down toward me so close I need to tilt my head to face him. It's an intimate position, and I can't help but think of last night with him as I stare into his stormy green eyes. *Was it just last night?* Our days are so jam-packed; I swear it was at least a week ago. *Jesus.*

I roll my eyes at him, sigh, and cross my arms

over my chest, careful of my cast. This at least puts a barrier between us. "You. Know. What." I'm not putting up with his bullshit anymore. I've had it with his back and forth games.

"What?" He shoves his hands into the pockets of his jeans, shrugging his shoulders, almost contrite. "That dude was literally leering at you like you were dinner. That shit can't stand."

I throw my head back in shock, and anger flares through me. "Excuse me?" I can't believe he has the gall to be jealous after the way he treated me last night. "Even if he was, which is debatable, what the fuck is it to you? It's got nothing to do with you and is none of your fucking business, Matt."

He jerks back as if I slapped him with my words, and his reaction confuses the shit out of me. *Why would he ever think he's entitled to be jealous over me?*

"I can still look out for you..." The torment behind his eyes as he says this rips something inside of me, but memories of what he said to me last night push their way to the front of my mind.

"Oh, wow. Do you look out so closely for all of your groupies? Or am I getting special treatment?"

"Sam..."

"No. *You* do *not* get to call me Sam." My throat tightens, and I can sense the threat of tears rising. I *hate* that I cry when I'm mad. *I fucking hate it.* "You don't have that privilege. And I told you last night not to come near me unless we were working. Well, we are not working, so stay the fuck away from me." I turn to leave, but he grabs my arm and turns me to him. The touch of his hand sliding on my skin makes the hair on the back of my neck stand on end.

"Samantha. I did not mean to suggest that you were a groupie last night..."

"Really? Because I allegedly "played the oldest trick" in the good old groupie handbook, if I remember correctly. That's way more than a suggestion. And not one I appreciate." He's still holding my arm, and I yank it away from him. I can't let him weasel his way into my good graces with his electrifying touch or smooth words.

"I said the wrong thing last night. I'm sorry for that." He does appear remorseful, but we've been here before. I can't keep doing this dance with him.

"What about the "fake connection" that I supposedly planted? Are you sorry you said that little gem too?"

His eyes fall away from mine to the floor, and he nods. "I am, actually. I'm very sorry for everything I said last night."

Did he just apologize to me? What is up with him? What is he playing at? I throw my hands up, "Dude. I did not buy a ticket for this roller coaster." I start backing away from him slowly. "I thought we connected, but I was obviously wrong. My bad. Let's move on. Some harm, but no foul. Okay?"

I don't wait for him to respond and head back to

the bar and then the lobby. On my way to the elevators, there's a bustle of a crowd outside. Several small groups mill about, either wearing or carrying Incendiary Ink or Indigo King swag. There are a few Sarah Lawrence fans in the bunch, which makes me smile to myself, glad my friend is represented.

"Tour pass?" A man from security standing in front of the elevators asks.

"Excuse me? I'm going up to my room for the night, thanks." I try to reach past him to push the Up button, but he blocks my way. *What the hell?* Nobody told me about a new security protocol.

"Sorry, ma'am. Only passes allowed upstairs."

"When did this change? I don't have my pass on me. It's up in my room." I am not in the mood for something else to go wrong on this tour. First no room, and now I can't get to the one I did snag. I reach in the back pocket of my jeans and fish out my hotel room key card. "See? Room key."

"Again, sorry, ma'am. I'll need to see a tour pass..."

"She's okay to go up." Matt's voice comes from behind me, and I turn to watch him flash his tour pass to the guard.

"Yes, sir." He steps aside and pushes the Up button for us.

"You knew about this?" I ask Matt. Reluctant to talk to him, but curious how he thought to carry his pass with him. *He's in one of the fucking bands, for Christ's sake.*

"Yeah. I knew."

"Well, I bet most people in the bar right now will be spending the night in the lobby. Kinda shitty to spring it on people like this." *Can they do this? Without any notice whatsoever?* It doesn't seem right.

Matt shrugs but then seems remorseful again as if he had anything to do with it. The elevator arrives, and we step on. Before the doors close, the fans outside surge forward, calling Matt's name, trying to get close to the windows. Several security guards step up and hold them back. *Wow.* I guess the tour craziness officially started. *I wish I had my camera. That would have been a great shot to mark the beginning of the tour.*

"You okay?" Matt's voice breaks me out of my mental film directing.

I shake my head a little to lose the documentary cobwebs but don't answer him. I said all I was going to say to him tonight. I'm not beholden to him now just because he got me upstairs. I should have had access anyway. Even though being in this confined box in such close proximity to him raises my pulse to an insane level, I refuse to give in to it.

The elevator jerks to a stop on my floor, and the doors open. Matt calls after me twice as I step out and head to my room. I ignore him.

twenty

THE MORE YOU IGNORE ME, THE
CLOSER I GET

MATT

I wake the next morning before the sun comes up after a shitty night of tossing and turning to an itinerary pushed noisily under my door. I'm a light sleeper anyway, and any kind of noise in the hallway triggers my senses. I roll out of bed and groggily shuffle over to pick it up. Three fucking pages of a long laundry list of press interviews and VIP fan meet and greets bracket our soundcheck and rehearsal in the middle of the afternoon.

The first interview isn't for another few hours yet, so I throw on sweats and head down to the hotel gym to sneak a quick run in. With all of the sitting around we're going to do today, I'm going to need it, and it would be dumb for me to attempt running outside the hotel since our location isn't a secret anymore.

The lobby is empty except for security, so

Samantha's prediction of a bunch of crew having to camp out here proved wrong. I find the gym and use my room card to open the door. The room's bright lights surprise me since I didn't expect anyone to be here this early. And no one is. The gym is empty. The back of my neck prickles, and I don't know why. The room is entirely empty. *Fucking hell.* Jax has me so torqued my paranoid ass is jumping at shadows.

I head to one of the treadmills and throw my earbuds in, playing our setlist as loud as I can stand it. I need it loud to block out my thoughts that run faster than I do. I'm on the third song and starting to work up a sweat with a steep incline when my phone dings with a text message. *It's not even 6 AM, and I'm getting a text?* I slow down to a jog, pick up my phone, and almost trip when I check the screen.

> JAX: Bro. Isn't it way too early to be running?

Instantly, I straddle the tread and yank the safety cord to stop it. There's no way to see me in this room outside of the standard surveillance camera in the upper corner. There isn't a single window in here. *How the fuck could he know I'm running right now?* At least I know I'm not just being paranoid about Jax. While his text isn't directly threatening, the message is clear: he's got eyes on me somehow. *But how?*

I didn't clock anyone in the lobby except for

security; not even the desk clerk was visible. From what I remember walking down here, none of the groups of people from last night were outside either. That doesn't mean someone in their car in the parking lot couldn't observe my walk through the lobby. *Fuck.*

I send a quick text to Taylor:

> ME: Tay, light up fire watch.

Fire watch is another basic term for guard duty. It's usually boring as fuck, but lighting up a fire watch means reinforcing it with more bodies. Less than a minute later, I receive a thumb's up emoji in response from him. I hate how easily I can fall back into the service lingo after all these years, but don't take too much time to think about it. I need to focus on what the fuck Jax is doing.

More than the question of *how* Jax could know what I'm doing, I need to know *why*. He's got to be going to some fairly long lengths to get anyone close enough to me to find out what I'm doing. Shit, he might be here himself now, and Denver was just a smokescreen. The thought of him being nearby makes my blood run cold. A cursory search of the internet only pulled up a Facebook profile that hasn't been updated in years, and a smattering of court records for petty crimes throughout the South. He's at least consistent in keeping his life of crime.

It's a start, but I need more information. I thought I had more time. I shoot another text to Taylor:

> ME: Need background and status. Jaxon Holloway. Male. 35. Last known Wimberly TX. ASAP.

Again, Taylor responds in the affirmative moments later. I'm cashing in a *lot* of old favors with this, but fuck it. *If not now, when?* My stomach starts to churn, and a bitter taste rises in the back of my throat. I shake it off and head back out to the lobby, keeping to shadows initially to spot if anything is out of the ordinary before going out into the open. I can't believe I'm skulking around the hotel like I'm in some fucking James Bond movie or something. Nothing is out of place, and the people I track seem to belong.

The elevator doors open, and out walks Samantha, dressed like she's about to take off on a run. Sure enough, she's putting in her earbuds and heading to the front hotel doors. *Shit. Why does she have to be a daily runner like me? Can't she run every other day?* I shove myself out of the shadows to catch her attention.

"Samantha! Hey. How's it going?" I jog over to her and stand between her and the doors, blocking her from leaving.

She stops short and glares at me, squinting slightly. She looks like she just rolled out of bed, but she's still fucking gorgeous. If Jax knows so much about me, he might know about my involvement with her, as little as it may be. My concern for her safety outweighs my desire for her at the moment, and I need to somehow keep her in the hotel if I can.

"Move," she says, dismissing me and trying to step around.

I echo her movements, still blocking her way. "I was hoping I'd run into you... I thought we could grab breakfast or something." I rub the back of my neck with both hands, trying to hide the sudden lie.

Her crystal blue eyes study my face so closely that my soul feels laid bare to her again. *What is it with her eyes? Fuck.* She's going to be able to tell I'm lying.

"I'm going for a run." She steps right, then quickly left and around me, actually passing me with a fake. I would be impressed if I wasn't so worried. I have nothing left to stop her from going, so all I can do is follow her.

"I'll go with you."

She peeks back over her shoulder, contempt in her expression and voice. "No, you won't."

"Sure I will," I say, keeping on her heels but scanning the parking lot as we go.

When I bump into her, I finally stop.

"What are you doing? I didn't invite you to run with me, and I don't want you to." She takes off across the parking lot, heading to the street.

I follow behind her but don't completely catch up. "I thought we could hang out," I call. *My god, this is so fucking lame. Hang out? An actor I am not.*

She stops again, but this time I avoid a collision. Pulling out an earbud, she regards me. "What are you doing? I said no. Boundaries, man."

"Fine. I'll just follow you then." I'm not letting her out of my sight out here.

She stares at me for a long moment, taking my measure and studying me. Sighing, she shrugs and resumes her run, not looking back.

After a quarter-mile of following her, I conclude that this is the way to run with her from now on. The view from behind is absolutely extraordinary. At about the half-mile mark, I detect someone running behind me. Glancing back, I catch one of Taylor's guys trailing me. *Jesus. What a sight we must be.*

Our running convoy arrives back at the hotel about an hour later. The parking lot is still clear, and Samantha stops at the concrete bench she uses to stretch out, so I do the same. The guy who followed me keeps his distance, going through his own cooldowns, remaining alert.

Samantha quirks an eyebrow at me before heading inside. "You're an odd bird." She shakes her head and goes into the hotel.

I let out a long breath, relieved that the run at least went without incident. I nod at the guy who followed me in appreciation for the escort, and he gives a barely perceptible nod in return. Once I'm cooled down, I head in for a shower before the press junket starts. Before I reach the elevators, I get a text.

JAX: She's pretty.

I halt in my tracks, my blood pounding loudly in my ears. I search around for any kind of sign of someone watching me, but I don't see a god-damned thing. *Hurry up, Taylor.*

twenty-one

MY HERO
SAMANTHA

I don't know what the hell that was, and I don't think I want to know. That is the strangest run I've ever gone on. Even more bizarre than the one where Matt ran into me and broke my wrist. *Who was the guy running behind Matt?* I think he was one of the security guards, but I can't be sure. I'm sure we looked crazy, running in a stupid line like that. It felt like being in track and field back in high school.

Stranger still is how Matt is being kind to me today. That makes zero sense to me. He was more than clear what he thought of me the other night. *And today, he wanted to grab breakfast and hang out? What the hell is that all about?* I can't keep up with his mood swings from one day to another. I get such a strong feeling from him that something is wrong, something terrible, and he's afraid to tell anyone. I don't know what that something could be, but it keeps driving Matt to distraction. There's a deep dark secret in that man, and part of me wants to either help him hide it or expose it to the light and free him once and for all. He's wound so tightly, he's going to break.

None of this should be my business with how he's treated me in the past, but the small glimpses I nab of the real Matt pull at me so hard I can't stop myself from caring about him and what's going on with him. He's obviously being tormented by something, but how do I convince him to share what that is without completely alienating him?

And do I want to? Do I believe he meant what he said when he basically called me a groupie? He did apologize for that last night, and he looked like he meant it, but is that enough? Why am I caring so much about this? I'm newly single. I should be focusing on enjoying this time and this tour, not getting wrapped up in Matt's mess.

I take a quick shower and then grab a quicker breakfast before heading to the venue to meet with the production coordinator to discuss where I'll be positioned and where I'll have access for tonight's concert. The band has a ton of press to do today, so I won't encounter them much until the show.

As I'm heading to catch the next shuttle from the hotel for my meeting, Vanessa calls out to me. When I turn to her, I notice the entire band following along, presumably heading out for their interviews. I give them a small smile but avoid eye contact, focusing on Vanessa instead.

"Hold up," Vanessa waves at me, trying to jog across the lobby in her pencil skirt and high heels. She is so not dressed for her on-the-go job; it's almost laughable. I hold my breath, hoping she doesn't wipe out on the tiled floor. She makes it to me unharmed and holds out a small rectangular box. "I'm glad I caught you. Here. Your glasses were delivered this morning."

I can't stop the smile that spreads across my face. I missed my glasses so much, I don't know how I functioned the last couple of days. "Oh my gosh, thank you so much, Vanessa. You have no idea how glad I am to have these."

"Just in time for the big day."

I tear open the box, pull the glasses out of their case, and put them on. *Amen and hallelujah, I can see again.* I blink playfully at Vanessa. "Oh wow. You're a woman."

She laughs. "Har har."

"Seriously, though. Thank you for getting these here so fast. I do appreciate it. I swear you know magic."

"I'll never tell," she says coyly. "I'll meet up with you on the bus after the show."

They exit the hotel with me, and Matt holds the door open, his green eyes burning something fierce over me as I walk past him. He's studying me in my glasses, and I try my best to ignore him, but something stirs within me under the weight of his stare. It's all I can do to not stare back at him. I dare a glance, but he quickly shifts his eyes and scans the parking lot as if looking for someone. *So much for that idea.*

The meeting with the production coordinator takes way longer than I anticipated, and I scarcely have time to run to the hotel to grab my equipment and head back to the venue before the show starts. I don't even have time to eat. I rush around my room, packing up my camera, extra batteries, memory cards, and other equipment, and I head out again.

When we arrive at the venue, the throng of people pressing to enter the front gates is something to behold. I instruct the driver to let me out and pull out my camera to start filming. I ask a few fans to talk to me about their love of Indigo King and their music as they head in. The teenage girls fan-girling over the guys in the band are pretty amusing.

"Oh my god. Ryan is soooo hot!"

"No, Jude is the hottest!"

"Matt is hotter than both of them combined!"

I can't help but smile at them as they start

fighting over which one is hotter. They're all not wrong. The entire band is unreasonably good-looking. They all definitely hit the genetics lottery, and in my mind, Matt especially. I thank the girls and tell them to enjoy the show and keep an eye out for the documentary later in the year because they might be in it.

"Oh my god, does that mean they'll see this? Like, watch it?" The youngest, with pink streaks in her hair and Jude's self-declared biggest fan, asks.

"Yeah. Most likely." I smile at her.

"So, they'll see me? And know who I am?"

"Absolutely. And, do you know what else? You're so close to them right now. You're probably breathing the same air."

"No way. I never thought of that." She looks like she's about to faint.

"Way."

All three of them shriek so piercingly I think something in my brain breaks. I can't help but laugh to myself as I grab my gear and head around to the backstage area. I remember being that young and into bands so passionately like those girls. It seems like forever ago now. I can almost remember the feeling of infatuation. It sucks to grow up sometimes.

The sun has lowered into the horizon, leaving a beautiful burst of colors beyond the surrounding mountains. Being the first unofficial summer weekend, the evenings are still chilly, and I'm glad I thought to grab my jean jacket to bring along with me. I shrug into it as I approach the back area, squeeze through the small crowd congregating along the fence, and head into the gate.

"Pass?" A security guard steps in front of me, blocking my progress and pulling me up short.

"Oh, sorry," I mutter and reach inside my jacket to grab the lanyard hanging around my neck, but my hand only finds my shirt. I feel around, thinking maybe it got twisted around while I put my jacket on, but the pass isn't there. *Fuck. Where is it?*

"Ma'am, do you have a pass or not?" The guard growls, growing impatient with me.

"I do. I have one. I'm here filming a documentary on Indigo King. I'm here all weekend with them, I swear." I glance up at him, pleading with my eyes for him to believe me. If I can't get in, I can't film the show. *The first fucking show of the tour. Damnit.* "Maybe it's in my equipment bag. Let me check."

He glares but gives me a curt nod to go on with my search, though his skepticism is growing by the second. He's about to kick me off the grounds.

I dig through my bag while at the same time racking my brain to remember the last time I saw the pass. *Fuck!* I know I had it at the hotel and can picture it on top of my dresser where I put it when I got back this afternoon. I don't imagine myself picking it up again as I left.

"I was just here this afternoon, meeting with the production coordinator about the documentary I'm filming. Can you call him?"

"No, ma'am. Either you show a pass, or you leave. We don't call people."

"I swear I'm with Indigo King. Or, more specifically, Blackmore Records. They're the ones paying me." I'm rambling. *Fuck, I'm rambling.* I'm about to go into full-blown panic mode. I need to find a way inside. I pull my phone out of my pocket and send a quick text to Vanessa:

> ME: Help Van! I'm at the back gate and can't get in. Lost my pass. Can you help?

"I just sent their manager a text. You should be hearing something about letting me in." I give him a weak smile. My confidence is shrinking as the time ticks by with no response from Vanessa, but I think to hit record on the camera hanging over my shoulder to catch if anything interesting happens. Fucked up situations like this can make for good TV.

"Ma'am, I'm going to ask you to step back. With no pass, you need to be on the other side of the fence."

I look back over my shoulder at the growing crowd of young fans leaning into the fence behind me, hoping for a glimpse of their music idols. Some older women, too, clearly hoping for more than a glance.

"Please. Believe me. I'm just here to do my job, like you."

He is thoroughly unconvinced and grows impatient with me and my antics and groveling. Another guard comes by, noticing his partners' displeasure with me.

"Is there a problem here?" He asks, towering over me, using his size to intimidate me.

"This woman claims to be filming a documentary of one of the bands but doesn't have a pass."

"I have a pass." I correct. "I just can't find it. I sent a text to the band manager, Vanessa Mercer, and she should be clearing this up shortly."

"No pass, no entry. No exceptions." The new asshole announces rudely, grabbing my bicep hard and forcibly directing me to the fenced area. "Nice try, ma'am. This isn't the first time we've seen that ploy from a groupie. Almost convincing, though." He shoves me a little harder.

"A what? A groupie?" I yell in disbelief. "Are you fucking kidding me?" I'm half tempted to haul back and punch this asshole in his ugly face. "You think I'm a fucking groupie?" That makes twice in the same amount of days that someone has either insinuated or directly called me a groupie, and I really don't fucking appreciate it.

The first guard must realize I'm about to go off

on his friend, and he grabs my other arm to help drag me out of the gate. I'm trying my best to wrench out of their hands, but they are fucking strong and grab me tighter, to the point of real pain.

"Let go of me! You're fucking hurting me!" I'm starting to make a scene, but I don't give a shit. I am beyond pissed. Not only for the 'groupie' thing but because they are hurting me now.

The people on the other side of the fence, who were dead silent as I was initially manhandled and dragged, now start cheering loudly. *What the actual fuck? How rude can you possibly be? Cheering at someone actually being hurt.* I am so pissed; the tears are about to start, making me more pissed. The cheers turn into screams of pleasure. I swear, if my wrist wasn't broken, I'd go off on every single one of these assholes.

"I said let her go," a deep voice yells behind me, and I'm suddenly freed. However, I'm not ready for the release and fall backward on my ass, barely avoiding landing on my bad wrist. The next thing I know, Matt is leaning over me with a worried expression and his hand outstretched. He's not acknowledging the crowd currently chanting his name behind him.

My blood is boiling over. I'm still on the verge of going berserk on everything and everyone around me, including Matt, but I grab his hand and let him pull me up. I give the security guards the dirtiest look I can muster without shooting flames out of my eyes, which I swear to god I could do right now if I tried hard enough. They are very purposely avoiding looking in my direction now.

"Fucking groupie..." I mutter. "Assholes."

"What's that?" Matt leans down to hear me over the nearby crowd.

"Apparently, I must really look like a fucking groupie. I should get it tattooed on my forehead," I yell at him, and it feels good to yell, even if only out of necessity. "That's twice in 48 hours." I grab my equipment bag and storm off, heading toward Vanessa, who I find not too far away to secure another fucking pass. *Jesus Christ, with the passes already.*

Matt doesn't say anything, or at least not that I can catch. I left him behind me without another glance back. I don't know what end of the relationship spectrum we're on at the moment since the mood changes hourly. I lack the emotional fortitude to cope with him after that ordeal. Being called a groupie by that guard struck a nerve in me that Matt exposed to air the other night. The one guard said this isn't the first time someone had posed as someone like me. Crazy, but creative, if I'm honest. Good on her, whoever she is. Or was. However, she is *not me*.

twenty-two

PEACEKEEPER

MATT

The show that night, our first of the tour, is fucking amazing. We performed for the largest crowd we've ever played in front of, and we're all still buzzing from the adrenaline rush it gave us. We've finished up our meet and greets with the fans and are preparing to get on the bus to stop back at the hotel and then head to Denver. Every once in a while, I catch Samantha out of the corner of my eye filming, but she's not obtrusive. If I didn't somehow sense her presence 24/7, I would never know she was there.

Jude is trying to sneak his new flavor of the week onto the bus with us to at least go to the hotel, but Ryan is preventing that from happening. This could turn ugly. Interestingly enough, they don't care that Samantha is recording everything they're doing and saying. I'm tempted to let whatever happens to play out on its own.

"Dude, just because you now get your dick wet on the regular doesn't mean the rest of us can't." Jude slurs his words, obviously inebriated. He's nose to nose with Ryan, who is amazingly unfazed about his personal space being violated.

"Jude, you are drunk, and your friend is even drunker than you, which I'll give you, is an impressive feat." His voice is barely over a whisper, and I have to strain to hear him. At least he's trying to keep the fight on the down low. "You know our rule about drunk people on the fucking bus."

"Yeah, yeah. If they're not one of us, they're off the bus," he grimaces. "But Pam isn't that drunk, I swear. She can keep her cool. Right, Pam?"

Right then, as if on cue from the Gods of Comedic Timing, the sound of retching comes from behind us, and we all turn to see Jude's new friend, 'Pam,' puking her guts out into a nearby trash can. If it weren't so pathetic, it would almost be funny.

Everyone checks back with Jude for his reaction. His shoulders slump as if he's just thrown a game-losing interception, and he rakes his fingers down his face. "Fuck me running."

Ryan slaps him on the back, empathizing with him. "Sorry dude."

"Well, this is a bad fucking omen for the tour if I

ever saw one." Jude hauls himself onto the bus behind Ryan, leaving his 'friend' to fend for herself.

"Jude! Hey!" I yell at him. "What about your friend here?" He waves a dismissive hand and steps onto the bus. "Dick." I head over to the woman, who thankfully stops throwing up and is using the bottom hem of her Indigo King shirt to try to wipe up her face and hair. Not the classiest thing I've ever seen, but probably one of the better uses of our T-shirts.

"Sorry about that," she mumbles, looking around with glassy eyes. She's attempting to apologize to everyone around her, but absolutely nobody is paying attention to her but me. I scan the area and find Samantha still filming her. Okay, maybe two of us are still watching. And the whole world by way of her camera. *No biggie.*

"Are you going to be okay?" I ask her. "Did you come here with anyone that can take you home?"

"Huh?" She's trying to focus her eyes on me, but I can tell she's having a hard time. *Why do I have to clean this mess up? Fuck.*

"Where are the people you came here with?"

"Oh! You said that already." She wipes at her mouth with the back of her hand, swaying slightly. I ready myself to catch her should I need to. Her high heels look mighty precarious. "I said, my friends are right there." She points vaguely to an area with a crowd of people.

I glance over and don't see anyone overtly looking for her. *Damn it all to hell.* Finally, I wave down one of the security guards, rummage through my wallet, and thrust a hundred-dollar bill at him. "Could you make sure this woman gets home safely, please? We need to bail."

The guy looks a little stunned as he examines the money, then eyes the disheveled woman warily. "Suuuure?"

"Thanks, man." I slap his shoulder with gratitude and head back to the bus. Out of the corner of my eye, I sense Samantha's camera following me as I walk away. She's captured the entire incident from Jude's starting to my finishing. It takes everything in me to not acknowledge her or the camera. And now I feel like I'm fucking acting or something. *It's fucking bullshit.*

Later that night, when we're on the road to Denver, and I think almost everyone is asleep, I head to the front area of the bus to grab a drink and check my email. I'm hoping Taylor sent a report by now. I find Samantha alone up front on one of the couches, headphones on, and reviewing her recordings. She sees me but ignores me completely, not even a nod or a tip of her chin. *Fine.*

I grab a water bottle from the fridge and sit at the table with my back to her. If I were to face her way, I'd end up staring at her instead of looking at my phone, which is an inevitability I want to avoid right now. Taking a long swig of water, I open the email app on my phone. Sure enough, I have a message from Taylor. My thumb hovers nervously over the icon for the attached report. *Do I want to read this? Open this can of worms? Open this wound that's been scabbed over for years?* I don't think I have a choice. Not now that Jax is inserting himself into my life again. I need to know what I'm up against now.

I open the report, and a full-color photo of my brother fills the screen. A chill runs down my spine at the sight of my only living relative. The lead actor of my nightmares. Right away, I notice the family resemblance between us. There was never a question of whether we were related or not. It was evident to everyone. The only thing in common between us now besides general features is his shaggy brown hair like mine. Jax doesn't look so good. In fact, he looks downright *horrible*. His cheeks are sunken, and his body is emaciated. His eyes are bloodshot and empty of any life. Whatever drugs he's on have taken their toll. The picture of him is at a gas station, smoking a cigarette like a fucking idiot. Same old Jax. Zero consideration for anyone's life but his own.

I scroll down to view more of the report:

CHAPTER TWENTY-TWO

NAME: Jaxon Michael Holloway

AGE: 35

LAST KNOWN RESIDENCE: 717 Rockwood Drive, Wimberley, TX 78676

CURRENT LOCATION: Colorado Springs, CO (Transient)

Fuck. I stop reading and drink some more water. He really is heading to Denver. That was the main thing I wanted to know; if the threat of him showing up was real. Sure enough, he's heading my way. I hoped he was bluffing, but Jax doesn't bluff. I should have known that much. Unfortunately, this confirms that he's got help on the inside somehow. Something in the criminal history section further down the page catches my eye.

CURRENT INVESTIGATION(S):

(OIG - Social Security fraud) Conspiracy/Theft of Public Funds/Obstruction/Resisting Executive Officer (Hays County) Obstruction/Resisting arrest

Unfuckingbelievable. The fucker never learns. At least I'm not there to take the fall for him this time. This time, he'll pay for his own crimes.

twenty-three

NIGHT VISION

SAMANTHA

I caught some amazing moments on camera tonight, and as I go through my memory cards on the bus as we head to Denver, excitement courses through me at what this film can be once complete. This could be fantastic.

I'm still riding the buzz of the evening when Matt shows up, dampening my mood instantly. I avoid his gaze and pretend I don't even notice him. I have my earbuds in, so it's a plausible excuse. Plus, ignoring him is now my modus operandi as a general rule, so this shouldn't surprise him. I *definitely* didn't notice that he's shirtless and only wearing an old pair of sweats. He grabs a water bottle from the fridge and sits with his back to me. Something in my chest tightens, and I'm not sure why I'm reacting this way.

There seems to be this residual energy between

us crackling and sparking whenever we're close to each other, and it still makes zero sense. I should hate his guts. Especially since he treated me so shitty as he did. I don't know what it is about him, but I want to believe deep down he didn't mean what he said and he's actually a good person. I have no clue why I think that, but I don't know why I won't accept his apology either. Maybe I'm trying to prove a point, or maybe I'm being stubborn as always. That's probably the most likely.

I sneak a glance up at him, sitting in the booth, intent on something on his phone. This could be a perfect chance to catch him unaware of my filming. As quietly as I can, I raise the camera and zoom in on Matt. His strong, broad shoulders are hunched and tight, as though he's beyond tense. My fingers twitch with the desire to go and massage his shoulders to work that tension out of him. The memory of how his skin felt when I ran my hands down that back makes my toes curl. *Not fair. Coming out here, flaunting all that muscular goodness in my face. Asshole.*

While I wasn't intending to spy on what he was doing, I can't help but catch the picture he's studying on his phone. The photo is of a man who looks remarkably like Matt but a hell of a lot worse for wear. *Is he a relative?* Sarah didn't think he had any family, but there's no denying Matt is related to whoever that is, despite his run-down appearance.

He scrolls up and down, bouncing between the

photo and the text beneath it. I zoom in a little more, guilt sitting on one shoulder, yelling at me, while my artistic justification sits on my other shoulder, saying this is for the film. I know I'm being nosey, but fuck it. He's holding the damn phone out for everyone to see. I can't help my camera was pointing and zooming in his direction right then. *Really*.

Perhaps the guy in the photo is why Matt is so hurt and afraid but won't talk about it. While they may be related, it appears they've had two entirely different lives. Where Matt is strong, confident, and generally nice, the photo guy seems weak, but not just that - something about his eyes makes me shudder involuntarily for some reason. They match Matt's, but they're *dead*. There is a gaping hole behind those eyes where a soul should be. I pause the recording and study the photo. The more I look at it, it feels as though someone is dragging a sharp icicle down the middle of my back.

I try to spot if I can glean anything from Matt's expression as he silently stares down at his phone. Other than the extreme tension in his shoulders, there isn't any outward sign he's upset. Of course, that doesn't mean shit. And with his back to me, I can't read anything about him. Strangely, he's not even bouncing his leg like he usually does.

The night is catching up with me quickly, and I can't help but yawn, hopefully unnoticed. My eyes are getting dry and itchy the more tired I become. I rewind and check out what text I can make out from Matt's phone, my guilt still not outweighing my curiosity yet. All I can make out is a name - Jaxon Michael Holloway. *Hmm. I wonder who that is.* Only one way to find out. I shut off my camera and pull up the search engine on my phone, typing in the name. A long list of news reports fills the search results regarding a bunch of crimes this guy's committed. No mention of a relative named Matt I can find. I'm still intrigued about who this guy is since he's got Matt wandering the bus at night, looking at his picture so intently when he should be sleeping. Like I want to do now.

twenty-four

REARVIEWMIRROR

MATT

So it *is* money Jax is after. *Figures*. He probably thinks he'll be able to lawyer up and out of the fraud charges or maybe try to pay it back. He's got a seriously rude awakening coming because he's not getting a single fucking red cent from me. I think I've calmed down a little now after the initial jolt at seeing his picture when I first opened the report. At least I have an idea of what I'm up against with Jax and his possible motives. I can prepare myself at least somewhat, though fuck if I know how.

I need to catch some sleep before we get to Denver, or I'm going to be useless tomorrow. I shut my phone off and move to exit the booth, and I can hear Samantha lightly snoring on the couch behind me. I stop to watch her for a minute. Rare is the moment I can study her without her hackles being raised. Not that I blame her. I don't. I was a total dick to her. And all because she was a bit insightful and saw through my bullshit. It wasn't fair. I'm still in awe of how open she is. I have never met anyone like her before. Not only is she beautiful, but she knows who she is and is confident enough to tell everyone else to fuck off. I admire that kind of bravery in a woman. Self-awareness is fucking sexy as hell.

With her glasses still on, it's difficult to make out her eyes since they reflect her phone, which is propped up on her stomach. She shouldn't sleep with her glasses on. She just got them back today and could roll over and break them.

I search around for a blanket and find one in the corner. As quietly as I can, I try to cover her. She stirs a little, and her phone slides down. I pick it up to put it on the console next to her and can't help but see the screen. Search results for Jaxon Michael Holloway fill the open page. *What the actual fuck? What the hell is she doing looking up my brother? Did she see my phone somehow?*

She must sense me hovering over her because she wakes up with a start, but I don't move away. Instead, I hold her phone screen up to her startled face. "What the fuck is this, Samantha?"

"Wha-?" She's pushing back in the cushion to move her face away, clearly confused.

I relent and pull the phone back. "Where did you get this name? How do you know about Jaxon Holloway?" I'm trying to keep my voice down, but this is difficult, with anxiety and adrenaline flowing through me.

"I...it was on your phone..." Her voice is barely a squeak.

"You were spying on me?" I'm trying to keep quiet, but the words come out like a hiss.

"No! I mean, kind of...but, no." She's tripping over her words. "I didn't mean to, but when I was filming you, I saw what was on your phone..."

"You were filming me?" *Jesus Christ. Was nothing sacred?* "What the fuck? Do I have no privacy?"

"I thought it was a poignant moment of quiet for you after the noise of the show..." She's recoiling from me as if she thinks I'm going to attack her.

I hand her phone back and sink onto the couch across from her, elbows on my knees and hands in my hair. *What the fuck do I do with this now? How do I handle her knowing about Jax?* She can't know who he is to me. Our names are different.

"Is he your brother?"

Fuck me. This girl. I rake my fingers across the back of my neck, trying to release the tension that keeps building, but it doesn't work. I'm caught. I'm fucking caught. By Samantha Fucking Fisher. When I met her the first time, I knew she would be my downfall. And I was right.

I glance up at her, knitting my fingers together and leaning forward. *Where the fuck do I start?* "Yes. Jaxon Holloway is my brother." My voice sounds strange. As if the words themselves are covered in cobwebs from not being spoken in so long.

"Oh, I didn't know you had family."

"He's not family."

"But you just said-"

"He's not my family. Not anymore. Not for a long time." I need to stress this point to her. That this discussion goes no further and ends here.

"Okay..." Her expression is of concern, tinged with a bit of sadness and not of anger as I'd expected with my harsh tone. I don't know what to do with that, so I do nothing. I hold her stare, trying to express my life story to her without having to tell her any of it. I wish I could download my nightmares onto a fucking memory card and hand it over when I need to explain why I am the way I am. Life isn't fair, though. It never is.

"I haven't seen or talked to him in eight years." She sits up but says nothing, interested in my story, so I go on. "To sum it up... we didn't have a great childhood. And when I turned 18, I changed my name and left and never looked back. And now, since my face is all over the fucking place, he's found me. He's expecting a reunion in Denver."

"When you say your childhood wasn't awesome..." She's now leaning into the aisle across from me, copying my stance, meeting my gaze with compassion that hurts to see, let alone receive. At least it's not pity.

I wring my hands together, picking at the callouses on my palms, trying to find the words and the nerve to tell her the truth. The last time I talked about this was my interview for an exception to join the Marines with a criminal record. And even that was only the second time I told anyone. "We never knew our dad. Well, I didn't. I guess Jax had a couple of years with him, but he took off for good once I came along. I always got the feeling my mother blamed me for that. Anyway, she was a heroin addict who overdosed when I was 10."

"Oh, Matt." She reaches out to put a warm hand on my knee, and I push through, trying to keep the momentum.

"Up to that point, we had protective services on our doorstep every other month, it seemed like, but they never did anything. Jax would always smooth things over with them. He's quite the conman. Always was. After she died, we were forced to move in with our grandmother, who died herself a few years later. Then we were on our own. I'll just say Jax isn't role-model material." I start to feel light-headed. Talking about this is easier than I thought it would be, but it's also the hardest thing I've ever done. And I'm not even close to telling her everything.

Her eyes glisten, the unshed tears magnified slightly by her glasses. "I'm sorry." And she means it. I can feel it in her simple touch and those simple words. I have to swallow hard to hold back my own tears.

"So, yeah. Jax is not a good guy. And now he's threatening to meet up in Denver."

"Threatening?" Her brow furrows, and her head cocks to the side.

I take a beat before answering. This is the high-level overview, and I'm teetering on having to give her details. I'm not sure I'm ready to do that yet. I don't know if any of this is putting her in more danger. But then, she should know she might be involved now if Jax's voicemail is any indication.

"He's left voicemails, indicating that he's learned about you somehow." My voice quivers as I push the words out.

"About me?" Her hand on my knee slides off, and she catches herself. I nod, avoiding her eyes. "What does he even know about me?"

"I don't know exactly. And I also don't know how he got my cell number in the first place. Very few people have it, so someone within my circle is not as loyal as I think they are."

"What did he say... about me?" Her apprehension is palpable, and I wish I could grab it and crush it.

I shake my head at her, not wanting to scare her any more than this already does. "I shouldn't..."

"Matt, I deserve to know if I'm in danger."

"I would never let anything happen to you. I swear. I hired my Marine buddy's security company..."

"Marines?" The lines on her forehead deepen the longer we talk, and my stomach sours. "You were in the Marines?"

Fuck's sake. Why not tell her your whole fucking story? Once upon a time, there was this kid from a really shitty family, who had a really shitty childhood, blah blah blah. I sigh heavily and plant my face in my hands. The word vomit needs to stop.

"Yes. But that has nothing to do with anything happening right now, other than the security company."

"Remind me to circle back to that someday..."

"Sure thing. Top of my list."

"No need to be snarky with me."

"Sorry."

"So, does this explain our crazy train run this morning? And the new pass rule at the elevators?" She seems amused and not concerned for her own safety at all. She definitely is taking this a lot better than I thought she would. I should have known she'd take this all in stride. It takes a lot to faze her. I just happen to fuck up a lot on a grand scale with her.

CHAPTER TWENTY-FOUR

"Yeah," I can't help chuckle, picturing it again. "That was pretty crazy."

"So, what are you going to do about Jax? Should I be worried?" She leans back on the couch, tucking her legs under her. It makes her seem so small, and I want to pull her close to me to protect her. She's not scared, but that drives me to want to do it even more.

"There's not much I *can* do, unfortunately. He hasn't made an explicit threat. So outside of the beefed-up security, I need to wait for him to make a move." I run my sweaty palms back and forth on my thighs, willing the tension in my muscles to unfurl its grip on me. "And Samantha, you can't tell anyone about this. Even the guys don't know about Jax or my past. I've gone to lengths you'd never believe in keeping these things to myself. I'd like to keep it that way."

Her eyes bore into me, again capturing the vulnerability and brittleness of my soul in her reflection. I don't know how she does that, but it unnerves me to no end, but not always in a bad way. She almost looks offended that I would suggest her indiscretion. Something about how she can see right through me makes me feel safe for the first time in my life. Like, I finally have someone else on the planet who understands me. And even though she still doesn't know everything, the fact she knows a little and hasn't run for the hills is a comfort I've never felt before. I don't really know how to handle it.

"Of course. You don't need to worry about me."

"Well, I do."

"I meant I won't tell anyone."

"I know. Thanks for that."

She nods and stares out the window at the passing blackness, and the hum of the tires on the road beneath us has a calming effect on us both. The sensation of a thousand pounds being lifted from my shoulders overtakes me. The act of telling someone just a few of my secrets has untied knots cinched years ago, and the release, combined with tonight's show, makes my muscles weak. I can't help but yawn long and loud, covering my mouth with my hand sheepishly as she gives me a wide-eyed look.

"You should go to bed and get some sleep." She takes her glasses off and sets them on the console next to the couch. Grabbing the blanket and wrapping herself in it snugly, she asks, "You'll need to be sharp tomorrow, no?"

I study her for a second, still in awe of her magnificent grace under pressure. I shake my head at her. "You're something else, you know that?"

Her lips quirk into a smile. "Something else is better than nothing else."

I stand and head back toward the bunk area but turn to survey her once more. She's leaning over her phone, presumably going through the search results on Jax some more. I'm not a praying person, never have been, but something in me throws out a wish, no, a demand, to the universe to protect her at all costs.

twenty-five

HONEY DON'T THINK

SAMANTHA

We arrive in Denver late the next morning, which leaves little downtime for the rest of the day. The band is whisked off to visit radio stations and other news outlets, and I tag along this time, getting priceless behind-the-scenes footage. Despite the tension between them during Jude's drunken incident the night before, it's as though nothing happened, the way they're joking around with each other. Matt seems to be in better spirits compared to the last few days, but I can still sense he's on edge. He's allowed that, considering what he's going through. He is constantly checking his phone, which is obvious to me but not so much to everyone else. Or, at least they don't show they care.

Matt does appear to look around me more than usual, not necessarily at me directly, but at the actual area around me. I'm well aware of the security guard that seems to have become my shadow for the day. It would be hard not to notice him lurking around like he is. He's not trying to be discreet but instead is clearly making himself known. Part of me wants to acknowledge the guy and befriend him; that's my nature, to be friendly. But the other side of me doesn't want to admit he's there or that I even know why. I would love to be able to deny that any of the last week has happened. A third and final side of me wants to be coy and laugh the whole thing off, making him carry my bag to give him something more 'useful' to do than standing too close and looking around. What a job. Standing and looking. I could do that. Obviously, there's more to it than that. I have difficulty coming to terms with restrictions like this forced upon me. While those restrictions haven't been spelled out to me explicitly, I know they're there, and I respect them. I know they're needed in this situation. It doesn't mean I have to like it because I certainly don't.

After the quick press rounds, we arrive at the Red Rocks Amphitheater, and the whole area is breathtaking. I make sure to capture the stunning rock formations making up the natural acoustic wonder. Technically, this venue is smaller than the other outdoor locations we'll be visiting, but the majesty of the surroundings makes it seem gigantic.

The backstage area is actually a maze of tunnels under the stage, and on the way, we pass through a stairwell full of markings of prior bands that have played here. Ryan is given the honor of putting a sharpie to the wall to commemorate Indigo King's visit, and he does a decent job copying the band logo on the cement.

I set up in the underground cafeteria area to conduct Ryan and Jude's individual interviews before the show. Ryan goes first, and his excitement to play here is nothing less than contagious.

"I mean, U2's *Under A Blood Red Sky* was recorded here. That definitive record fucking made them. No doubt about it. So many iconic people have played here. It's crazy that we're about to. I just hope the rain holds out." His manic rambling is adorable. He's like a kid in a candy store with an American Express Black card.

"I know you only have one show under your belt, but how does it feel?" I ask.

"It's an adjustment, playing to bigger crowds, but it's fucking amazing. Sorry. Amazing. You can edit out my swearing, right?"

I laugh. "Why would I do that?"

The red rising up his neck to his cheeks is hilarious. "Fuck if I know. Shit... Fuck... Never mind..." He ends up laughing with his head buried in his hands. *Yup, that's totally staying in.*

Jude doesn't have such reservations about his

potentially offensive language during his interview. When discussing the possibility of rain during their set, he let loose.

"Let it fucking rain. Fucking bring it. We're not afraid of any god-damned weather. We're fucking Indigo King." Jude will always be Jude.

Matt comes into the cafeteria right after Jude leaves while I'm packing up my equipment, getting ready to meet with the production coordinator to discuss positioning here. I was not expecting him at all. He 'doesn't do' individual interviews.

"What are you doing?" He looks confused, but I'm the one confused about why he's here.

"What do you mean? I'm packing my equipment to move it."

"What about my interview?" He quirks an eyebrow at me, and I light up inside like a Christmas tree at the thought of him sitting and answering my questions.

"Are you being serious? Since when are you agreeing to be interviewed solo?" He's got to be joking. He's made it abundantly clear he wants no part of this documentary and has only begrudgingly participated so far. For him to voluntarily show up like this has me shaken up. *Is this because of our talk about his brother last night?*

"Since I decided to not be a baby about things." He steps up close to me, invading my personal space, filling it with his presence, soap and cologne, and everything that is *Matt*. I have to force myself to not faint away on the spot. Then he starts lifting his shirt up, and the thrum running through every muscle in my body has to be visible. *Surely, everyone saw and felt that too, right?* "Don't you have to mic me up?" His deep voice travels through my ears and straight to my core. *Yup. Called it. I'm totally going to faint.*

I swallow hard and raise my gaze to him, dragging my eyes away from his sculpted stomach right in front of me. When my eyes meet his, I can tell he's as affected as I am right now, and I can't move, even though I should. If I was smart, I'd step back from him. But I'm not smart. No. *I'm fucking dumb.* My hand involuntarily reaches out to touch his waist, and the jolt that hits me when my fingers brush his skin hits him too, and he visibly shudders.

My eyes close, and I lean into him just as he wraps his strong hands behind my head, pulling me into a warm kiss. His tongue slides into my mouth and meets mine, dancing slowly, steadily, patiently. He places his other hand along my jaw, and his thumb gently caresses my cheekbone with such care my breath hitches. Everything about this is so tender, nothing like our previous fevered interplays. Something deep inside me melts, and I reach up to run my fingers through his hair, bracing the back of his neck and pulling him deeper into the kiss.

A groan from low in his throat escapes, and his

hands drop to my hips, gripping me tightly and drawing me even closer to him. The hardness in his jeans against me lets me know exactly how close he really wants to be. This makes my own moan slip between us as his mouth leaves mine and starts moving down my neck to the dip in my collarbone. Each time his lips graze my skin, stars shoot behind my eyelids.

"Oh. My." Vanessa's voice only a few feet away shocks us back to reality, and we instinctively jump apart. My body instantly feels his absence, and I mentally curse Vanessa's timing. "Sorry about that. Didn't mean to interrupt."

"It's okay, Van," I say, readjusting my glasses, turning to her, and stepping in front of Matt to help hide the bulge in his jeans. It's the polite thing to do. "What's up?" He puts a hand on my shoulder, reestablishing our connection, and it means a lot he would do that in front of Vanessa.

She doesn't miss it, and I can tell she's biting back a smile, but it's playing in her eyes. If she winked at me right now, I wouldn't be surprised, but she restrains herself.

"Nothing. There's someone... I mean. I was... checking on things." She backs up to the door, waving her arms nonchalantly as though she didn't walk in on us making out. "Looks like everything here is...great. So, I'll just..." She points to the door and then runs out of it, her high heels squeaking on the tile floor.

"Thanks for the cover." Matt chuckles behind me, lowering his hand to my waist and turning me to face him. He runs his fingers through my hair, tilting my face up to him.

"It was the least I could do after that kiss." I can't help but eye him a bit warily. The kiss was amazing, but I'm not sure what it meant, and I don't want to ask. I'm afraid of upsetting this precarious peace between us or whatever is happening. Everything involving him is so fragile.

A crease between his brows grows deeper as he watches my thoughts churn. "I should leave you alone." He sounds so defeated, so resigned. "I'm not sure why I can't. With everything going on, I should stay as far away from you as I can. Actually, you should stay away from me. I've never been anything but bad news to anyone. But there's something about you that keeps pulling me in. When I'm around you... I don't know."

"It's the same for me too. I can't stop thinking about you, even when you're an asshole." If we're admitting our attraction to each other, there it is.

He laughs and bends to touch my forehead with his own. "It's not going to be easy. I will always be an asshole. And full disclosure, I'm pretty fucked up all around. But at least I'm self-aware."

"Ha! Full disclosure, I already knew that about you." I know he's only half-joking and really does believe that about himself. I search his green eyes, and he doesn't flinch or look away. He meets my gaze, almost challenging me to doubt him, but I don't. Things have changed. I need to admit to myself things are different now. And I'm tired of fighting him. I don't want to fight this thing between us anymore either. I only hesitate for a second before nodding. "Okay."

twenty-six

ME AGAINST YOU

MATT

She's going to regret this. As soon as she said, "okay," the knot inside me that unraveled last night after telling her part of my story just retied, and this time double-knotted itself for good measure. I'm fucking insane getting involved with her right as Jax pops back onto the scene. I know she's in danger. He's already threatened her. *What the fuck am I thinking?*

Sure, I warned her I'm an asshole, but that's a generic disclaimer that every guy should stamp on his forehead, for Christ's sake. The bad news part doesn't even begin to cover it, and it does all my issues a disservice in the description department.

I'm tempted to tell her all this; take back everything I said, and run out of this cafeteria as if chased by a pack of rabid wolves. Those crystal blue eyes of hers hold me in place, though. Not that I mind being held here entirely, to be honest. I could fall for Samantha and swear I'm well on the way there. *Could she ever fall for me? Would I ever let her in enough to know the real me? Do I even know who that is anymore?* So many questions swirl around in my mind as I lose myself in her eyes. Those deep pools of clear blue.

She leans into me again, lifting her mouth to meet mine, and her warm body presses into me, driving me to distraction. I reach around and grab her ass, pulling her close to grind against me, and the pain of my need for her is exquisite. I wonder if we can find a room with a lock on the door…

The buzzing of my phone in my back pocket forces me to pull up for air. "Sorry," I mutter as I reluctantly look down at the screen.

JAX: Here.

"Gotta go. We'll do this later?" Walls up, shutters down. I give Samantha a quick peck on the cheek and leave the cafeteria without looking at her or answering her subsequent question about what was going on. I have no idea what 'Here' means, and I don't know if I want to find out. *Here at the venue? In the city? Backstage with us? What the fuck?* The adrenaline racing through me leaves a bitter taste in my mouth.

I find the security detail assigned to Samantha

posted outside the cafeteria. He appears capable enough, but I can't take any chances. "Are you one of Taylor's guys?" I ask him as I glance around. He nods at me and keeps his gaze alert to the surrounding area. I pull up the photo of Jax and show it to him, "This guy is not to get within 50 yards of Samantha. Understand?"

"Yes, sir." He studies the photo quickly but closely.

"Stick to her like glue. She'll probably try to shake you at some point. Don't let her."

"Yes, sir." He repeats.

"Thanks." I turn from him as I dial Taylor's number and head toward the green rooms. He answers on the first ring.

"Matt."

"Tay, that guy I had you run the background and status on - Jaxon Holloway, he's a threat."

"Imminent?" He doesn't sound surprised, but Tay is top-notch at his job. He probably knew from the report request that Jax would be a problem.

"Unknown. Just received a text that said, 'here.' I don't know what that means at this point."

"Gotcha. What kind of threat are we talking about? Physical? Weapons?"

I sigh and run a hand through my hair, then grip the back of my neck. There is so much I don't fucking know. It's pissing me off. "Again, I don't know. I've got one of your guys assigned to

CHAPTER TWENTY-SIX

Samantha Fisher directly since she's been specifically threatened."

"Understood." Taylor pauses for only a second, arranging his thoughts. "I'll blast his photo to everyone, make sure everyone's got eyes out for him. What's our end game? Authorities? Or out of bounds?"

'*Out of bounds.*' That is an excellent way to put it. Another way of saying we'll handle it ourselves, presumably with our own form of justice. *Man, that is so fucking tempting.* While I like the sound of that a lot, I can't think that way. That's how Jaxon thinks. Everything he's ever done in his life is out of fucking bounds.

"Play it straight for now. But that might change with the circumstances."

"Understood." He hangs up, and I stop to look down at my phone, studying the text from Jax again. Those four simple letters in a row, H-e-r-e, can strike terror into my soul. My first instinct was to shift away from Samantha and make myself a moving target. *Was that the right thing to do? Or should I keep her close? What the fuck is Jax doing? Should I meet up with him and get it over with?* My head says that's a perfectly terrible idea. My best bet will be to keep ignoring him and keep him away. We're not in Denver for long anyway. *What could he possibly do between now and when we leave?*

I turn into the Indigo King dressing room, and a voice makes my blood run cold.

"There he is. Matty! What's up, bro?"

In front of me is my worst nightmare come true. My brother Jaxon is sitting on the couch next to Jude, *as if he fucking belongs here*, just chilling with the guys. I think my heart actually stops, and the blood drains out of my head, leaving me dizzy and breathless. *This can't be happening. This is not happening.*

"Matt! You should've said your brother was coming to the show. When I got his text that he couldn't reach you, I had to help, obviously. I went to tell you he was here, but you were... busy." Her laugh resonates off the walls, and my ears ring as if hollow. Vanessa looks ecstatic like she's done something charitable. She has no idea what she's done. My eyes don't leave Jax's, and his don't leave mine. We're catching up on eight years of hate-filled glares.

"Yeah, man. You didn't tell us you had a brother." Jude is oblivious to the negative energy flowing between us. "Of course, you don't tell us anything worthwhile, but still." He chuckles to himself, but it dies a slow death on his lips as he finally reads the room.

"I don't have a-" Before I can finish my sentence, two security guards rush into the room.

"Mr. Sturridge, we just got the order from Taylor." One of them says, breathless from running.

"We didn't know who he was when we let him through. Our apologies, sir." The other one does sound apologetic but also angry. *Good.*

I tear my eyes away from Jax to acknowledge them with a nod. I should have been more specific with Taylor about Jax from the beginning. *This is my fault. This is all my fault.*

"Should we remove him, sir?" The first one asks.

"Remove him?" Vanessa sounds shocked. "But Matt, he's your brother."

Ignoring her, I nod again at the guards. "Do it."

They move toward Jax, who jumps up and around the couch as if he's going to make a run for it. *What the fuck is he thinking?*

"Whoa. Dude. Is this how you treat your older bro?" He chuckles and flashes a wicked grin at me. "We've got so much catching up to do. It's been such a long time since we've seen each other. Too long, man."

I clench my fists and step toward him, ready to beat the shit out of him if I get the opportunity. *Please, give me the chance to pay him back.* I still can't speak. I'm caught between rage and terror, and my throat closes completely. I can hardly breathe, so there's no way words could come out.

Two more security guards come in, apparently alerted to the situation somehow, and move to circle around Jax, penning him in and preventing his escape.

"Seriously, dude?" he scoffs like he can't believe I'd throw him out. The guards close in on him, and he throws his hands up. "Alright! Alright. I'll go. But Matt, I'll be in touch later. We really do need to catch up."

I don't miss the threat in his words or his eyes as he walks out with the surrounding guards, pulling him away. He holds my stare with a warning that leaves me seeing red. Once he's out of sight, I turn and punch the nearest inanimate object, a wall. Luckily it was an interior plaster wall and not one of the outer rock walls. I pull my hand out of the hole I just created and glance down at my hand. Blood pools on my knuckles and then runs between my fingers. *Fuck*. That's going to hurt.

"Well, shit." Vanessa comes up from behind and pulls me over to the sitting area, pushing me gently into a chair. "Let me find a first aid kit or something." She runs off to search.

Jude leans forward on the couch, elbows on his knees, staring at his hands. "Dude..."

"I don't want to talk about it." An edge catches my voice that I didn't intend, but I leave it there. The pain in my hand is starting to reach my brain, and I flex the bloody fingers, testing its functionality.

"Are you going to be able to play?" He doesn't

seem offended by my reaction. That's Jude. Rolling with the punches. Literally.

"I'll play. Don't worry." I refuse to let Jax's appearance and my subsequent stupidity stop me from doing what I love and what I now need to do: playing music and beating the shit out of my drums.

twenty-seven

LOOK AFTER YOU

SAMANTHA

I'm about to head upstairs when I spot Vanessa running straight at me, yelling something about a first aid kit. I step aside to let her through, and a security guard suddenly pushes me back into the cafeteria after Vanessa. He isn't exactly gentle about it either.

"What are you doing? I need to head up to the stage area." I yank my arm out of his vice-like grip, which, in all honesty, hurts more than his holding me.

"You'll need to wait a minute, Miss." He turns around to face the doorway and either blocks my view to the hallway or shields me from view out there; I can't tell which. Until I can.

There he is. Jaxon Holloway. He's noticed me as well, and his dead eyes pierce mine, making the hair on the back of my neck stand up. The guards surrounding him aren't gentle with him either, tearing the tour pass off from around his neck and hauling him down the hall, presumably to an exit of some sort. As I watch him pass, the guard in front of me tries to move me further into the room, but I resist as much as I can. I can't look away from the nefarious being in front of me. Like he's a car accident on the highway, and I'm a rubbernecker. I need to check out what this guy is all about for myself. This asshole that Matt seems so terrified of for god-only-knows reasons I'm not sure I want to know.

I only grab the quickest of glimpses of him as the guard finally wins out on pushing me away, and he makes the most of it. He actually winks at me and blows me a kiss. It was not him being flirtatious. It was downright sinister. My skin crawls so acutely I want to jump out of it and under a rock somewhere.

"What are you doing to her?" Vanessa is staring at us like we're doing some sort of interpretive dance she doesn't understand. Her head even tilts to the side as she watches the guard move me away from the doorway, never turning away from it. I swear he reaches for a weapon he doesn't have and curses under his breath.

Once we're out of sight and the apparent line of fire, the guard turns and examines me from head to toe. "Are you alright, Miss Fisher?"

"I'm fine."

"Why wouldn't you be fine?" Vanessa asks, confused. "What the heck is going on around here?"

"Didn't you see him?" I point to the now empty hallway.

"Who?"

"Matt's brother, Jax."

"Oh, yeah," she sighs as though it's not a big deal. "I'm the one that let him in."

"You what?" I can't keep the incredulity out of my voice. Hard to believe she'd do that without talking to him first. "Where's Matt? Is he okay?" I start to move to leave, but the guard still blocks me. I glare at him.

"Yeah, yeah." Vanessa is nonplussed about my newly imposed captivity. "I didn't know they didn't get along. Shit. I didn't even know he existed until today. As soon as I saw him, I knew they were related. You can't deny the resemblance."

I bite the inside of my cheek. Matt's story, and whatever Jax's role in everything is, is his to tell. Not mine. As much as I want to fill Vanessa in on what I know, I can't. I promised Matt I wouldn't, and I'll keep my word.

"Right." I can't think of anything else to say in response.

"And now Matt's gone and punched the damn wall, and his hand is bleeding like crazy… Like I don't have enough to worry about, he's got to destroy the damned venue. The label is going to go ape shit when they find out." She's rummaging through cabinets, opening drawers, tossing their contents out of her way as she goes. She pulls out a large red nylon bag with a white cross. "Bingo. First aid kit."

I follow after her as she heads back down the hall to the dressing room, my personal bodyguard hot on my heels. Matt must be freaking out. For him to have punched a wall, he's got to be going through it, and in a huge way. This must have been the text he received when he was with me. I can still picture his face going blank as if he put a mask on at that moment to hide every feeling he was having. Punching a wall sure isn't hiding, so maybe he's allowing himself to sort through his emotions with this.

We make it to the dressing room, and a small crowd gathers around Matt. Ryan and Sarah are there, along with Jude and some guys from Incendiary Ink. I follow Vanessa as she pushes through to where Matt is sitting, anxious to find out if he's okay, both physically and mentally, after the run-in with his brother.

Our eyes only meet briefly since he quickly pulls his gaze away from mine. An ache starts to grow in my chest to want to hold him. Just pull him into a hug and protect him. He wouldn't want that, though, so I keep my distance. He lowers his head, looking down at his hand, and his head suddenly shoots up. "Samantha, no-"

My gaze follows his to examine his injured hand, and I see it. The blood. *So much blood.* Streaking across his hands and down his fingers and splattering the floor and the coffee table. He hasn't done anything to try to stop the blood from flowing...

Matt lurches toward me with his bloody hand, and my throat closes, cutting off any words I might have said. My vision tunnels, and the tortured expression on his face reaches me. It's the last thing I see before the world spins out of control and my knees give out from under me. *Fucking blood.*

This time when I come to, I'm not in an ambulance or hospital at least. I am, however, surrounded by rock stars hovering over me with worried looks on their faces. I immediately sense the heat on my neck travel up to my cheeks as the embarrassment blooms within me.

"Sorry about that," I say, trying to sit up slowly. I'm on the dressing room couch and still a little woozy and lightheaded. "At least you all know I'm not a vampire. So, there's that." A few chuckles rumble through the group, and people start to disperse from around me, thank god. I search the crowd for Matt but don't find him. "Where's Matt? Is he okay?"

"He's fine." Sarah's sitting on the coffee table next to me. Someone cleaned up the blood on the floor and table. "Vanessa took him to get bandaged up... Out of your line of sight."

I flop back onto the couch. "Good call. That is one thing I hate about myself, fainting like that. Makes me seem like such a weakling."

She swats at my arm. "What? Girl, you are one of the strongest people I know. Get out of here. So you go a little wonky when you see blood. The way Matt caught you when you collapsed, it looked more like you swooned in front of him. It was kinda cute."

I roll my eyes at her. "Yeah, you have me perfectly summed up."

"I'm just saying you two would make a cute couple. You know... if you wanted to."

I can't hide the smile that emerges, and she gives me a look. "What?" And now I'm blushing. *Jesus*, my brain must be short-circuiting from everything that's happened in the last ten minutes alone.

"Nothing," she says, but the way she says it infers that it is most definitely not nothing.

Almost everyone then clears out to prepare to take the stage. The rumble of the crowd overhead is starting to make its way to us. Matt and Vanessa return, and he is thankfully blood-free, and his hand is wrapped with gauze.

"Are you okay?" We both ask each other simultaneously, then laugh at our awkwardness.

"I'm fine. Thanks for the swoon assist earlier. How's your hand? How are you?"

He gazes at me with a raised eyebrow. "Swoon assist?"

"Sarah said it looked like I swooned for you when I fainted. Or whatever." I shift away, embarrassed again. *Could I be more awkward? Geez.*

"Ah, I see." His eyes show amusement, but the rest of him is still all business.

"Are you okay?" I ask again. I know he's putting me off, but if I can coerce him into opening up even a little, I'll feel better.

"Yeah. I'll be fine. I just scratched it up. Nothing major." He's referring to his hand, but I wasn't. Not entirely, at least. I don't press him, though; he's got to be freaking out still from everything. "I need to go warm up. I'll catch you later at the hotel?"

He doesn't wait for me to respond, and he just kind of pats my shoulder before he leaves. It's a very different vibe than the one we had before his brother showed up. I hope it's not an omen of things to come.

I take my shadow of a guard with me back up to the ground level to position myself for the show. And what a show it is. *I think.* At least from what I hear. About two songs into Indigo King's set, the gauze on Matt's hand becomes a problem for him, so he rips it off and proceeds to bleed all over himself and his drums. The crowd goes freaking bonkers about it, but I don't. Luckily, Deputy Dog is nearby to catch me when I faint yet again and is nice enough to keep my camera rolling for me, so I at least film the show. Too bad I won't be able to watch it. *Fucking blood.*

twenty-eight

DAMAGE

MATT

After our set, the local on-call doctor for the venue checks out my hand and wraps it again. I'm instructed to try not to flex my hand as much as possible so it can scab over. *Whatever*. Despite Vanessa's protests, I skip the night's meet and greet and head back to the hotel to try to chill out. I should not still be this high-strung after beating the shit out of my drums.

The driver drops me off at the back of the hotel to avoid any possible run-ins with the press or otherwise, and I take to running up and down the stairs in the stairwell to expend the rest of my energy. When my knees finally feel like they're about to give in, and my breath is decidedly labored, I exit the stairwell on my floor and head to my room to shower and crash. I haven't been this exhausted in a long time, and with Jax removed from the situation for now, maybe I can sleep for a change.

I wave at the security guard prowling the hall, and when I enter my room, I discover that our bags haven't been delivered yet. *Shit. No clean clothes. Fuck it.* I really need a shower. I do the best I can using only one hand while holding the wrapped one out of the shower spray. When I'm drying off, there's a knock on the door, so I throw on my boxers, wrap myself in my towel, and spy through the peephole. A guy in a hat stands with his head down, but he's holding my bag. They must be delivering everyone's stuff now.

I open the door, ready to take my duffel off his hands, but instead of him handing it to me, it's brutally forced into my chest, and I'm pushed back into my room and against the wall, my breath nearly knocked out of me. I recover quickly and push back against the intruder, angling the bag away from him to expose him. His hat gets knocked off, and he staggers backward. *Jax.* Of course it is. *How the hell did he get my bag, let alone past security?*

I don't have time to ask questions because he pounces on me again, shoving me back into the wall with his forearm pressing into my throat, making it near impossible to breathe. What air I do get is filled with his alcohol-fueled breath. The acrid scent of stale beer and cheap cigarettes surrounds him. The smell instantly throws me back to my childhood, Jax in my face in this very position. He's using his entire body weight to lean into me, and he has leverage; I don't. *Don't let him turn you, whatever you do. Do not let him turn you.*

"Matty. You were fucking rude to me earlier. Not cool, man. Not cool at all."

My brain isn't working. It just doesn't work anymore. I've gone brain-dead. I've forgotten how words work. I've forgotten how my body works. All of my Marine training - *poof. Gone.* As I stare into those hate-filled green eyes that counterfeit my own, I can't move past my disbelief that he's here and this is actually happening. After all the lengths I've gone to for all these years, for him to just show up like this and be able to reach me so easily is seriously fucking with my head. All the years of preparation I've put in for this exact situation just go up in smoke. I'm reduced to my fucking ten-year-old self, vulnerable and defenseless.

"What's up, Matty?" He sneers. "Too good to talk to your big brother now that you're a huge rock star?"

"How did you get up here?" I'm trying to make out what's on the lanyard around his neck without being obvious, but he's blocking my view of it.

"I got friends in high places too, bro. And do you know what friends in high places do? They hand out favors. Isn't that right? Do you hand out favors to your friends?"

I stare at him, not responding as my mind races, trying to figure out who the fuck his friend in a high place is that would let this happen. For the life of me, I can't think of anyone that would know enough to sell me out like this. I shake my head at him, not wanting to give away any more than I already have.

"Well, I think you owe me a favor..."

"I don't owe you shit..." I growl between clenched teeth. My head is clearing, and I could maneuver out of this if I wanted to now, but I need to know what his game is. I need information.

"My poor baby brother goes to juvie and then disappears off the face of the planet. I thought you were dead, man. You've got no idea the emotional distress you inflicted on my poor heart." His voice drips with sarcasm.

"Yeah, in juvie because of you, dickhead."

He presses harder against my windpipe. "I did the best I fucking could with you, dickhead. Your going to juvie was the best thing that could've happened to you. You're just too fucking dumb to see that." Something behind his eyes shifts. "But that's all in the past now. Bygones are bygones, as they say. Juvie was a gift to you; now I'm here for the favor."

Part of me wants to keep letting him talk, but that shift in his eyes was malevolent, and my already bruised shoulder is screaming for relief. I push the arm on my neck forward by the elbow, sliding out behind it and behind Jax, who seems surprised at my escape. He recovers, turning back to face me, hands fisted in front of him.

"Look, man, you're making bank now. I just need a few large to get out of a situation, that's all. It'll hardly be a drop in the bucket for you. Give me that, and I'll be out of your hair. For good. Promise."

I can't help but shake my head and scoff at his so-called promise. Jax doesn't do promises. *Not that he keeps.*

"I don't know what makes you think I have money, but I can assure you, I don't. I especially don't have money to give to you. So you can get out of my hair anyway."

"Bullshi--"

A knock at the door breaks my attention for a second, but he doesn't need more. The next thing I know, my face is being smashed into the wall, my right arm bent behind me. Exactly where I did not want to be. I've been in this position too many times with Jax, and it never ends well. I can almost feel my arm break again in sympathy for the past.

He gets too close to my ear, his hot breath on my face. "Don't even think about making a sound," he hisses under his breath. I wasn't planning on saying anything or calling out. I don't want anyone else involved in this shit if I can help it.

I hold my breath as a second knock sounds, and

CHAPTER TWENTY-EIGHT

Samantha's voice calls out, "Matt? Are you in there?"

Fuck. No. Go away, Samantha. Run the fuck away.

"Should we let your girlfriend in?" he whispers, a low chuckle in his chest vibrating against my back. He digs his fingers into my raw knuckles, and I can feel the wounds open up. It's excruciating, but I don't cry out.

"Fuck you."

"Think she would? She is pretty..."

Hopefully, Samantha's long gone from the door because I shift and swing my free elbow behind me and into his cheek, the connection reverberating through my bones. This is enough impact for him to drop the arm behind me he's holding, and I'm able to turn and punch him on the same cheek. The knuckles on my right hand are now bleeding freely again, but I don't care. I keep hitting him with both fists, the blood on my hand mixing with the blood now on his cheek, his jaw, and his eye. I just keep punching. A voice is screaming far away, but I ignore it. I dreamed of this moment in every nightmare I've ever had. *Retribution.* He's not even fighting me back anymore, he's only trying to cover his head, so I aim lower where I can hit, where I can cause him pain. And the voice that was screaming is now crying, but I ignore that too. Jax is on the ground now, so I balance myself on the wall with my bloody hands and kick him as hard as I can with my bare feet, over and over and over.

Strong hands are on me, pulling me off and away from Jax, pushing me out of my room and into another one across the hall. I'm assisted to a chair where I sit down. Everything is blurry; my eyes are full of tears. I must've been the one crying before. That means I was the one screaming too. I wipe at my eyes with the backs of my hands and see red for a minute as the blood from my knuckles mingles with my tears momentarily. Once they're clear, I stare down at my hands; both of them now display open wounds. I've really done a number on them. *I hope Samantha doesn't see this*, I think. What an odd thought. *But I know she doesn't like blood...*

Samantha... It was her at the door before. I glance up, and it's Jude sitting on the corner of his bed, a concerned expression on his face. I'm actually relieved to see him instead of Samantha.

"I am not going to ask what the fuck, because that's your business." His face softens, as does his voice. "But I will ask if you're okay. Are you okay?"

I stare up at him, trying to gather my thoughts enough to answer him, and it's so damned hard to think straight. Every thought seems to be an echo from a few minutes ago. "I don't know, man."

"Fair enough. We're still early days into the post-brawl decompression. You able to get in there and clean yourself up?" He nods his head in the direction of the bathroom.

I glance down at myself, blood and sweat everywhere. "I need another fucking shower." I stand to head that way, but it dawns on me that I don't know how things ended. "What about Jaxon? What happened to him?"

"Security is dealing with him. Samantha got them to check the situation, and they heard you going off. I just got back, and they handed you over to me, so I missed all the excitement."

"We're going to need damage control from Vanessa."

"Don't even worry about that shit yet, dude. Go take a shower. I'll deal with Vanessa."

The consequences of what happened are starting to weigh on me as I head into the bathroom and lock the door behind me. *What the fuck did I just do?* I look into the mirror, at the bruises blooming on my neck and cheekbone, at the blood smeared under my eyes. Blood and bruises, things I've seen too much of in my lifetime, mostly my own. But tonight is different. Everything is different now. When I study my reflection in the mirror, I don't see myself. *I see my brother.*

twenty-nine

HERE FOR YOU

SAMANTHA

After Jax gets hauled away for the second time, I call housekeeping to come up and clean up Matt's room. I'd do it myself, but I know I wouldn't be able to handle what I would see. I tip them as they leave since I'm still in the hallway. I've been pacing the entire half-hour they've been in there.

Jude's come out a couple of times to give me updates on Matt, once when he was in the shower and a second time when the doctor came by to tend to his hands again. He's keeping me away for my own good, and I understand. The last thing I want is to be a distraction with my damn passing out all the time.

"So are the guards multiplying, or are we witnessing binary fission?" Jude asks, eyeing the additional guards walking around.

"Binary fission? Really?" I shake my head at him. Jude is the most complex of the Indigo King guys and the hardest to pin down. Inside his crass, rough-edged exterior lives an encyclopedia of random knowledge waiting for his run on Jeopardy!.

"What? When an organism splits into two..."

"I know what it is, Jude. I was merely commenting on your use of the term in this situation."

"The context was fucking spot on, Sam. What the hell?" He furrows his brow in mock confusion, but a smile plays on his lips.

"Never mind. Forget I said anything."

"That'll be the first rule of Sam's Club," he chuckles to himself.

"What?" He's lost me.

And now he's laughing in earnest. "Sam's Club - like Fight Club, get it? The first rule of Fight Club is you don't talk about Fight Club. So, the first rule of Sam's Club is to forget Sam, *you*, said anything."

I'm not seeing what's so funny, so I cross my arms over my chest and wait for him to laugh himself out. This takes longer than I anticipated, as he doubles over at one point and needs to wipe tears from his eyes. He finally does a laugh/long sigh thing and pulls himself together.

"Are you done?" I ask, unimpressed.

This throws him back into laughter, and the

guards down the hall are staring at us in curiosity. I give them a small wave and shrug. I know precisely what Jude is going through. He's got a case of slap happiness. It happens when you're thoroughly exhausted or in the aftermath of a particularly stressful situation, and out of nowhere, something inappropriately hits you as the funniest thing in the world. Your brain tells you this is not that funny, but you can't stop laughing.

Unfortunately, I'm still in the middle of my own stressful situation, so I can't join him yet. I'll need to wait until I witness for myself Matt is okay before I go off the deep end like Jude.

"How about now?" I ask.

He leans over with his hands on his knees, bracing himself for another onslaught of self-amusement. "I think so..." He holds his breath with his cheeks puffed out and exhales slowly. "Yeah. I'm cool now. Sorry about that." He wipes at the front of his shirt as though it got dirty while he was laughing. *Yup. Complex.*

The doctor exits Jude's room, and we both stare at him expectantly. He's an older gentleman with a haircut and mustache belonging somewhere in the 1970s. Giving us both a curious look, he nods. "He'll...be okay..." And with that, he takes off down the hall toward the elevators, anxious to run away from us crazy music people.

Jude and I glance at each other as if we were expecting a little more than what we got. Today's been seven kinds of weird, and it doesn't show any sign of letting up.

The door to Jude's room opens again, and Matt appears and just as quickly disappears back behind the door. I did happen to catch he was only in a towel, but that was it. *Damn, open the door again, please.*

"Jude, go grab me some clothes." Matt's voice says from the other side of the door.

A sparkle in Jude's eye flares as he crosses his arms and taps his chin with a finger, contemplating either a witty comeback or refusal. Maybe even a challenge. But Matt must be able to see him because his voice rises and is all business. "Don't mess with me now, dude. Just get me some fucking clothes, or I'll start touching your books."

That puts a damper on Jude's mischief, and he turns into Matt's room without a second glance. Jude must love his books. *Noted.* Something to ask him about in his interviews.

I go up to Jude's door and place a hand on it, trying to feel Matt through the oak. "Are you okay?" My words come out hoarse and quieter than I intended, but I think they're loud enough for him to hear. The sound of the anger still in him hurts something deep in me. Not anything of my own, but the parts of Matt that are in me now; memories, thoughts, ideas, cares, hopes, they all hurt for him. I've never felt this before. I'm not entirely sure I like it.

"I'll be fine, Sam. You can go now. Thanks."

Jude comes out of Matt's room with his entire duffel bag, and I move out of his way, so he can go back into his own room. Before he shuts the door, Jude peeks his head out. "Thanks for the help, Sam. I'll make sure he doesn't break anything else." And boom, I'm summarily dismissed.

I stand there for a minute, not exactly sure what just happened and feeling all kinds of foolish to still be here, out in the hallway by myself. Well, along with the security guards who are now staring without actually looking at me. Sensing their attention on me gives me goosebumps, so I rub my arms and head down the hall to my room.

Once there, I sit on the end of my bed, contemplating everything that's happened in the last twenty-four hours. And a *lot* has happened. Matt opened up to me a little about his brother, Jax. Matt and I made out. Jax showed up. Twice. Causing all hell to break loose. And now Matt's flipped a switch and is back to being cold to me. I think that covers everything. It's hard to believe how much has happened so quickly with this tour. It is kind of crazy. It can't be normal. *Can it?*

I do know Matt's yo-yo relationship style is fairly routine, at least. I've figured out that much. *Do I want to be in that kind of relationship?* This new and powerful empathy I'm feeling for him is throwing me for a loop. And my desire even right now to go down the hall and take care of him is so not *me. But is that so bad? To want to take care of someone?*

Perhaps if that person keeps pushing you away, you should learn how to take a fucking hint.

And here's my devil's advocate. Hello old friend. What if he's pushing me away because he's hurt?

He can only heal himself. You can't "fix" him. Don't fall into that trap.

And if he doesn't need fixing but needs a friend instead?

Then be his friend. Not his lover.

Friends with benefits?

What's the benefit of getting hurt? Because you know you would.

Probably.

Odds are, he won't change. Most people can't. Or won't.

But I don't want him to change. I want him to be a whole person. He seems so lost sometimes.

Not your job to find him.

No, but I could be there for him while he does it himself.

He doesn't seem to want you there for that.

True. Can't argue the lack of want on his side. This

does appear to be a one-sided effort. So, why am I bothering? Why can't I leave it alone?

Because you're you, and you're going to do whatever the fuck you want anyway.

He called me Sam...

thirty

MY BODY IS A CAGE

MATT

The night is long, and I don't sleep much. What sleep I do steal is full of nightmares about Jax. Jax getting to me. Jax getting to Samantha. Jax hurting me. Jax hurting Samantha. Combinations of all the above. None of them ended well. Actually, I don't know how they end; I wake up in a cold sweat on the verge of screaming before it gets that far. Even when I wake, I can't tell if I'm still dreaming or not. The mere fact my brother is back in my world again is a fucking nightmare on its own.

I finally give up on sleep and roll out of bed for the day around six o'clock. Despite being completely exhausted, my anxiety is through the roof, propelling me to need to move. Before I go anywhere or do anything, I call Taylor to find out what happened to Jax after I was pulled away last night. He does not sound happy when he answers.

"If it isn't His Royal Highness of Pain-in-the-Assland."

"Hey, Taylor. How's it going?"

"I had easier gigs in Afghanistan. And you would know you were with me."

"Yeah, yeah. I like to keep you on your toes. Nothing you can't handle." I try to keep my tone light, but it's so hard. "So what exactly broke down yesterday? Have you done a post-mortem yet?"

He's quiet for a second before he responds. And when he does, it's with trepidation. "I don't know how to tell you this, Matt, but you have a fox in the hen house over there."

"Oh? Who?" This piques my curiosity but confirms my suspicions. I knew there had to be someone on the inside helping Jax.

"Still figuring out that little detail." He sighs heavily, his frustration coming through without a word spoken. "I can pretty confidently say the problem is not your immediate crew, but that's as far as my confidence goes. There is one thing..." He fades out. Hesitating.

"What is it, Tay? Don't hold back on me now."

"Well, it might not mean anything, so I don't know if I want to read into it or not."

"Fucking tell me what it is already, dude. You know I hate when you do this. You're overthinking."

"No. I'm being thorough. There's a difference."

"Fine. Whatever. Just tell me what it is." I can't

take much more. Taylor's investigative skills are top-notch, but he tends to chase dead ends in an effort to be 'thorough.'

"The tour pass Jax had, was not an Indigo King pass. It was an Incendiary Ink pass."

His words hang in between our silences before smacking me upside the head. That makes zero sense. *Who the fuck would Jax know with the Incendiary Ink crew? Or the band?*

"...I don't understand. It was a legit pass? Not a fake?" A counterfeit I could understand and would expect from Jax. Otherwise, not so much.

"Scanned as real." He sounds apologetic, but to me, this is excellent news.

"Okay, this is crazy. But, okay. At least it's not my circle."

"I figured, but I need to dig deeper. So far, your brother's not talking."

This catches me off guard. "Wait. What? Are you holding Jax somewhere?"

Taylor is quiet again for a long minute. "Of course not. He's still in the hospital, but we're... with him."

"Are the police involved?" This is the last thing I need. If Jax presses charges against me, this might turn real bad, real fast. Indigo King's entire existence could be in the balance.

"No. No law enforcement. We've convinced him

it wouldn't be in his best interest to pursue that route, considering his own actions."

I let out the breath I was holding. "Okay. That's a relief. So, what's the plan? I have a free day but don't know the schedule yet. We've probably got press, but I'm not sure if they'll want me to participate with how I'm looking at the moment." I know Vanessa will want my balls on a platter after last night. She gave me space after everything happened, but that could be bad as much as good.

"Just sit tight, man. I'll keep you updated throughout the day."

"What are my options for getting out of my room since Jax is in the hospital? I'm dying for a long run if I can swing it."

"The best we can do is monitor the stairwell again. With the Incendiary Ink connection now in the mix, we'd prefer to keep you close." He sounds sympathetic, but I understand. He's stretching his ranks thin as it is. "I know how you get, so sorry for the cage, but it's for the best."

"Are you still keeping an eye on Samantha Fisher?" I don't care about myself right now. I need to know those I care about are safe.

"Yes, sir. No change there."

"Cool." At least that's one less thing for me to worry about, though I still will. I'm not kidding myself about that.

We hang up, and I prepare to hit the stairwell for

a workout before everyone wakes up. As I'm opening the door to leave, I almost run into Vanessa, holding up a fist, ready to knock on the door, clutching a stack of papers to her chest. She doesn't drop her fist right away, and I'm afraid she's going to use it to hit me for a second. Something in her eyes flares bright when she sees me, and I almost flinch.

"Matthew. You're awake." Her tone is flat. Unaffected. And she used my full name. *Not good*.

"Unless I'm sleepwalking..." I try to joke, but it doesn't work. She is not amused.

"We need to talk." She shoves past me and into my room, not waiting for an invitation.

"Come on in..."

Taking a seat at the small table, she looks around as if inspecting the room. I think she's looking for damage from the night before. Lucky for me, there is none. I did enough damage at Red Rocks itself. I'm sure I'll hear about that now and how much this will cost me to fix.

I sit on the end corner of my bed, waiting for the wrath to be unleashed. Vanessa doesn't let loose on us very often. Or at all. She puts up with our bullshit for the most part, but we don't give her too much hassle to deal with. I brace myself for the onslaught anyway.

"What did I tell you the other day?"

I can't gauge her temperament with that question. It's too mild, and her inflection is unreadable. I also can't tell if the question is rhetorical. I stare at the gauze around my knuckles, picking at the loose cotton threads along the edges and avoiding eye contact at all costs. When I don't answer, she goes on, but now her voice is soft and full of compassion.

"I said you could talk to me about anything. And I meant it."

I nod. "I know, Van." I still stare at my hands, not wanting to face her. Vanessa has been with us since day one, and she's witnessed all of our ups and downs. But nothing like this. Nothing close to this. Last year, even Ryan's alcohol-fueled meltdown didn't get this bad, but she supported him with zero judgment. I shouldn't expect less from her now. But I wish she was mad. I'd rather have yelling and screaming or even fists flying than this. I don't deal with this well at all.

"So, I guess that means you just don't want to talk about it then, right?" She almost sounds offended or hurt, so I look up at her, and sure enough, her eyes are pained. *Goddammit.* I didn't realize this would affect her this way.

"Van...c'mon..." *Fucking rage at me. Tell me how worthless I really am. Give me another reason to feel this shitty. Tell me how disappointed you are in me. Anything but this.*

"Matt, you guys are like the brothers I never wanted, but you're my family. You know this." A smile gentles her features, and I can't help but briefly smile back. "So I wanted to apologize to you personally for letting Jax in last night. I should've talked to you about it beforehand. You never mentioned him, so I thought there was going to be a nice surprise reunion or something... Obviously, I was wrong. And I'm sorry for that." Now she's getting misty-eyed, and I need to look away again. *Fucking hell*. Nobody should apologize for any of this but me.

"I don't blame you, Vanessa. Not at all. Jax would have weaseled his way in another way and, in fact, did just that later on. It's what he does. He uses people. I'm sorry he used you like that to get to me."

"Well, what did he want? I assume from the aftermath it wasn't a well-intentioned visit."

"Money."

She hisses through her teeth in disgust. "What a dick."

This makes me laugh and shake my head. "That's one way to describe him."

"Will you tell me about him someday? About why your relationship is what it is?" Her curiosity is never self-serving. She wants to know so she can help, and I love that about her. But it's also why I'll never tell her about Jax or my childhood. Knowledge can be power, a weapon, or a shield, but it can also be a wound. It can be an open sore that festers, and I would never want to wound Vanessa like that.

"Maybe." I lie. "Maybe."

227

thirty-one

BREATHE ME
SAMANTHA

I wake up early to go for a run since there isn't much to do today. Running appears to be the go-to exercise for people on tour since we're kept like caged rats most of the time. I only planned to go through the footage I have to mark clips for the final cut. I've been trying to do the work as I go instead of having a ton to go through at the end of the tour.

As I leave my room, I catch Vanessa coming out of Matt's room, and she turns to give him a long hug. I turn away quickly and hurry down the hall the opposite way to take the stairs instead of passing them to reach the elevators as I planned.

Okay. That happened. It doesn't mean anything. There's a rational explanation for why Vanessa left Matt's room this early and gave him a long hug in the doorway. Completely rational. They are friends.

They've known each other for a long time. Friends hug. *It's normal. Totally normal. But this early? Really?* I didn't take a good enough look to see if either of them was recently waking up from a wild night of sex.

And if it wasn't sex, but he was just hugging a friend who was comforting him, what is my issue then? That he didn't turn to me for comfort? That he basically brushed me off last night? None of this should be about me. Matt is going through some really crazy shit right now. So, I'm jealous of Vanessa being either a friend or a lover? Or both? What the fuck, Samantha?

Why am I getting upset? I don't have any claim on him. We have no commitment or agreement between us. He's free to fuck around with whoever he damn well pleases if that's what he's doing. As do I...if I wanted to. I just don't happen to want to at the moment. No big deal. That doesn't mean anything is unfair. It's just how it is. I like to think if I keep saying the words, 'no big deal,' they'll sink into my subconsciousness and have some meaning instead of being random words said in a particular order people accept as a standard phrase.

I hit the exit door to the stairwell a little too hard, but I don't care. I also don't care that two security guards are now following me down the stairs, calling after me to stop. *Fuck that, and fuck them.* I was planning on a run, and what I saw makes me want to run even more. *Good luck stopping me.*

I come across Zach in the lobby, the roadie from Incendiary Ink who bought me a drink the other night before Matt showed up and scared him away. He was decent enough but most likely not my type. Of course, I didn't spend enough time with him to make a judgment either.

"Hey, Sam," he says when he sees me. "Heading out for a run?"

"Hi, Zach. Yeah, thought I'd give my legs a bit of a stretch before my day starts." I'm polite but continue toward the doors. He falls into step alongside me.

"Mind if I join you?" he asks, keeping up with me, whether I agree or not. "It's a beautiful morning."

I glance at him out of the corner of my eye, but nothing seems amiss about anything he's doing. I think I'm just unnerved by the whole Matt/Vanessa hug thing. I'm still processing that moment, and it's making me uncomfortable. It's got nothing to do with Zach.

"Sure. I wouldn't mind some company." I flash him a quick smile as he opens the door for us.

As we start our run, we're followed by security, as I had a feeling we would be. Zach, however, was not expecting company.

"Wow. What's with the watchdog?" Looking over his shoulder, he glares at the guard running behind us. His tone is more pissed off than it should be. *I could see being a little annoyed, but pissed? It's a bit much.*

I glance back at the gentleman following us without complaint, alert as ever, and give him a small wave. He nods but doesn't wave back. "Only a precaution, I'm sure. Doesn't Incendiary Ink have its own security?" Surely they have their own 'watchdogs.'

"Yeah. The band does. Not the rest of us, though. We're just peons." He's starting to breathe heavily, and we've only been jogging for five minutes. Not even running yet. I hope he isn't expecting me to go easy merely because he joined me. Because that is not happening.

I shrug noncommittally. "It must be a label thing for the documentary I'm filming. Protecting assets or something. I don't know."

"Assets, huh? You got that right. Your assets are pretty amazing."

I can actually feel his eyes scan my body with lascivious admiration, and it makes me feel slimy or dirty the way he does it. Not attractive at all. *I need to lose this guy.* I was being nice, but it's time to move on. Besides, I've got shit in my head to clear out before I go back to the hotel. Specifically, Matt. And Vanessa now too. *Great.*

"I'm going to do some sprints. I'll catch you later." And before he can utter a single protest, I'm off and running away. My muscles stretch and ache with the strain and its delightful agony. My lungs burn as I reach for air when I slow. Glancing back, I spot the guard, but no Zach. He must have given up and turned around. *Perfect.* I got a weird vibe off of him anyway. Not necessarily nefarious, but definitely creepy.

I slow back down to a jog as I turn around and head back to the hotel, crossing paths with the guard, but we ignore each other as he falls in behind me. At least he's not breathing down my neck. That would be weird. Maybe make me run faster, but I'd rather not utilize that incentive.

My thoughts turn back to Matt and Vanessa hugging in the hallway, and I still don't know what to think about that. I examine my reaction to it; I was jealous. I *am* jealous. I'm not going to fool myself on that front. Jealousy comes from hurt and betrayal. But I have no right to either emotion, *so how do I stop reacting this way?* Perhaps it's normal since I have feelings for Matt. *Shit. I have feelings for Matt. When the fuck did that happen? I have been with my body the whole time, so I should know when things like this happen, right? Fucking feelings.*

I'm supposed to be rebounding from Nick. Bouncing all over the fucking place and not landing anywhere important or serious. Yet, I am catching feelings for the most unavailable person I've ever met. Not only is he closed off emotionally, but he's also maybe got a thing for his tour manager. And my friend. I can't begrudge Vanessa happiness; she deserves it. She's a sweet person. But it would be kind of shitty since she knows I like Matt. At least, I think she does. I guess I wasn't clear enough about it to stake any claim on him. *Jesus Christ. What was I supposed to do? Mark my territory?*

This is getting me nowhere. Fast. I need to let it go and move on. I have other things to focus on, so I should work on those. I don't need the distraction of a relationship right now. And if this reaction of mine is any indication, falling for Matt would be the stupidest thing I could do.

My guard and I get back to the hotel, and Zach is nowhere to be found. Hopefully, he's given up on any pursuit of me. That's a dead-end he should know about by now. After stretching out and cooling down, I get my tour pass scanned, head inside, and take to the stairwell again to push one last burst of energy out of me. Ignoring the guard posted inside who wasn't there when I left, I make it as far as one flight up before I hear someone else on the stairs. I stop and lean into the railing to look up and see who it is.

It's Matt. *Of course, it is. Shitballs.* I'm tempted to turn tail and head back out to the lobby and the elevators, but I stop. I need to be able to coexist with this man, whether it pains me or not. I need to move on with my life too. I won't be able to do that if I'm constantly running away or avoiding him. I take a deep breath and push myself up the stairs. I only need to go up four flights, so hopefully, we won't cross paths.

No such luck. As soon as I start up again, Matt flies down, nearly running into me again. He's shirtless because, of course, he is, and he's got his earbuds in, so he probably didn't notice me in here. *Damn him and his fine bare chest.*

"Samantha. Sorry. I didn't know you were here." *So, I'm Samantha again, am I?*

I can't look at him. I can't talk to him. *What is there even to say?* My heart and brain are in the middle of a brutal war for power, and it's still a stalemate. I move to pass around him, and he steps the same way, so we end up doing the awkward, stupid dance you do when you just want to get fucking past someone and the universe hates you.

He laughs a little, but I don't. I stop moving and wait for him to make way for me. "It's cool," I mutter, keeping my gaze down, not wanting to meet his green eyes, which slay me every time they catch me. Once he's out of the way, I ease past him, making sure not to touch any part of him. When the smell of his sweat, mixed with his cologne, hits me, it makes my stomach do a little flip inside. *Stupid stomach. Stupid girl.*

I sprint the rest of the way, ignoring Matt's calls after me. I'm ignoring everybody today.

thirty-two

PIECES
MATT

"Samantha, hold up." I catch up to her as she pauses in front of her door, the key card hovering at the ready to unlock it. She's back from a run, it looks like, and her long ponytail is sticking to the damp skin of her back. Her sports bra reveals her amazing stomach, which makes me want to reach out and glide my hand over her bare skin. I need to stop myself from gawking at her as I approach. She is simply stunning, and it's hard not to stare. She, however, is still not looking at me at all, like in the stairwell. No, she's actively *avoiding* looking at me or my general direction, for that matter. I lean against the wall next to her door, careful not to stand too close. She's obviously upset about something, so I want to give her space. "Is everything okay with you?"

She takes a deep breath and then turns the

fakest smile on me. Being an open book, her eyes display the Herculean effort that actually goes into that facade. "Yup. Everything is just peachy! Catch you later." She slides the key card into the lock, and the mechanism whirs, allowing her to open the door.

Before she can step inside, I put a hand on the door, holding it open. She has the option to go in if she wants, but I need to know what is going on with her. "Samantha, talk to me." I don't understand why she's being like this. I thought we had made some ground up yesterday. *Did my fight with Jax scare her off?* I can understand how that would happen. It can't have been easy to witness me in such a state last night. Maybe she figures it's best not to be involved with someone so violent, like me. Punching walls. Beating brothers.

She sighs and crosses her arms over her chest, leaning against the wall on the other side of the door in the hallway, so I let her door close softly on its own. She stares at my shoes, her lips pressed into a flat line. Something has seriously got her down.

"What do you want to talk about, Matt?" The sickly sweet tone in her voice lands sour on my ears. "And don't you own any shirts?" She glances up at my bare chest and then quickly away as if caught looking. All's fair, I guess, since I ogled her.

"We could start with why you're mad at me?" It's as decent of a place to start as any. I ignore the shirt comment. Any reply will either be snarky or suggestive, and I get the sense she's not in the mood for either.

At my question, she pierces her gaze into me, but I don't look away. If she's as intuitive as she professes to be, she'll realize that I have no clue what her problem is with me. She searches my eyes completely, and I let her see all of me, not holding back a thing. Letting the roller coaster of the last few days play out in my thoughts for her to study. Her own face shifts and changes as she goes through it along with me. She gets all of my fear, all of my rage, all of my shame and embarrassment, and lastly, all the concern I have for her.

After a minute of scrutiny, she blinks, "I'm not mad at you. I don't know what I am." She moves her focus to her shoes but still remains closed off.

"Well, what's going on?" Despite my better judgment and efforts, I can't *not* care about her. I can't seem to stay away from her either, even though, for her own good, I probably should. Something about her makes me think it might be worth the risk. "Talk to me."

"I want to take a shower and chill out. It's been a crazy few days." And she's back to avoiding me. I can tell something is wrong, though, but I'm not sure if I should press the issue or not.

"Are you sure? Something is definitely bothering

you, and I have a funny feeling it's to do with me somehow."

She hesitates, arms still crossed, and lets out a deep sigh. "Fine. I thought our kiss yesterday was the start of something between us, but I guess I was wrong." She finally glances back up at me, awaiting my reaction, but I'm merely confused.

"What are you talking about? I thought the same thing."

"Matt. I saw Vanessa leaving your room this morning."

"And?" This is making less and less sense. I don't understand why seeing Vanessa would upset her.

"And? And I saw the hug you guys shared. It was pretty intense, but I wasn't like spying on you or anything. I was just heading out for my run and briefly saw you guys. I don't know what the hug was about, but it was pretty early in the morning, so it obviously made me wonder about the two of you together. And then, too, if it was just friends, then I'm still sort of jealous because you didn't turn to me, or whatever because you brushed me the fuck off last night after everything. And then, on my run, I decided I didn't have any right to be jealous of any of it. It's not like we're a thing. And it's not about me right now. And great, now I'm derailed. Fuck."

Wow. So that was a lot. She thinks me and Vanessa hooked up? Ugh. The thought creeps me out. Not because Vanessa is ugly or anything, far from it. But we all think of her like our sister. I can't stop the small laugh that escapes, and I smack my hand to my mouth to contain it, but I'm not fast enough. Samantha does not see the humor in this and moves to unlock her door again.

"Shit. I'm sorry. Really." I contain the laugh but not the smile. "Nothing is going on with Vanessa and me. She's like a sister to me, to all of us. That would just be weird." She gives me a dubious look, unsure whether to trust me or not. "I swear. Vanessa came by this morning when she was handing out the itineraries to check on me. And there was nothing in that hug. Believe me."

"I do. I just got too deep in my own head. Overthinking everything like I always do."

"I didn't mean to brush you off last night either. Things were just out of control, and I wanted to keep it away from you."

I step closer to her, and she doesn't move away. Even a sweaty and disheveled Samantha is gorgeous and irresistible. But she's going to regret me. I just know it. She's going to realize what a monster I am eventually and run for the hills. *Then why am I doing this? To her? To me? The heart wants what the heart wants. That's why.*

"Okay. Good. I mean, I knew you were an asshole but didn't think you were *that* big of an asshole." The hint of a smile plays on her lips, and I can't tear my eyes away from them. I want those lips on me. *Now*.

"I *am* an asshole, so we're clear." I lean in slowly, testing the waters, and without objection, press my lips to hers, and she responds with enthusiasm. I do love how bold she can be. She takes it farther, backing me into her door, the wood cold on my back. Pressing against me, when our bare skin touches, our kiss electrifies, sending jolts of heat lightning throughout my body. No one else's touch has ever done this.

Her mouth opens to me, and our tongues meet, arousing an intense need within me. This isn't enough. I need more. More of her. All of her.

"I'd say get a room, but you guys already have rooms. You're choosing not to use them, why?" Jude's voice cuts in from down the hall. I didn't hear his door open. Or perhaps I did and ignored it. *Whatever*.

Samantha rests her forehead on my chest, still breathing heavily, as I am too. I put a hand on the back of her neck, holding her to me, letting her know I do not want to stop what we started.

"Fuck you, Jude." I grin at him. "And no, I'm not volunteering."

"Damn. You stole my line," he laughs.

"Too bad."

"You might want to grab a shirt for the meeting, hot stuff."

Shit. I got so carried away with Samantha I forgot about the meeting this morning. We're supposed to discuss the Jax incident, and I'm not looking forward to it. "I will. I'll be down in a few."

Jude heads to the elevators, and I glance down at Samantha, who is pulling away from me.

"You should be going. You don't want to be late." Her cheeks are flushed, and I can't tell if it's from embarrassment or the fervor of our kiss. Either way, it's very attractive on her, making it even harder for me to leave.

"I should, but I don't want to." No sense lying about it.

She raises an eyebrow at me. "Go. Text me later. We'll grab food or something."

"Or something sounds fantastic," I say, kissing her neck, the salt of her skin delicious.

"Matt...you need to go...your meeting..." she whispers, lightly pushing my chest.

I reluctantly pull back. "Fine. But note that I'm leaving under heavy protest."

"Duly noted."

She unlocks her door, enters her room, and gives me the sexiest look I've ever seen. It's full of angst, need, hunger, and every carnal desire in one look. It takes everything in me to walk away once the door closes instead of knocking or breaking it down to touch her again.

No. Instead, I need to go to a meeting to talk about

my fucking dickhead brother. I'm hoping the label hasn't heard about the fight between Jax and me or that he ended up in the hospital. I can only imagine the bad press that would ignite. It would not be a good look for Indigo King to employ an abusive drummer who can't control himself. Not the bad boy image I want for myself either, to be honest. I never wanted that stereotypical perception of me. Not that I give two shits what anyone else thinks, but it would reflect poorly on the band and that I do care about. So, on to damage control.

thirty-three

HUSH
MATT

When I enter the small hotel conference room, everyone is waiting for me.

"Glad you could join us, Rocky," Jude smirks while swiveling left and right in his chair. "Or, should we call you Romeo?"

"Shut it." That's the best I can do. *Pathetic, really*.

"Romeo?" Ryan's eyebrows go up in inquiry. "Is romance in the air for our young, strapping percussionist?"

"Don't you start too," I mutter. *Man, my comebacks are shit lately*.

"Boys, settle down. We've got some serious shit to talk about." Vanessa knows how to whip us into line; treat us like the little lost boys we are, and we pay attention.

I have to stop smiling to myself at Samantha, thinking there could be something between Vanessa and me. The idea is too preposterous. How she could jump to that conclusion is beyond me, but then I never could figure out how women's brains worked. Still waiting on that particular breakthrough.

"Sorry, Van," Ryan says. "Let's jump to the important shit then. What's up?"

Vanessa looks over her laptop directly at me, a cautious expression on her face. "A situation came up in the past hour we need to talk about. We've been given an ultimatum by your brother Jax."

I stiffen at this, sitting up straight in my chair. *That motherfucker.*

"What kind of ultimatum?" Jude gets the words out before I can.

"He wants Two Hundred and Fifty Thousand dollars within forty-eight hours, or else he will go straight to *Blindsided Magazine* and the police and report the assault by Matt as unprovoked and a pattern of abusive behavior."

The silence that follows is deafening. *I knew it. I fucking knew it.* This was always his Plan B. If I wouldn't straight up give him the money, he would create a situation where I had to. This is it. This is where I'm kicked out of the band. Something this huge can't stand. We'd never survive this kind of bad press, not in a million years. We're too new. We're still making a name for ourselves. Shit, we're still proving ourselves to the haters we're not some fly-by-night one-hit-wonders.

They're all staring at me expectantly, maybe waiting for me to quit. I should step down. Bow out. Save them the hassle of firing me by leaving now.

"Guys... If you want me out... I completely understand..."

"What?" Ryan is incredulous. "We know this is all bullshit."

"Fuck that noise, man." Jude is equally nonplussed. "You're not going anywhere, so shut the fuck up with that."

"We'll figure something out," Vanessa chimes in, nodding her head in agreement with the guys. "So kick that thought out of your head. I wanted you to know what we're facing. Now that you know, any initial thoughts on how you want to handle this?"

Ryan leans forward on the table, intense eyes on mine. "This is your shit show, man. However you want to play this, we'll support you one hundred percent."

My mind hasn't had time to catch up with everything said, from Jax's demands to the band not wanting me to quit; it's all too much.

"I was born Matt Holloway. Not Matt Sturridge," I blurt out. I'm not sure where this is coming from, but an overwhelming need to put everything out in the open where it can breathe takes over. "I changed my name after I got out of juvenile detention and before I joined the Marines. I didn't want my brother Jax to ever be able to find me again."

CHAPTER THIRTY-THREE

"And then you had to go and get famous like the idiot you are," Jude snickers.

"Why were you looking to keep away from your brother so badly?" Vanessa's eyes are pained again, and it's hard to look at, so I shift my gaze to the tabletop, examining the wood grain. *How much do I want to tell them?* My god, there aren't more than two people in the entire world who know about this, and it was almost a decade ago that I told them. This is the exact situation I wanted to avoid. I didn't want anyone else getting pulled into this shit, and here we all are, right in the middle of it.

I must be taking too long to answer because Ryan states, "Family first. Always. But now *we're* your family, and we're here for you. Whatever you want or don't want to tell us is fine."

I nod, still staring at the table. I know these guys are my friends. My chosen family. We've always been more than bandmates to each other, even from the beginning. And with this shit hanging over our collective heads now, I owe it to them to explain. I owe them the story of how we got here. After taking a few deep breaths, I start in.

I tell them about our absent father and our drug-addicted mother, about our neglectful grandmother, and how we were basically left to fend for ourselves most of our lives as everyone in authority eventually disappeared one way or another. I let them know about the sibling abuse I suffered at Jax's hands repeatedly and my frequent visits to the emergency room because of him. And how I shamefully never told anyone because he convinced me foster care would be a million times worse. I tell them how Jax continued to cash our grandmother's Social Security checks after she died but used that money for drugs instead of food or rent and how he's facing charges now on the same issue. And then, I explain how I ended up in juvenile detention.

"I couch-surfed with the few friends I had as much as I could get away with my first two years of high school. I'd stay with Jax if I needed to but typically only went to his place when children's services would check in on us. Jax persuaded them to let him be my guardian after our grandmother died. He was able to collect welfare and food stamps for that, and of course, he used it all for drugs and alcohol too."

Vanessa puts her head down on the table, hiding her face. I can tell she's crying. But Ryan and Jude both don't turn away. They don't flinch. The anger each of them is displaying is palpable, and I appreciate them more than ever before. This is the right thing, telling them my story. I should've done this years ago.

"When I was sixteen, Jax got promoted to the neighborhood drug dealer and got in a fight with one of his customers on our front lawn. It got out of hand, so I broke things up. Jax had cut him pretty bad with a broken bottle. The guy was so out of it, though, he probably didn't know what was going on. Someone had called the cops, and Jax shoved the broken bottle into my hands before they showed up, telling me I would be let off easy since I was a kid. They'd throw me into the foster system if he got put away. They'd slap me on the wrist and let me go if I fessed up to it instead of him. So like an idiot, I did. But I didn't get a slap on the wrist, and they didn't let me go. I got two years detention for aggravated assault."

"Jesus," Jude mutters under his breath. Ryan shakes his head. Vanessa still has her head down.

"The only people that know about this are my detention center counselor and the Marine recruiter I interviewed with to get an exception to join with a criminal record. Oh, and I told Samantha a little. Not all, but some."

"How long were you in the Marines?" Ryan's voice is muted, intense.

"Five years total active duty, including boot camp. I did two deployments to Afghanistan. That's where I met Taylor, my friend whose security company has been helping out since Jax showed up." Everything is coming out so easily now. I thought I was better off keeping this shit bottled up all these years, but it was remarkably simple to say out loud. And I'm floored by how chill everyone is, for the most part. Vanessa still hasn't lifted her head off of her folded arms yet. I'm starting to worry about her.

"Damn, I feel like I should be thanking you for your service, but it feels way too weird." Jude gets up from his chair and starts pacing behind Ryan, his hands shoved in his pockets.

"Nah, man. It's cool." I don't need thanks. That's not why anyone joins the Marines.

"Wait - so *you* hired the extra security who's been locking shit down?" Ryan asks, surprised. "What the hell, man?" He seems offended.

"Well, yeah. When Jax popped back onto the scene, I thought it prudent to put up some reinforcements."

"So, instead of telling us what the threat was, you just hired more security to protect us from it? That's kind of lame, dude." He is definitely offended, but I hear him.

"When you put it like that, it sounds bad..."

"You should've told us. I think we had a right to know your brother was a danger."

I still cringe at Jax being called my brother, even though technically he is. "He never threatened you guys. Just me, and maybe Samantha."

Vanessa finally raises her head, her eyes puffy and swollen from crying. "He threatened Sam? Does she know this?"

"Yes. She knows. And it wasn't a direct threat, just an implication. Which I know isn't any better, but..." I put my hands up defensively. The mood shifts, and I don't like where this is headed. "Look, this all happened really fast, like, only the past couple of days. I haven't had time to digest it, let alone deal with it properly. I think that's obvious." I turn my hands so the knuckle side faces them, showing them the scabs and scars of how I dealt with it *very* incorrectly. "Cut me a little slack here."

They all focus their attention on my beat-up hands for a brief moment, then away, acknowledging my situation. I understand their concern, but it's exactly why I didn't want to involve them if I didn't need to. And I didn't think Jax was a direct threat to them. His problem is with me, not with them. I see now he considers the entire band a golden ticket of some sort, so I was wrong not to let them in on everything before now. Keeping things from them was selfish of me. *Who would've thought keeping your past a secret would be greedy? Certainly not me. I thought I was doing the right thing.*

"Okay, so let's think about what we're going to do now." Vanessa wipes under her eyes, removing the remnants of tears. She's back to business and in manager mode. "Any suggestions?"

The three of us stare at each other, and none of us offers an answer.

"We just took in a lot of very major information about Matt here." Jude waves an arm in my direction as he continues to pace. "I think we need a little time to ruminate on the situation before making any decisions."

"You and your two-dollar words," Ryan chuckles.

"Screw you, that's at least five bucks."

"Well, guys, we don't have much time to respond." Vanessa checks her phone and stands quickly. "Right, I need to make some calls. The clock is ticking, and thanks to me, you three now have a totally free day, so do your ruminating or whatever, and let's reconvene at dinner."

She leaves the conference room, and the three of us consider each other, not saying anything. None of us wanting to be the one to open the conversation.

After a few unproductive minutes like this, Jude paces his way to the door. "Well, this has been lovely, but I need food if I'm going to be asked to think. I'll catch you guys in a bit."

Ryan gets up from his chair, following Jude out the door. "I need to find Sarah. I'll text you in a little while, Matt." At least he doesn't sound mad at me anymore, so there's that.

I'm left alone with my scars and my thoughts. Thoughts that are wounds I've reopened, leaving me drained of everything. What a fine fucking mess.

thirty-four

BREATHLESS

SAMANTHA

I wait in the lobby for Matt to leave his meeting, thinking we can grab some lunch when his meeting is over. Vanessa exits first, her head buried in her phone. Her eyes are red and puffy like she's been crying, and a pang of guilt hits me for ever thinking she and Matt had something going on. I should have known better. Everything's been so amped up around here it was easy for my imagination to run away with me. She gives a small wave as she keeps walking and talking on her phone intently. *What was the meeting about that has Vanessa crying? This can't be a good sign.*

A few minutes later, Jude exits, his hands shoved in the pockets of his jeans, looking equally upset. He hurries by me without even seeing me. His mind is obviously somewhere else. Ryan follows behind a little while later, stopping once he exits the conference room and looking around like he's a bit lost. He runs both hands through his hair, exhaling a deep breath. Noticing me, he comes over to where I'm sitting.

"Hey, Sam. How's it going?" He sits on the couch across from me.

"You tell me. Everyone is pretty intense walking out of your meeting. What happened in there? Is everything okay?"

He eyes me, considering his response carefully. "Yeah. Intense is a suitable word for it." He looks around, surveying the surroundings. "Everything is for Matt to tell you if he's going to. It's not my place. We still need to meet again later to continue this discussion."

"That sounds ominous." My stomach clenches with worry about whatever is happening for everyone to be so freaked out. I almost want to pull out my phone and start recording this as it might be important somehow, and maybe I should capture it. But I have the sense whatever this is, it isn't meant for public consumption either.

His gaze meets mine, strained and fierce. "Yeah. It is." He stands and gazes down at me, his demeanor cautious. "Keep an eye on him. He's going through some heavy stuff at the moment. He seems to trust you, which is weird for him but awesome."

I nod. "Okay. I will." What an odd request. *Keep an eye on him? What is he going to do?* "Should I be worried? You're kind of scaring me." The knot in my stomach tightens even more as my thoughts race.

"Nothing like that. I mean, I don't know, be careful with him."

I'm unsure how to take what he's saying, but I nod again. The conversation is getting weirder the longer we speak, and I'd like it to stop now. *What does he mean 'be careful with him?' Why wouldn't I be 'careful?' Does he think I'm out to hurt Matt somehow? That's crazy.*

Ryan studies my response, and my face must show my thoughts. Stupid horrible poker face. "I didn't mean to imply you wouldn't be." He runs a hand down his face. "Fuck. I don't know what the fuck I'm saying right now, so I'm going to shut the hell up and find my girlfriend. Forget everything I said. I'll see you, Sam." He rushes away toward the elevators to escape this awkward discussion and thank god. I couldn't take much more. I've never seen Ryan so concerned or upset. I really need to find out what their meeting was about.

I wait for Matt to come out next, anxious to find out what has everyone so damned freaked out. I don't know who else is in the conference room with him, so I don't go in. I don't want to interrupt anything so important. After about ten minutes, I run across the street, security in tow, to grab a cold lunch for the two of us. Matt is in the lobby when I get back, looking way too serious but apparently waiting for me.

"I saw you leave, so I was hoping that was what you were going for."

"I didn't know how much longer you would be, so I figured food would be on your mind when you got finished. Want to find somewhere quiet to eat and talk?"

"Sure." He grabs the bag of food, takes my good hand into his, and pulls me toward the elevators. But he doesn't stop on our floor. Instead, we go to the top floor and through an exit that opens onto a rooftop patio. While the view of the surrounding mountains is breathtaking, the best part is there isn't a security guard in sight.

"Wow. I didn't know this was up here. This is gorgeous."

"Yeah. One of Taylor's guys told me about it." He sits at one of the couches surrounding a crystal fire pit. The sun is warm, but the breeze is still cool up here. We take our time eating, making small talk, not ready to jump into the heaviness we both know is ahead of us. When we're done and talking becomes unavoidable, I broach the subject of the band meeting.

"So, you were the only one that came out of the meeting not upset. What did you do to everyone in there?" I smile, trying to keep things light as long as I can. I'm well aware it won't stay this way.

A hint of a smile plays on his lips but doesn't entirely form. The sadness in his eyes takes over his face. "It was kind of brutal for them. They learned all the details of my sordid past."

"All the details?"

He nods and proceeds to tell me everything he told the band. Some of it I knew, and some of it, the heartbreaking sides, I didn't. I can't stop the tears that run down my cheeks as he tells me about his abusive childhood, but I don't interrupt him. I know how hard it was for him to start telling his story. I want him to be able to finish on his own terms.

I hold his hand firmly throughout, allowing him to squeeze my fingers however tightly he needs to as he talks. He never cries. His eyes fill with tears a few times, but he holds them back. I'm doing enough crying for both of us.

"The issue now for me is how I reacted. Beating Jax up like that... I swear I feel like a fucking monster. *Worse* than him. I just lost it. I almost don't even remember it; I was so far gone. It felt good for only a second, if that. Afterward, I just felt empty. Hollow. I still do."

"Oh, Matt." The torture in his eyes is heartbreaking. "You are *not* a monster. I think your reaction was understandable. Maybe it's not the right thing to do, but it's understandable why you did it." Surely no one would blame Matt for going off on his brother after everything he's done to him. And for him to blame or punish himself for everything is insane.

"And now Jax is threatening to go to the police and the press unless we give him a quarter of a million dollars," he finishes with a deep sigh.

"Wait, what?" That last sentence throws me off-kilter. "What on earth can make him think he'll get away with this?"

"I don't know. He's always had balls bigger than his brains. Plus, it's what he always does. Sees an opportunity and takes advantage of it."

"Well, he can fuck right off with that idea." I am livid Jax would think he could do this to Matt. I don't care if it's my place or not; I just can't watch it happen. He's been through way too much as it is. He deserves some peace.

He laughs lightly, wiping another stray tear away from my cheek. "Well, alrighty then. Maybe I should sic you on him."

"Do it. Well, wait a few weeks for my cast to come off, then sic me on him." I gaze down at my cast, considering how many things have changed in so short a time. Despite our super rocky start, I can feel myself falling for Matt. It's probably the dumbest thing in the world for me to do, especially since I'm fresh out of a long-term relationship, but I can't stop myself from feeling for him. *Intensely*. The protectiveness I have for him is the strongest I have ever felt for anyone and is what most surprises me.

Sure, I'm attracted to him; he's a tremendously handsome guy. Anyone with two eyes and a brain would be. But his willingness to be vulnerable after all he's been through is so admirable. I'm honored he's thought enough of me to tell me his story.

"Now, I need to figure out what to do about Jax." He leans forward, rubbing the back of his neck. Then he stands suddenly and starts pacing the length of the fire pit, his nervous energy bubbling over. "And by dinner time, too. Like I need another deadline."

"You're not actually considering paying him off, are you?" I can't believe that's even an option. *Who has that kind of money to throw away?*

"I don't have a lot of options. I need to think about the band. I have some money set aside, and I can borrow the rest... I think the label and attorneys could get involved."

"No, Matt. Once you feed that demon, he'll come back hungry for more." I can't just sit while he paces, so I stand up and join him. We must look like idiots stalking around the damned fire pit. "There's got to be another way."

"Samantha, if this gets out to the press-"

"You might help other people in your situation," I say slowly, an idea starting to form in the corners of my mind.

"What? Help who?" he stops pacing, looking at me expectantly.

I hold up a finger while the idea solidifies before

expressing it aloud. It might work *if* we time things right. *And* if Matt were willing... "If you went to the press with *your* story, you would neutralize him. But you'd have to tell everything, Matt. *Everything.*"

He nods slightly, stopping to think but not thoroughly convinced yet. I can tell the idea is challenging for him. I don't blame him. It's a scary thing to do if he agrees to it.

"Just think of all those other kids out there with brothers like Jax who think they're the only one going through the same thing. Imagine if they knew they weren't alone. We could find resources to amplify for helping others like you. Sibling abuse is a real issue that I don't think many people know about. You could shine a light on the subject and rid yourself of Jax for good at the same time." My heart is racing, hoping this is a doable idea. "And you wouldn't have to hide anymore..."

The pacing starts again, and my heart sinks. He hates the idea. It would be so perfect, though. He would be helping so many others, if not himself.

At last, he walks up to me, cups my face in his hands, and leans down to kiss me sweetly on the lips. He pulls away and gazes into my eyes, his features so intense I get lost. "You're a genius."

I can't help but grin back at him. "It's about time you admitted it."

thirty-five

YOU'RE GOING DOWN

MATT

We meet in the hotel restaurant for a late dinner before we're all supposed to head off to our next stop in Albuquerque, and I tell everyone Samantha's idea about beating Jax to the press to neutralize him. She's even filming our dinner, with my blessing for the documentary. I don't want the film to be all about me or this situation, but it is a part of what's happening, so we're writing our history in real-time. We may as well document it as it happens. Plus, I just like having her nearby. It's comforting.

"Are you sure that's how you want to handle this?" Vanessa's concern is written all over her face, her brows furrowed with worry. "I have the label on speed dial if we want their lawyers to handle everything. Just say the word."

"It's up to these two if they're okay with this option. It could get messy, but I don't see a downside here." I turn expectantly to the rest of the band for their input.

Jude and Ryan stare at each other, weighing the idea between them. After a silent conversation, Jude gives him a slight nod and then turns to me.

"If this is what you think is best and can handle it, we've got your back, man." He holds out a fist for me to bump, which I do, careful of my beat-up knuckles. "I'm not afraid to say it, but you've got the biggest balls of all of us, dude. Kudos."

"Agreed," Ryan says, holding out his own fist for me. "And I hope you're right, and it does help someone else. That would be fucking amazing."

"Cool. Thanks, guys. It means a lot." This chosen family of mine surprises me in the best ways so often, I sometimes can't believe that I'm so lucky. Sure, there are times I want to strangle each and every one of them, but more often than not, I'm nothing but grateful for this family.

"I know exactly who should do your story." Vanessa starts going through the contacts on her phone, ready to arrange everything. "Henry March at Rolling Stone Magazine would be the perfect writer to cover this. If I remember correctly, he lives in the southwest somewhere, so he's probably not too far away." She stands and starts heading to the exit of the restaurant. "Let me see if I can get a hold of him and what his schedule looks like. I'll be right back."

I take a deep breath. "Okay. So this is happening." The edge of a panic attack threatens to push through my current calm. My palms are sweating, and I wipe them on the front of my jeans before starting to tap out a nervous beat on my thighs.

"Buckle up, buttercup. It could be a bumpy ride." Jude waives down our waitress and orders a refill on his beer, giving her a sly wink before she walks away. *Such a player.*

It's so hard to sit here and not acknowledge Samantha mere feet away from me since she's filming. Out of everyone around me, she's the one I want to talk to the most. I've had years of talking to Ryan and Jude, so they're barely interesting anymore. She interests me. Not only is she drop-dead gorgeous, but she's intelligent, caring, talented, and sexy as hell. *Holy shit. I'm falling for Samantha, aren't I? Or am I too far gone already?*

I need to consider this carefully. I have been nothing but a train wreck on steroids since she met me, yet there she is, looking at me in a way I've never been looked at before. *Could she possibly feel the same way about me?* That can't be true. After how downright dickish I've treated her, she's got to be being polite, or at least playing it cool. *She can't be catching serious feelings for me, can she?* I can't dare to dream that big. Not yet anyway. I've only just released my demons from their cages; I don't know how they will react to the outside world yet. This could be a bigger nightmare than the one I've been hiding.

Vanessa comes back in, waving her phone. "Good news. We're all set. Henry will meet us in Albuquerque tomorrow afternoon before the show."

I can't help but clench my fists at her announcement, and I don't know what the reaction means. I can't tell if I'm angry or excited, or both. I'm undeniably nervous; I do know that much. This is fucking crazy, but I can't turn back now. Wheels are in motion.

Later in the evening, we all pack up and start on the road to Albuquerque. The tension between everyone is palpable. It's not negative energy, more like electrified anticipation bouncing between us.

Samantha and I hang out in the lounge area of the bus until the small hours of the night, going through her footage so far. She's trying to distract me from the oncoming storm, and it is so appreciated. Plus, I'm learning a lot about her job, which is extremely interesting. Well, when she describes it, it is.

We end up falling asleep together on one of the front couches, legs tangled, her head on my chest, trying to avoid each other's bumps and bruises as best we can. *And I didn't have a single nightmare.*

Before I know it, Vanessa is waking us up because we're at the hotel already. I feel like I just fell asleep. We have a full day of press, not including my interview with Rolling Stone before the show tonight, so it is going to be an extremely long day. One that I am not looking forward to at all.

I manage to get through all of it without completely losing my mind. Even the interview with Henry goes smoother than I thought it would. Talking about my childhood is getting easier the more often I do it. I never thought that would be the case.

This interview is a little different, though. Reporters demand proof and sources, so I have to share details, including things like my medical records with him. Thank god for electronic health records that I can just pull up for him. His reaction to seeing my x-rays is brutal to watch, but I survive it, just like I survived how my x-rays got that way. At the end of the interview, he asks the one question I've been dreading:

"So, even with the alleged sibling abuse you've suffered in the past, you mentioned an incident with your offending brother that happened recently. If I'm correct, the wounds on your neck and hands show evidence of a physical altercation of some sort. Do you care to address that?"

I stare down at my hands, still a fucking mess, carefully considering the question. Vanessa and the label's lawyers instructed me not to admit to anything during this interview, but that still doesn't sit well. So, I need to walk a fine line between admission and explanation. I can only hope I don't trip myself as I go.

"If I've learned anything through all this, it's that violence doesn't ease the pain. It doesn't fix anything. And actually, it probably causes more trouble than it's worth. More often than not, you end up hurting yourself more than the other person." *And prove yourself to be the monster you always feared while at it, don't forget.*

Henry is gracious and thanks me for the time. And Samantha gives him the list of resources she pulled together for others in a similar situation to use in his story.

It was so helpful to have her there during the interview. Even though she was doing her own job filming it all, it was extremely reassuring to know she was there, and I could look to her when needed. We haven't heard from Jax at all today, and technically we have until tomorrow morning to respond to his ultimatum. However, he's got a little surprise headed his way, as Henry's article should be online sometime tomorrow morning.

Now I just need to drink all the coffee in the Albuquerque vicinity, and perform with high energy I don't have in front of thousands of people. No problem. I'm a pro.

thirty-six

OUT OF TARTARUS

SAMANTHA

At the amphitheater in Albuquerque, it feels like we're in the middle of nowhere because we basically are. There is very little around this venue except for the open desert and mountains. It's beautiful, especially at sunset, but so barren it's almost like we're on our own planet out here. I set up my camera on the side of the stage instead of out in the audience. The stage here is gigantic, so Ryan and Jude will have room to roam, and I'm curious what they'll do with all the space. Matt is the high-energy one, but the other two can give him a run for his money if given the opportunity to. Well, tonight's their chance. This should be a great show.

Matt comes by before the gates open, moving like he's twenty pounds lighter. It's a subtle change in him, but it's dramatic at the same time. Telling his story and having everything out in the open must be so liberating for him, I can only imagine. After everything he's gone through in his life, to finally put the past in the past where it belongs reflects in his whole being now. He even smiles openly on occasion. If I thought he was hot before, his newfound confidence cranks that up to eleven.

He comes up behind me, sliding his arms around my waist and resting his head against mine. "Are you as tired as I am?" he sighs. He's got to be exhausted. He must be completely drained with all the interviews he fielded today and the important one with Rolling Stone. I was with him all day, and I'm tired from documenting everything, but I don't have to be "on" like he does during those interviews. Even though I'm working too, I'm only a bystander. My job is literally to be the fly on the wall. He doesn't have it so easy.

"I'm tired, but probably not Matt Sturridge tired." I hug him against my back, and we start swaying a little to the music on the sound system, enjoying a rare peaceful private moment.

"Well, Matt Sturridge will be sleeping the sleep of the dead tonight." He straightens his back and scrunches his face up. "Wow, talking in the third person is the strangest thing. Don't let me do that again."

"Matt Sturridge doesn't like it?" I laugh.

"No. He most certainly does not." He shudders violently, expressing exactly how much he doesn't like it. I love seeing him so easygoing. It's so refreshing. I knew he had it in him somewhere, he just needed to find it, and it appears he has. "I need to go. I'll find you after."

"Have a good show. Remember to pretend not to see me."

"That's not even possible." He turns me around and plants a solid kiss on my lips, wrapping me in his arms and leaning back, causing my feet to leave the ground. I can't help but kick my feet in protest as I giggle. Silly Matt Sturridge is damned attractive as well. *I will never survive this man.*

Watching his evolution over the last few days has been incredible. He's gone from a completely shut-off asshole to an open and vulnerable, caring human being. Still flawed. We all are. But he readily admits his flaws and works to fix them, something not many guys would do. I think I've officially stopped fighting my feelings for him. Despite the rough road that got us here, and we *are* here, I believe we are at a place where things can actually grow. I honestly don't know how we got here, but I'm not going to doubt it anymore.

When the crowd starts streaming in, a low buzz fills the air, but the vibe is different from usual. I can't put my finger on it, but it's off somehow. I take my spot on the side of the stage. There are a few other camera jockeys in the area from local media outlets that I greet with a smile and a wave.

After Sarah's set, one of them, a tall female with cropped dark hair and perfect makeup, sidles up to me as if we're friends. I've never seen her before, but she seems nice enough. She's got an Incendiary Ink press pass around her neck, so I should probably be friendly to her. "So, you get to follow three hot and talented musicians around and get paid for it. What a horrible job you have." She smiles, and the only thing I can think is, *my, what big teeth you have.*

"Yeah. It's the worst." I go along with her obvious sarcasm.

"And hazardous too, apparently." She indicates the cast on my wrist. "Is it true Matt did that?"

"It was an accident, but yeah. Matt knocked me down while we were running." I realize how that all sounds, and make sure to follow up. "Like I said, it was a complete accident. No one was at fault."

"Oh, of course," she nods. "And the cheek...was that the same incident? You've been through the wringer! You should earn hazard pay."

I laugh nervously, "Yeah, but I'll be fine." Suddenly I'm not liking this chick's questions. She's being awfully nosy. "I'm sorry; what's your name?" I flash a smile, but I'm sure she can tell how fake it is with my horrible acting skills.

Indigo King is about to take the stage, and Ryan strums a few test chords on his guitar from the opposite stage wing. Typically, the crowd would go absolutely nuts at that, but it sounds more like a mixed reaction tonight. Maybe Indigo King isn't as famous in Albuquerque as they are in other cities.

"Rose. Rose Kelly." She shouts into my ear as she pulls a business card out of her bag and hands it to me. "Thanks, Samantha," she chirps as she waves and walks away.

I eye her warily but shove the card in my back pocket and start recording. I can't let the bad feeling I got from her interfere with my job. And something is in the air tonight. Such a negative current runs through everyone; I can almost physically see it.

The band starts playing their usual set in earnest and is still getting a varied response from the crowd. Nothing like the rabid admiration that they had in the last two shows. I turn the camera on the crowd to see if I can glean what's going on. Several people are sharing their phone screens with people next to them. *What the hell are they looking at? They're here for a concert, not to stare at their phones.*

After three songs, the guys sense that something is happening, but they obviously don't know what it is either, so they play on. It's not like they can stop and ask the crowd what their fucking problem is. I've seen videos of them playing rough crowds before, and Ryan is usually an expert at winning them over, but this is an extreme case.

"There you are," Vanessa pants, rushing next to me, almost tipping over in her heels as she comes to a stop. "We've got a serious problem."

The band is at the interlude, where Ryan introduces the members to the crowd. Jude is up first, and the crowd goes nuts, cheering his bass solo as usual.

Vanessa pulls up something on her phone and shows it to me. It's an article on *Blindsided's* website, and the headline makes my heart stutter:

ROCK DRUMMER STURRIDGE ENJOYS HITTING MORE THAN DRUMS

Under the headline is a photo of Jax, bruised and cut up, taken after his fight with Matt. The asshole reneged on his blackmail deal and went to the press early. *Shit.* I glance up at Matt as Ryan introduces him, and some of the crowd actually boos him. *This is unbelievable.*

I don't know if he hears the negative reaction because he always gives his all, and he performs a flawless drum solo. He may not hear the crowd with his ear monitors in anyway. That could be a good thing. Ryan and Jude definitely hear it, though, and they look at each other questioningly, but all either can do is shrug and play on. They have no clue that Jax's story is out in the world, painting their drummer as a monster.

It kills me to watch them now, knowing what I know. Vanessa clutches me tightly, the same anguish in her face that's most likely on mine. She's so protective of all of them; this has got to be devastating for her. I squeeze her hand on my arm in support, not knowing what else I can do but document everything. Make sure the real story gets told.

Sarah joins our huddle next, her phone open to the article and her face stricken. At one point, Ryan examines our group on the side of the stage and looks as if he understands that something is terribly wrong. He cuts their set short by two songs and goes straight into their finale. Matt and Jude don't argue about the change in the setlist and join in finishing up their set.

When they're done, they exit to our side of the stage, and I move to grab my camera to catch all of this reaction because it's what I'm here to do, and this is important. Matt gives me an odd look as he takes note of my movements and then the stances of everyone around him.

"What is going on?" He doesn't ask. He *demands*. It is so hard to record this and not reach out to him. I feel like I'm betraying him somehow, and my heart is shredding.

Vanessa steps up to him tentatively, opening her phone to the article and showing him. Her outstretched hand shakes, and she doesn't say a word. Ryan and Jude crowd around Matt to read over his shoulder.

"Are you fucking kidding me with this shit?!" Jude yells at the night sky, his arms spread wide. The grief and anger in his voice are sobering.

Matt doesn't say anything. After reading the article, he calmly gives Vanessa her phone back, then leans over with his hands on his knees and his head down. Ryan is next to him, rubbing his back as he leans over and whispering softly enough, so no one else hears what he says. Matt nods in agreement with whatever it is and straightens.

Vanessa steps in and gives him a hug, which Matt accepts readily. This time there is no twinge of jealousy from me. I know better now than to think there's anything beyond friendship between them.

I notice then that all the other press people that were on this side of the stage are all gone, and increased security is in their place. I wonder when and how that happened. Maybe Matt's friend Taylor monitors the situation and reacts before he needs to say or do anything. I also worry about who the security is really for now. Jax can't get anywhere close to us. *Is it for the angry crowds that are now turning on Matt?* I don't even want to think about the possibilities for harm that now opens.

Matt breaks from the group and steps over to me, ignoring the camera. "Let's go do an interview." His face is stone, jaw clenched, and lips a hard line.

I shut the camera off, put it down, and hug him. "Are you sure?"

"I need to talk about this, and we may as well officially document it."

thirty-seven

RIVER CHILD

MATT

Samantha sets up her camera in the lounge area of the bus later that night as we barrel down the highway toward Phoenix. I'm happy to put Albuquerque at my back. That was not fun. Everyone agreed to give us space for this interview. But Ryan and Jude want to join later to make sure their thoughts on the whole situation are heard.

My favorite part of doing interviews with Samantha comes when she approaches me with a mic. I lift my shirt for her before she even needs to ask and give her a wink causing a fierce blush to rise on her cheeks. She doesn't back down, though, as I knew she wouldn't. Bold as always, she steps up and winks back. As she tapes the wire to my skin, she's slow and deliberate, taking her time and driving me absolutely crazy.

CHAPTER THIRTY-SEVEN

She pats my chest and looks up at me earnestly when she's done.

"You're sure you want to do this?" *Those blue eyes.* So much concern and worry are conveyed in them. I feel bad for putting her through this, but I know she's taking it all in stride. I think she could handle anything. Well, except blood. Or needles.

"I'm sure." The proverbial cat is already out of the bag. I may as well go big or go home.

"Okay then." She moves back behind the camera and starts recording. "So tonight's show in Albuquerque didn't go so well for you. Do you want to talk about what happened this week leading up to tonight?"

Damn, she's diving in headfirst. Okay. "Well, a lot of this will be covered in the article in Rolling Stone tomorrow, so I don't need to go through everything in too much detail. I didn't hold anything back in that interview. But..."

"But...?" She's so damned encouraging. I hate it, but I love it.

"But... my brother, Jaxon Holloway, who was attempting to blackmail me for a quarter of a million dollars, beat me to the press regarding a recent altercation between us."

"Are you denying you were violent with him?" Her eyebrow raises as if this question is more for her than for the film. *Fair enough.*

"Not at all." I swallow hard. This is where

Vanessa and the lawyers are going to lose their shit. "I most certainly beat the shit out of him. But it wasn't the right way to deal with the situation. Let me be clear. I am not sorry Jax was hurt. He deserves all he got and then some. What I am sorry for was how I responded. And for the record, he surprise-attacked me in my hotel room. It began as self-defense. It...got out of hand." I almost forget that part all the time - that he attacked me when I was vulnerable. Not like I need reminding of the incident, but I tend to focus on my own actions.

"And what about his accusations that you have a history of violence toward him? And this was a continuation of a pattern of behavior?"

"It's total bullshit." I shake my head in disbelief at it. It's insane for him to hint at something like that. "I'll be honest with you. I never raised a finger to Jax my entire life until that night. Even with everything he did to me, I *never* reciprocated. I didn't want to be a monster like him." *And yet, I still feel like one. All the damned time.*

"Anything else before I grab the guys?" She's verging on tears and wants to distract from it. *And I hit another step on the way down as I fall for her.*

"Come here." I motion for her to sit by me. She moves to stop recording, but I stop her. "No. Keep it going. Please." I suddenly need to let her know what my thoughts of her during all of this have been. I grab her hands as she sits across from me.

"Matt. I'm supposed to be behind the camera. Not in front of it." She runs her fingers through her long hair and puts her hand up to the side of her face to hide it from the camera. I reach out and pull her hand back down.

"You should never hide your beautiful face." Her expression turns to shock, which I'm not surprised at, considering our crazy history. I don't know where any of this is coming from. I think the dam inside me has been breached, and now I can't stop telling people how I feel.

She places the back of her hand on my forehead, pretending to check for a fever. "Are you okay, Mr. Sturridge?" She laughs, and the sound fills me up. "Maybe we should check for a concussion. I do believe you just complimented me."

"Hey, I compliment you." I join her infectious laughter. "I called you a genius yesterday. It was yesterday, right? My days are starting to run together."

"Oh, okay. I stand corrected. One compliment."

"Seriously, though. I want it documented that the idea of going to the press and getting my story out was your idea. You convinced me that by telling the world of my experience, I could maybe help someone else going through the same thing. So in the off chance it does help someone, thank you."

The blush growing on her face is so fucking cute; I'm glad we're still recording. She hides her face again and shrinks away from the camera, most likely out of the shot. She would know where the frame is. I try to pull her back, but she's strong and is determined.

She performs an acrobatic roll off the couch to move away from me, giving me inappropriate ideas, and ends up behind the camera again. "Okay. Ready now for Ryan and Jude?"

I laugh but nod. "Ready."

I might be reading too much into her resourceful escape, but I hope she was only being camera shy and not uncomfortable with what I was saying. I'm getting a little bit too forward and open, which is total insanity because that is so unlike me. I should tone it down, though. I don't want to scare her off. I just need to stop the fucking oversharing.

The rest of the guys come up to the lounge area, and Jude starts in before he even sits down, getting his face up close to the camera.

"Listen up, people in documentary land. Let it be known that that man right there," he points back to me as I start to laugh my ass off even though he's dead serious. He's gone right off the deep end. "That man would normally not hurt a hair on anyone's head. So get that thought right out of your fucking minds." *Okay. So Jude apparently had some beers in the back of the bus after the show.*

Samantha is highly amused by his alcohol-fueled antics, and her distinctive laughter is a balm for my weary soul. Being the utterly sober one of us, Ryan merely shakes his head and smiles. There isn't much else to do with that kind of display.

"Do you want to add anything to Jude's statement, Ryan?" Samantha sneaks in between giggles, desperately trying to compose herself but finding it as hard as I am. Our eyes catch, and a current flows between us that is undeniable. The heaviness of the day's events turns into vapor when I gaze into her eyes, even from across the room. Or bus, as it were.

Ryan is still considering Samantha's question. He's always deliberate with his words, making sure he thinks before speaking. Something I should start doing.

"I thought about this since we got on the bus," he starts. "Guys like us in rock 'n roll bands always seem to get a bad rep. Like we're expected to be fucking assholes, drinking, whoring, or getting into fights all the time. But we're really not like that at all."

"Here here," Jude chimes in, sitting on Ryan's lap. This is getting out of hand now. And Ryan is trying to be so serious. The contradiction is hilarious. "However, I am a bit of a harlot, so *some* stereotypes do apply...well, to *me*."

"I mean, for fuck's sake, Jude here reads *The Lord of the Rings* books like every other month. And he makes us watch the damned *extended versions* of the movies all the fucking time."

"What? You like those movies too. Admit it." Jude lays his head on Ryan's shoulder like a little kid. Ryan isn't bothered in the least.

"And Matt was a god-damned Marine for chrissake. He served our country and deserves our fucking respect. Not fucking boos because of some fucking lies in a gossip rag. C'mon people. Wake up."

"I think you forgot to say "fucking" one more time." I can't help but tease him at least a little bit. I'm still floored by the support from these guys. Public displays of affection aren't usually my thing, especially with guys. But these two are showing their character, and I appreciate it greatly.

"Fuck you, man," he replies as he pushes Jude off him. He instantly cringes, knowing what's coming.

"Are you volunteering?" I ask with a grin.

Jude swears, "God damn it, I was ruthlessly pushed to the floor and missed my cue."

Samantha rolls into her sweet laughter again, and we all join her. After today, this is not how I thought the day would end. Never in a million years.

thirty-eight
KILLING TIME
SAMANTHA

We do indeed sleep the sleep of the dead on the way to Phoenix and arrive at our hotel in the early morning. We'll be here for a couple of days before moving on to Los Angeles. Today is full of press for the guys, so I'll be my typical fly-on-the-wall self I'm getting used to.

I arrive at the interview space set up in one of the hotel's ballrooms. Sections are cordoned off for each band, and the press will make their rounds throughout each all day. Catering set up a table with drinks and snacks, and the guys are grabbing what fuel they can before the junket starts. They are all aware today will mostly be about the Matt story. The Rolling Stone article still hasn't hit online yet, so it will be a rough start. Vanessa is on standby near me should they need rescuing at any point. Each reporter only gets between ten and fifteen minutes each. Vanessa makes the call to move them out if they're running long.

"That's strange...." Vanessa murmurs, heading to the opening of the surrounding curtains. I follow her to check out what she thinks is so odd. Peeking outside the Indigo King entrance, we see a line of reporters stretching out of the ballroom. The other two bands have no reporters waiting. *Well, shit*. A rough start isn't even the beginning of how bad this morning will be. "Holy hell, we're in trouble."

Ryan comes up behind us. "What's going on?"

"Well, you guys are definitely the top story today," Vanessa steers us back to the seating area. "Indigo King is the only band with press waiting, so prepare yourselves."

"No shit?" Jude's smile is growing.

"Not a good thing, dude." Matt's eyes are full of worry, and his knee suddenly won't stop bouncing. I wish I could calm him somehow. While he was more open yesterday, it might not be the same today.

"Okay, well. Here we go, boys. Remember to be on your best behavior." Vanessa instructs and returns to the opening to wave in the first reporter with a stiff smile.

"Yes, mother," Jude grumbles, not quite under his breath, but there's no bite.

The man who enters the area appears to be super excited he's the first in. He takes his seat across from the band and pulls out his phone to record the interview.

"Good morning, guys," he starts nervously. "Larry Moore, *Rough Cutt Magazine*. My first question is actually for Samantha in the corner over there. You are Samantha Fisher, right?" He turns and looks directly at me, and I'm too stunned to answer aloud, so I nod at him and glance around at everyone in confusion. *Why is he asking me a question? Is he allowed to do this? This doesn't seem like it's supposed to be allowed...*

"Sir, your questions should be directed to the band...." Vanessa's confusion is more irritated than surprised like mine.

"I just want to confirm your voluntary statement to *Blindsided* that Matt broke your wrist and also injured your cheek there?" He points to my scraped-up cheekbone.

"What?!" Matt sits up, ready to jump off the couch, his head swiveling between this Larry person and me. Ryan holds him back. *For now.*

The guy presses on, aiming his phone's camera at me. "Can you confirm that was indeed your statement to *Blindsided*?"

"This is bullshit." Matt turns to Vanessa, who doesn't appear to know what to do in this situation. She's not the only one.

I finally find my voice, but it shakes and hardly

carries any volume. "They must've taken what I said out of context...." *What did I say? And, to who?*

"So, Matt didn't break your wrist or injure your cheek? They are obvious injuries, Ms. Fisher. I can see them myself."

"Fucking hell," Matt says, breaking free of Ryan and standing, his fists clenched. "What the fuck are you doing?"

"It was an accident." I can't catch my breath. *This can't be happening. They've got it all wrong.* "It was a simple accident...." I'm so angry at this asshole for insinuating Matt hurt me on purpose. Nothing could be farther from the truth. And I would never say anything like that. Furious tears blur my vision.

"Weren't you the first of two people Matt put in the hospital just this week? The other being his own brother?"

"I swear to god," Matt steps forward, his jaw tight, definitely intimidating. Larry turns his phone on him, capturing everything.

"That's enough." Ryan jumps up, pushing Matt back gently. "Larry, right? Listen, Larry, if you don't have questions for the members of Indigo King, we're going to ask you to leave."

"Oh, I have questions for you guys as well." He smirks, and his whole demeanor screams *douchebag*. He's not nervous anymore, that's for sure.

"Fine. We're happy to answer your questions *for*

the band." Ryan pats Matt on the back, easing him back onto the couch slowly. Matt still looks like he will pounce on the reporter any second, but he's glaring daggers at me. I still can't breathe.

"Were the two of you aware of Matt's propensity for violence when he first joined the band? Or is this a new revelation for you both?" He has the nerve to look sincere with the question.

All three lurch off the couch and in the reporter's direction amid a slew of curses and threats, but Vanessa slides in between them to prevent anyone from getting to him.

"That's enough time for *Rough Cutt Magazine* today," she grabs his shirt, pulls him out of his chair, and drags him to the exit. "I'll be in touch with your editor, and you can consider your press pass with Indigo King revoked until further notice." Despite his continued protests about his allotted time, she hands him off to the security guard stationed at the opening for removal.

I still haven't moved from behind my camera, and my vision is still blurred with the angry tears flowing down my face. I can't stop trembling. The shaking is coming from somewhere deep inside me as if my soul is frostbitten, and it's spreading every-where. *Where the fuck did this come from?*

"Sam?" Matt's voice breaks through. I guess he's been trying to get my attention for a while, but I spaced out, trying to comprehend what just happened.

I look up at him, but I can't read him like usual. Any progress we made in that department vanishes. His mask is back, and his emotions are walled off again.

Vanessa comes up and puts an arm around my shoulder. "Are you okay? What the hell was that about?"

"I...I don't know." I can barely think straight with everything that happened in such a short time racing through my mind. I wipe at my tears with the heels of my hands, smearing mascara all over my face, but I don't care. It's too much.

"Did you talk to *Blindsided*?" Ryan asks, his tone accusing. "Did you say those things?"

My heart plummets. They think I did this on purpose. They think I would betray them that way, or I would betray Matt. Vanessa's arm drops, and she steps back to examine me. They all doubt me. I can't believe this.

I raise my eyes to Matt, searching for anything to show me he doesn't believe I would do this. *Nothing.* The wall he's constructed between us is now freshly mortared and set. Impenetrable. I can almost hear pieces of my heart hit the floor as it shatters. That's it then.

The tightness in my chest becomes too much, and I can't breathe. I'm suffocating. I sense the blood draining from my head, and I need to get out.

"Samantha?" Vanessa moves to put a hand on me, but I flinch away. They're all standing way too close.

I spy the exit out of the corner of my eye, and I instinctively take off, nearly tripping on my tripod as I go. Their accusations propelling me to escape faster. I try to dash past the line of reporters waiting to interview Indigo King, but they recognize me, and some of them step in my way as I try to get away. Camera flashes blind me as I'm swarmed and bombarded with questions.

"Are you okay, Samantha?"

"Did Matt threaten you? Is that why you're trying to run away right now?"

"Was this the first time Matt beat you?"

I charge through them all, forcing my way through and past until I'm free to move again. I can hear their questions follow me, but they don't pursue, thank god. Once in the hallway, I spot a side exit and rush through it to a parking lot. Each step away from the chaos behind me pulls my heart-strings taught to the point of snapping. Each measure of distance growing between us makes me come apart that much more, to the point I end up huddled under a tree on the edge of the parking lot, crying my eyes out.

Not only was I accused of saying Matt was

violent with me by those reporters, but Vanessa and the band believed I would say such a thing. I don't know which is worse: the fact the press is printing the lies or that everyone I trusted believes them. The way Matt looked at me was so cold and with no emotion. Like he expected me to betray him all along. *I'm crushed*. I thought we were beyond shit like this by now, but I was so wrong. So wrong. This is not the first time I've been wrong about a guy and not the first time I've been wrong about Matt. *Will I ever learn my lesson with this guy?* The thought makes my heart skip. *Fucking heart.*

Shit. I left my camera and everything back there. I can't believe I ran out of there like I did. I most likely made things worse for the band by doing that. *But what the hell was I supposed to do?* I could tell by the look on Ryan's face he'd never believe I had nothing to do with the *Blindsided* story. He'd already made his mind up.

Speaking of which, I pull my phone out of my back pocket and pull up *Blindsided's* website. Sure enough, there I am on the landing page. The headline reads, *A History of Violence*. Underneath is a close-up of my injured face from yesterday in Phoenix. *Fucking hell.* Not only is there a picture of me from last night, but there are pictures of me from when the accident happened. One shows me in the lobby of our hotel, crying with blood streaking my face. I scroll past that one quickly.

Who the fuck was there with a camera? I don't remember anyone taking pictures. Then a picture of Matt and me behind the food trucks in Salt Lake City, with him looking mad as hell and me looking scared. Flashbacks to when I woke him up, and he startled come rushing to me. Again, I can't recall anyone with a camera pointed our way, but I wasn't exactly looking for anyone either. *What the fuck is going on?*

I'm getting my breath back, and my tears are starting to slow, at least, when a car pulls alongside me and the tinted window rolls down. It's Zach from Incendiary Ink's crew.

"Hey, are you okay?" He's genuinely concerned. I shrug and pull the hem of my shirt up to wipe my face, which I'm sure is a mess. "You look like you could get out of here for a few. C'mon, let's escape for a little while. Forget about this shit show for a few hours."

Something in me hesitates, but the thought of getting away from everything, even for just a few hours, sounds so inviting. I could use some time to sort my thoughts and emotions. This could be a perfect way to do that.

"Just for a little while," I say, getting up slowly. "I don't want to be gone for too long." I'm not sure why I'm saying this; I shouldn't care how long I'm away from everyone. The longer, the better should be the correct answer.

CHAPTER THIRTY-EIGHT

"No worries. We'll come back whenever you want." His smile seems sincere.

As I move around the car and open the door to get in, Matt starts heading toward us, but he's far enough away I can't see the expression on his face. I'm sure he's still mad as hell at me, so I quicken my movements, buckling my seatbelt. "Let's go."

We wind through the streets of Phoenix, not saying anything for a long time, taking in the city and the sunny scenery. We're listening to music on the radio. I'm starting to calm down and get my bearings back. I am angrier at *Blindsided* than anything else. I understand everyone's side of it, but I'm caught. And I'm still so hurt they would believe I would purposely say anything to hurt Matt. I thought they all knew me better than that.

I appreciate that Zach's not pressing me to talk about anything. Until he starts talking out of the blue.

"Crazy few days, huh?" He's got that *'hey, we're in this together'* way about him that hits me wrong.

"Crazy is a good word for it," I say, not wanting to talk about details. He's not getting the hint. I stare out my window, trying to let him know I don't want to talk.

"I mean, Matty's been a dick since he was a kid, but I never knew he was so violent. I guess you don't really know people, huh?"

I whip my head around to stare at him. "You

knew Matt as a kid?" I'm trying not to sound too upset or surprised by this, but *what the actual hell?*

"Oh yeah. I grew up near the Holloway's in Wimberly. Jax and I used to get into some real shit back in the day."

"Interesting. He doesn't act like he knows you." *And that is weird.* If they basically grew up together, you'd think Matt would acknowledge him some-how. *Why wouldn't Matt say something about it?*

"Yeah, well, fame seems to have gone to his head in a big way."

"Were you guys close when you were younger?" I can't imagine Matt being friends with Zach. They are at opposite ends of any spectrum.

"Jax and I were. And I saw Matty here and there. Whenever he decided Jax's home was good enough for him."

Something pricks at my heart, and I open my phone, pretending to scroll through social media, but I hit record in my camera video app, turning it sideways so he can't tell I'm recording him. I don't know what it is, but if I had hackles, they'd be raised to the roof of this car right now. A sinking feeling comes over me Zach may be more involved in all of this than I know.

"Were you there when Jax hurt that guy with the broken bottle?"

He glances at me, gauging my attitude. Maybe he's surprised I know the story. I force myself to seem passively interested, not desperate like I am, for this guy to talk and speak the truth. To exonerate Matt of everything.

"Fuck yeah, I was. It was my mother who called the fucking cops." He laughs as though the entire incident didn't alter the trajectory of Matt's life forever. "Who knew he would convince Matt to take the heat for it, though. That was truly inspired. The mastermind was at work that day."

"Yeah, it sounds like it." I force myself to laugh along with him, but my stomach churns at the thought of Zach being there when Matt took the fall for his brother. "So you and Jax stayed in touch all these years then? That's cool." I need to appear okay with everything he's saying, but the knot in my stomach that he is involved in everything is only tightening the more he talks. It's getting harder to keep up a front.

"On and off. We connected again when Indigo King signed up with the Incendiary Ink tour a few months ago. I figured out that Matt *Sturridge* was Matty *Holloway* and got a hold of Jax since he had no clue what happened to him after juvie."

"Oh, that's nice." I'm forcing indifference I don't feel. My teeth are on edge, knowing this whole situation is wrong.

He laughs, and it sounds malevolent. "'Nice' is not a word I'd use to describe Jax." We turn onto another highway, making a circle of the city. "Diabolical is more like it."

"Diabolical? How so?" I look over at him from under my lashes, trying to be coy, but failing miserably. I need to keep him talking. He's not looking at me as I do this, so it's a wasted effort, *thank god*.

"His whole plan to get money out of Matty. Labels will pay out good money to avoid scandals like this shit." He waves to indicate my person. *Yup. I'm the shit.* "But I convinced him that would probably be a dead end. By all the meetings that were going on, I could tell that it wasn't going to go anywhere."

I don't respond for a while, trying to appear interested in the scenery out the passenger window. I don't want to seem too eager for information. My pretense feels like it's running thin, so I need to chill out for a while. Even though Zach is apparently super willing to tell me all about what he and Jax have done, it's such a tightrope I'm walking; I need to be careful.

When I finally glance back over at Zach, he's smiling to himself; *grinning* like the Cheshire cat from *Alice in Wonderland*. It's one of the creepiest smiles I've ever seen, and I have to suppress a visible shudder.

"What are you so happy about?" I finally ask. What an idiot. He looks like he wants to talk more.

"The sweet payday we got from *Blindsided*. It

helps to make friends with the press. Rose really came through for us. Fucking *twice*. Can you believe that?"

Rose? The chick from the side of the stage last night. *Damn.* I knew something was off with her. I start to feel nauseous remembering our conversation. I guess I did volunteer the information like the reporter said, but wow, did she take it out of context and leave out a lot of pertinent information. Guilt weighs on me like wet snow, causing me to shiver.

I can't help but cringe every time he calls Matt '*Matty*' too, and the reference to '*we*' now boils my blood. To think he's been involved this entire time is unreal. And I spent time with this guy. Not a lot, but enough to raise more suspicion against me for involvement in any of this.

I wish I was a better actress because I don't know how much longer I'm going to be able to keep up this farce. I know for a fact people can read me like a fucking book. I guess I'm lucky he's driving and needs to pay attention to the road and not me.

"Wow. How much did you guys collect for the lies?" *Shit. Careful Samantha.*

He shifts his gaze at me briefly, and I worry for a second he's figured out I'm only pumping him for information, but he doesn't seem worried at all. *He really is a dumbass.*

"$100K each story." He looks proud. "I got a $50k finder's fee too for access and hooking Jax up with Rose." His laugh makes my skin crawl, but I go right along with him.

"Damn. Nice job." *God, I hope I sound convincing.* I double-check that my phone is still recording. It still is. I can't believe what I'm hearing. *How can people be such assholes?*

"Yeah. Road crew doesn't really pay shit on these gigs, so you gotta make bank where you can, right?" He seems to think I'm crew, but whatever.

"Why'd you drag me into it, though?" I ask, wondering how he thinks I could be okay with that. "Couldn't you have done it without me?"

He winces, but not enough for me to think he's remorseful. "Yeah... sorry about that part. You were collateral damage, unfortunately." He reaches over and pats my hand, and it takes everything in my being not to shrink away and vomit right onto the floorboards of his rented car. "When the accident happened between you two, I knew photos might come in handy. Plus, the stories don't make you look that bad, just Matty."

"Right." I'm going to be sick. Playing along with this charade has taken every ounce of acting strength I had, which was not much to begin with. I have the sense if I'm forced to go much further with this, I'll expose myself. "Can we start heading back? My head is starting to hurt. Too much crying, I guess."

He gives me a disappointed pout. "Are you sure? We were just starting to vibe...."

I'm going to lose it if he thinks something is going to happen between us. *My god, I hate being a woman sometimes. Just because we listen to you doesn't mean we want to fuck you.* "I'm sure. Sorry, since the accident...." I leave it at that, not wanting to add any more to the stupid story but wanting to go back to the hotel and dissect everything that happened this morning. It is too fucking much.

"Oh, damn. Right. My bad." He looks a little contrite. *Asshole.* "No problem. I'll head back now. I need to be at the venue soon anyway. Let's grab a drink later, yeah? I've got cash now to show you a good time." I instantly need a scalding hot shower or a bath in a vat of lye. He maneuvers the car off the exit ramp and directs us back to the hotel, where I need to show all of this to everyone connected to Indigo King. They need to know the truth.

thirty-nine

KILLING TIME

MATT

Where the fuck is Samantha going with that asshole? And isn't he the creepy guy from the bar the other day? What the hell? I still don't know what happened in there. But Samantha taking off like that; it's so not like her. She's not one to run away from anything. Something isn't right at all. Could I have been so wrong about her? Was she somehow in on all of this? I can't believe that.

Just thinking about these questions makes something inside me twist and contort into shapes that shouldn't exist. She wouldn't be that malevolent, right? Shit. It was her idea to tell my side of the story with Jax. She wouldn't use any of that against me, right? Or did I misjudge her like I misjudged everyone else in my life? Did she see my demons and judge them unworthy herself? If she did, can I blame her? Am I not a monster just like Jax? Didn't I go too far? I did. And I know it. I am the monster everyone says I am, if not more so.

The sun beating on my shoulders burns through the cloth of my shirt as I watch the crew guy's car pull away, taking Samantha away with him. She had to notice me coming after her. *But why was I?* I don't know what to think.

"Matt?" A woman's voice says from behind me. I see Ryan's girlfriend, Sarah, when I turn. "What happened?"

"I'm not sure." I run my hands down my face, trying to gather my thoughts. I'm still taking everything in. "Actually, I have no clue what's going on right now."

"Are you worried about this?" She holds up her phone with a *Blindsided* article displaying Samantha's injuries under an awful cliché headline. *Where did those pictures come from?* I can't help but cringe at the sight of her hurt like that. Injuries I inflicted. Accidentally, but still. Knowing I hurt her so severely wrenches something inside me, I don't think can ever be untwisted.

"Of course," I say, honestly. *Who wouldn't be concerned about an article like this?* About someone you hurt and someone you trusted because the injury was accidental. Nothing more.

"Sam would never do this." She crosses her arms

over her chest, challenging me to doubt her. "And if you think she would, you don't know her at all."

I study her face, seeing her sincerity and belief in Samantha. Could she be saying this because of their friendship? Jesus, how deep into this hole of mistrust am I going to dig myself?

"I don't know what to think." I step past her and start heading back toward the hotel. I'm not going to solve anything out here. "Shit's gone out of control."

"Shit has? Or you all have?" She moves to stand in front of me, blocking my path. I have no choice but to stop and face her.

"What are you talking about? We all have?"

"Since your brother showed up, you guys have been jumping at shadows." Her exasperated tone strikes a chord in me. She's right. We have been on edge since Jax showed up. *One point to Sarah.* "You, in particular. You see problems where there are none. Do you really, in your heart of hearts, think Sam could do this to you? I mean, really, Matt. That girl cares about you more than she should, to be honest. She'd never do this to you."

"More than she should, huh?" I take that in. She's not wrong. *But can I be sure she wouldn't sell me out?* I want so badly to believe that. I want this feeling that I can't put my finger on to go away. I don't know if it's hurt or guilt or both, or if everything I'm feeling has nothing to do with Samantha; I'm just misdirecting it her way.

"Yes. More than she should. Because you're being an ass."

"I never claimed to be otherwise." I move around and past her, heading back into the hotel. "I get what you're trying to do for your friend, but I wish you would stay out of it. This doesn't concern you." It is admirable for her to stand up for her friend, but it might be misguided. Maybe she doesn't know Samantha as much as she thinks she does. *How close of friends are they?*

"You're wrong about this," she says from behind me as I open the hotel door and head back to the media circus waiting for me.

When I get back to the ballroom, I'm again bombarded by the press, still waiting in line. For now, Vanessa put all interviews on hold, so they don't have anything better to do than wait for one of us to pop up. I push past them, not commenting on anything thrown at me. I find the mood in our area has changed.

"What's up?" Everyone is staring at their phones with interest, not mindlessly scrolling.

"We're waiting for the Rolling Stone article to post," Vanessa says, not looking up from her phone. "Henry texted and told me it should be up in a little while, but that could mean minutes or hours."

Something in me cracks. Realization hits this is

now our reality, waiting for this or that article to ruin or boost our image. It's complete and utter bullshit. Whether or not Samantha had anything to do with the reports, this is not what I want Indigo King to become. Sarah was right about one thing, we *have* been jumping at shadows. This is no way to live, and how I have been living for way too long. It will be hard for me to *not* live this way, but I at least need to try. Now that I no longer need to hide, I'm not going to *start* hiding again, just from someone else.

"Is this who we are now?" I can't let this go without comment. "We achieve some fame, and now we're going to live or die by the press? Is this the kind of band we are? Or want to be?"

Everyone stares at me, shocked by my outburst. They all look uncomfortable, but no one says a word.

"Text me when it's over." I leave and go to my room to wait out our destiny being decided. *This is fucking bullshit.* I'm starting to understand why bands trash hotel rooms.

In my room, I thoroughly read the article with an eye for any hint Samantha didn't have anything to do with its being written. After just one careful reading, it's evident that she didn't. You can see the words being twisted beyond recognition. None of it sounds like her at all. The guilt taking over now, at ever doubting her, is crashing over me.

She'll want nothing to do with me, and I don't blame her. We were just starting to make real progress since I finally got my head out of my ass and allowed someone in. Only for me to regress back to my old ways of suspicion and doubt and pushing away. Recovery from this could be impossible.

After about an hour's worth of climbing the walls later, I compose and delete and compose again, a text to Samantha. Before I can delete it yet again, an incoming text pops up.

> SAMANTHA: Come meet me at the edge of the parking lot where you saw me earlier. It's important.

Important? I'm the one with important things to say. I hope I'm not too late to say them.

forty

DEMONS
SAMANTHA

Waiting for Matt to come and meet me, I need to figure out where my head is when it comes to him. I thought I was falling hard, but then this happened, and everything I thought I knew about him flew right out the window. So I'm back to square one, not knowing who he really is. It doesn't help he's shut himself off from me again too.

Why do I care so much about this? And, can this even be real after only a week? Surely, this is only infatuation or physical attraction. *But then, why do I want to shield him from every hurt that comes his way?* We're in such close proximity to each other at all times it wouldn't be out of the realm of possibilities to fall for someone this fast.

I send a quick text to my mother, the self-proclaimed relationship expert, and my match-maker extraordinaire.

> ME: When did you know you loved Dad?

> MOTHER DEAREST: The first time he admitted to being an ass.

> ME: Dad was an ass?

> MOTHER DEAREST: All men are. 😊 Does this question mean you might be in love with someone?

> ME: TBD

"Hey." Matt's voice startles me, and I drop my phone like a hot potato as if I was doing something I shouldn't. I swear under my breath and pick it up, dusting off the mulch dust with my shirt. It's already dirty with my ruined mascara from earlier, so why not. It's only an Indigo King shirt, after all. "You okay?"

I glance up at him, shielding my eyes from the sun behind him to take him in. He doesn't appear mad at me anymore. If I didn't know better, I'd say he was concerned. I wonder what happened since I saw him last to change that. "You tell me. Am I okay?"

He sits down next to me in the tall ash tree's shade, his hair ruffling a bit in the warm breeze as he leans back against the trunk next to me with a long sigh. I can smell his light cologne, and it almost undoes me.

"I'm an ass, Samantha." He closes his eyes and taps the back of his head lightly against the tree. I glance down at my phone to make sure he can't read my texts with my mother. *Nope. Weird.* My pulse increases by a couple of beats per minute.

"Not going to disagree with you there."

He laughs to himself. I'm glad one of us finds this humorous. "See, that's just it. You're honest to a fault. There's no way you had anything to do with those articles. For me to even think it for a second was completely insane. I'm sorry I ever doubted you."

This is not what I expected when I asked him out here. I pictured myself begging to be believed and crying tears of frustration. Not vindication and the threatening relieved tears pricking the back of my eyes. I blink them away quickly. I cried enough today, thank you very much.

"What brought you around to sanity?" I'm curious how he came to this realization.

"Time." He pulls his knees up and rests his arms on them, folding his hands together. "Please understand, I'm still new to this whole trusting people thing. Like, incredibly new. A matter of days, not years. I'm still learning how to even do it."

"Okay...I sort of understand that. But..."

"But I fucked up. I should've known better. I am sorry it took me so long."

I can read him again. I search his face for the truth of his words, and it's right there. The walls are gone. And those damned green eyes, so warm and full of regret, melt the chill in my bones a little bit. My heart aches for all he's said to be true. I think it is, but the ups and downs between us in this short time are dizzying sometimes, like now. It must be too much for him too, because he shifts his gaze away.

"Well, in the off chance you still thought I was involved, I recorded this for you." I open my phone to the video of Zach confessing everything and play it for him. As he watches, his face goes through several emotions, and he replays it twice. I'm surprised he's more confused than anything else instead of anger or fury.

"I have no memory of him from Wimberly." I can tell he's still racking his brain, trying to remember him with no results.

"That's what you got out of that?" I can't believe out of everything on the video, he's only concerned he doesn't remember Zach.

"No, of course not. But that's the surprise out of everything he said." He hands my phone back, and our fingers touch, making me jump and drop it again. *Jesus.* "Everything else was kind of expected. I wonder what Incendiary Ink is going to do with this, though. They'll probably lose their shit. They're already kind of pissed we're getting so much press. Even though it's been on the negative side lately." He shrugs as though not a big deal. I'm thinking it's a big deal.

"We should give this video to Vanessa." I start to stand up, but he reaches out to hold my arm, keeping me next to him. His touch forces a wave of emotion to skitter across my heart, but I'm not sure which one. Everything is so jumbled anymore.

"Can we talk for a minute before we do that?" The hand still on my arm, rough with callouses but warm, convinces me to stay.

I glance down at his battered hand and then back up at him, trying to figure out what we are to each other now, after everything that's happened. I have no clue, which makes me think we're nowhere. At least, for now.

"What do you want to talk about?" I'm so hesitant with him, and it's not right. I hate I'm like this with him now. It's not normal. Nothing with him is normal, though. This has been such a crazy relationship already; I don't know where any of this leaves us.

He takes a minute to collect his thoughts before speaking. I like he's being careful with his words. "Life hasn't been the same for me since I met you." This makes me laugh, which makes him laugh. We both know what he said is the understatement of the year, if not the decade. "Seriously though, with all the Jax and press bullshit aside, I realized today I do trust you, which is a huge deal for me, as you might have guessed. I only trust people I care about, and you're now on the shortlist." He slides his hand down my arm to twine his fingers with mine. "I want you to know I care about you."

We're both staring at our joined hands instead of at each other. This confuses me more, which didn't seem possible only minutes ago. Every day is like a roller coaster of emotions. I don't know if I want to stay on the ride.

"What does that even mean? The two of us together are nothing but a hot mess. And it's only been a little over a week."

"I know. That part is crazy. I swear it feels more like months. We sure know how to use our time wisely....."

"I don't know about wisely. It's not been all fun and games." I raise my casted hand to point to my banged-up cheek.

"Well, yeah... that part sucked. Sorry again."

"What do you want from me, Matt?"

He leans back, shocked by my forwardness. Well, if he likes my honesty, he's going to need to deal with what comes with it.

"Wow. Okay." Trying to compose himself and his thoughts, he squeezes my hand. "How about we start all of this over? We kind of jumped in headfirst without laying much groundwork. And I know I just mixed up a bunch of metaphors, but it made sense in my head before I said it. *Damn*, I need to shut up."

I giggle a little and squeeze his hand back. He's read my mind. We need to back this up and call for a do-over. "I think starting over would be a smart thing to do. While you trust me now, I'm not so sure I trust you...." More honesty to throw into the stew. "The hot and cold with you has been very confusing for me. Calling it mixed messages doesn't even begin to cover it. I don't want to keep going through that. Not when my heart is on my sleeve all the time."

He nods. "That's totally fair. And believe me, if I could go back and change how this all went, I would. I've been in my head so deep for so long, I guess my people skills need some work." His forehead creases with worry, and he looks at our hands, gently rubbing his thumb over my knuckles. The mere sensation of his skin sliding against mine, even so innocently, lights something inside me. "Are you saying you don't want to try again? Did I fuck things up beyond repair?" The concern deepens when he raises his gaze to mine, and I can feel myself being pulled toward him. Some gravitational force shoving me headfirst into his orbit, where I don't know where I'll end up.

"Not beyond repair, no. But there does need to be repair." While yes, I'm insanely attracted to this man, and the universe seems to be hellbent on us being together, I've been hurt, and it's not going to be instantly okay. Holding his hand now feels strange, considering where we were just a couple hours ago. "So long as you can acknowledge that, we'll have something to work with."

"I understand. I've got work to do, but I'm willing to do it." He eyes me warily for a moment, "I don't know what it is about you, but I just can't stay away, no matter how hard I try."

"You sound disappointed." I smile. "You really know how to make a girl feel special."

He groans. "I didn't mean it like that."

"I know. I'm just having fun torturing you. I think I've earned a little fun at your expense today."

"Fair enough. You have indeed earned the right to torture me as you see fit." His smile grows wicked, and I have to clench almost every muscle I possess to not lean in and kiss that smile off his lips.

I tap a finger on my chin with my free hand. "Does this mean we'll actually try dating?" The thought is crazy, but I think it might be worth trying, even on a hectic tour schedule. I can't deny my attraction to him either, both mental and physical. Whatever this is between us needs to be pursued and sought out.

"If you want to, sure." He smirks, then his lips twitch into a crooked smile. "Unless you just want to have incredible sex...."

"Incredible, huh?" I can feel a blush blooming. "Shouldn't incredible sex be part of the dating? If we're going to do this, I want it all. I want the whole fucking fairy tale."

"The whole fucking fairy tale? Geez. So demanding." His eyes twinkle as he smiles at me, and I question my life choices. Especially this one. "What fairy tale has incredible sex in it? I need to read that one."

"The one we'll write, I guess."

S ex-filled fairy tales put aside for the time being, Samantha and I head back into the hotel to show Vanessa the video she recorded. Once we do that, things start happening rapidly. Incendiary Ink and their management are shown the video of Zach's confession, and he's summarily fired. They leave any law enforcement involvement to those investigating the incidents with Jax in Denver to avoid any bad press on themselves. However, the Federal agencies going after Jax for the Social Security fraud he committed in Texas and ran away from have dibs on him, so local authorities in Denver will have to wait their turn for his crimes there.

While all of this craziness is happening, the Rolling Stone article hits the internet. We agree to do the press junket later this afternoon to give reporters time to read the article and check sources, etc., before bombarding us with half-baked requests for me to retell everything. Blackmore Records also put out a press release regarding Jax's arrest and Zach's dismissal and assumed pending charges. So the press has a lot to digest before they come at us guns blazing.

We only get a couple of hours to decompress and prepare for the onslaught. There is a lot of communication between us, the label, and different law enforcement agencies, making sure we have the latest status of the various investigations. Apparently, cooperation is the name of the game when it comes to the government.

In a surprise development, we discover the hotel in Denver had cameras in the hallways and captured Jax bursting into my room when he attacked me, so my self-defense argument stands for now. However, that means they also caught Samantha and me making out in the hallway. Nothing was said about it, but it's something to keep in mind going forward when feeling hot and bothered.

When we're done with the press for the day, I'm tempted to go for a run to expel the excess energy I've built up but decide on something else instead. I take my time getting ready and head to Samantha's room to surprise her. When she opens her door, she is, indeed, surprised to see me.

"You ready to go?"

She stares at me, mouth agape. "Huh?"

"Our date." I know she wasn't expecting our first date to be tonight, *but why wait?* I want to get this going as soon as possible. "You ready?"

"We didn't set a... huh?" She's thoroughly confused, and I can't help but enjoy her bewilderment immensely. "What are you doing?"

"I'm picking you up for our date, but I see you aren't ready." She's already in an oversized t-shirt and pajama bottoms, looking fucking incredible. *I wouldn't mind staying in either...* "I'll give you a few minutes. Meet me downstairs when you're ready. Keep it casual. Nothing fancy." I wink at her and walk away, smiling to myself because I know I've just thrown her off her game.

After all the emotion today, I don't want to just hang out in my room by myself or with any of the guys. I want to be with Samantha. Being with her puts me at ease, even though it also revs me up. It's a sweet combination that fights with each other yet compliments simultaneously. It's not anything I've experienced before, and it's addictive.

About ten minutes later, Samantha comes into the lobby, still a little confused and more hesitant. She really wasn't expecting this, and maybe I'm moving too fast.

"If you don't want to do this, just say the word." I don't want to force her to go out with me, for christ's sake. I want her to be a willing participant in this.

"Do I look like I don't want to go?"

"Samantha, your face is like watching TV with subtitles. You couldn't hide an expression to save your life." She blushes at this, and I can't help but reach out and brush her cheek with the back of my fingers, my skin yearning to feel the heat of the blood beneath hers.

"Hey, I did okay earlier with Zach when I was getting information from him." She's so proud of herself for that, and she should be. The recording she got today put a lot of the puzzle pieces together and helped with the investigation.

"That's true. But Zach is also an idiot."

"That is also true." She smiles up at me, her blue eyes large and expressive behind her lenses. "So, where is our big, not fancy date?"

"How do you feel about dive bars?"

"Is there any other kind?" She grins, and her face lights up, no longer anxious, which is a good sign.

"Great. I know the perfect place."

She quirks an eyebrow at me, but I smile back at her and pull out my phone to order a car.

The driver pulls up to The Wanderer, a decent-sized square brick building with folding chairs out front for the smokers. I tip the driver, and we exit into the warm desert night, stopping to take in the exterior of the building in all its dive bar glory.

"Only the best dive bars have no windows." She can't restrain the smile spreading on her lips.

I can't stop myself from putting my arm around her and kissing the top of her head. "Wait till you see the inside." The smell of her shampoo and lilac perfume and the feel of her so close flips a switch inside me, and I pull her into a hug. She hugs me back, and we stand holding each other in the parking lot of this dive bar for several minutes in silence.

The thought that everything I've been running from my entire life is now a non-issue is still hard for my brain to understand. It will take some time for me to get used to the idea that I'm genuinely not in danger anymore. On top of everything is Samantha, who I never saw coming into my life in a million years, yet here she is. *Here she is.*

"Thank you," I whisper into her ear.

"For what? I didn't do anything."

"But you did." I pull back and gaze down at her. "You did so much more than I could ever explain."

She laughs and grabs my hand, heading toward the bar. "Well, we've got all night for you to try."

Once we step into the bar, Samantha starts laughing, her hand placed over her mouth in a weak attempt at suppressing it. "This is perfect. You've been here before?"

"Yeah, we've been through Phoenix a few times." I lead her further in, past a few taxidermied animals hanging on the wall whose gazes seem to follow us wherever we go, past a huge fish tank situated in the middle of the room for some reason, and into the main bar where we face two pool tables and a long bar with a wall of TVs behind it. There's also the sound of karaoke singing coming from a side room somewhere. The regulars are out in full force tonight, but we snag seats at a small high-top table.

I order us some drinks and food. While waiting for our drink order, I lean on the bar and watch Samantha tapping her fingers on the table to the song some poor soul is attempting to sing. She tries to appear encouraging, or maybe it's hopeful, but cringes at a particularly sour note the singer hits, and she catches my eye and bursts out in laughter. Slapping a hand over her mouth to stifle it, I hit yet another step on the way down as I fall for her. *How many damn steps down are there? How can I not fall for this woman? She is the whole package.* Samantha is so open, honest, and unassuming that you'd almost think she was naïve, but she's far from it. Her confidence, boldness, and self-awareness are most attractive about her.

When the drinks arrive, I take them to the table, hand Samantha's to her, and lean in to kiss her. She reciprocates, meeting my lips lightly with hers, holding for a moment before we pull away, our eyes meeting. I'm drowning in the blue pools of her eyes, and I don't care. If I drown, I'll die happy.

She reaches up and taps my temple. "What's going on up there? You look a little lost."

"On the contrary, I think I've been found." I'm feeling bolder now. I'm still finding my way, but I don't want to deliver mixed messages anymore. Not with her. "You finally found me when no one else could."

"I still can't believe it's only been a little over a week. I feel like I've known you much longer than that."

"A lot has happened. That's for sure." If I think about it too much, my head will spin.

"Well, when we live like those guys," she points to the fish tank, "we're bound to get close pretty fast. Especially since I'm basically recording your every move."

"I actually don't mind that so much anymore, oddly enough." I scrunch up my nose at the realization. Now *that's* crazy.

"I'm growing on you, huh?" Her tone turns spicy, and there's a gleam in her eyes.

"You're doing something to me."

"Good things or bad things?" Again, with the sexy voice, this time adding a small bite to her lower lip. *God, she drives me crazy when she does that.*

"You need to be careful little lady, or I'll end up doing something to you, right here in this bar." And man, would I love to just find a dark corner or broom closet and take her completely. I gently uncross her legs and nudge myself in between, keeping it PG-13 rated but letting her know the idea is real.

"Don't threaten me with a good time..." she giggles, and it's the miniature version of her laugh and is even more charming.

Our food arrives, and we spend the evening talking about her and her childhood since the last few days have been all about everyone in the world finding out about mine. I enjoy hearing about her parent's love story and watching her light up as she talks about them. I don't even feel envious because they sound too perfect to be real.

We play a few games of pool, and I discover during the second game that Samantha is a damned pool shark. She plays inept so well during the first game I'm stunned when she runs the table in the second and third. This is especially shocking because she has such a horrible poker face, but she hid it so well. Then again, I was distracted by other parts as she leaned over the pool table. I quit after an utter humiliation in the third where I didn't even get to take a shot; she ran it and won from the break. It was a masterclass.

"What? It was helpful during college. And a great way to get free drinks," she shrugs.

"I'm sure your mere existence garnered you all the free drinks you wanted." I no doubt would have paid her tab if given a chance.

"I actually didn't take that bet very often. It always seemed to have strings attached to it I didn't want."

"You're letting me buy your drinks tonight."

"Yeah, but you're a big rock star who can afford it." Her devious grin is back, and it's difficult to not return the smile, despite the label.

And it turns out, I *don't* buy her drinks after all. When I go to the restroom before we leave, I come back to find our tab already paid for by Samantha.

"Well, damn. I've never had a woman pay for the entire date before." I joke. "I feel like I need to put out or something."

"Now you know how it feels then," she chuckles.

"Seriously though, thank you. That was very kind of you. Especially after everything I've put you through." And I mean it. Tonight was supposed to be about me making up for being an ass, but she hijacked my gesture.

"You can get the bill next time. But next time, I want something fancy." She winks as we head to the parking lot to wait for our ride.

"Fancy? Like button-down fancy? Or suit and tie fancy?" *God, please don't say tuxedo fancy.*

She arches an eyebrow, enjoying my discomfort at the thought of dressing up. "Hmm. How much do

I want to torture you...?" After thinking a minute while I squirm inwardly, she extends my torture. "I don't know yet. Let me think on it, and I'll get back to you."

"You're killing me, smalls."

"Sorry, but we're in LA next, and I don't know anything about it or what's good, so I need to do some research first before I can answer."

Seeing as it's my current hometown, an idea comes to me. "Well, I happen to live in LA... Do you trust me?"

"Of course not," she laughs, eyeing me warily. "What are you plotting?"

"It's a surprise."

"Oooh, I hate surprises!" She bounces on the balls of her feet and pretends to beat on my chest in frustration. She's too damned cute.

"Too bad, Vapor Girl. You'll just have to wait and see what I have planned." I pull her to me, wrapping my arms around her, forcing her to be still, but she's still a livewire of energy.

"Vapor Girl, huh? I forgot about that. Is that your plan? To give me the vapors?" She giggles again, probably a little tipsy at this point.

"It wouldn't be a surprise if I told you, now would it?" I kiss her forehead, and she leans into me, wrapping her arms around me tightly. *Yup. She's tipsy*.

When we get back to the hotel, I walk her to her

room. She's a little unsteady on her feet, but not too bad. She's keeping it together for the most part, except for the giggling.

"This is me." We stop in front of her room, and she pulls out her key card.

Before she can unlock her door, I turn her to me and pull her into a deep kiss. The taste of tequila on her tongue as we melt together is intoxicating. I cup her face with my hands and gently release the kiss as I pull away. It'll kill me, but I need to end this here. I want to do things right this time.

"Don't you want to come in?" Her voice is hoarse with desire, and my god, I can't believe I'm going to say no.

"I don't put out on the first date, sorry." My grin reflects in her own, and I'm glad she laughs.

"Well, you'd better put out next time, then."

"So demanding..." I place a hand behind her head and lean down for one more kiss.

I wait for her to unlock her door and step inside before heading down the hall to my room. She leans out of her doorway, watching me go, openly ogling me, and I'm loving the hell out of it because it's Samantha, and it's sexy as fuck.

Cold shower, here I come.

forty-two

THE BEST MISTAKE I EVER MADE
SAMANTHA

We have a week to spend in LA since the band is playing two shows at the Hollywood Bowl, and almost as soon as we arrive, Sarah wants to take me shopping for my next date with Matt. Seeing how I drunkenly demanded a fancy fairy tale date, I now need to *buy* something fancy to wear on said date. I don't know what I was thinking. Well, I guess I *wasn't* thinking, honestly.

The vintage clothing shops along Le Brea Avenue are perfect, and I could spend all day in each of them. There is so much to look at. Vintage, however, does not always mean affordable. One of the stores didn't even carry anything under $100, and I quickly turn Sarah around to the exit to head to the next one.

"What are you doing?" she laughs as I push her along.

"Did you see the price tags in that one? I'd like to not have to sell any of my internal organs to buy a dress for this date." I'm not cheap, but I'm sure a dress would be way out of my price range if the costume jewelry is expensive.

"Don't worry about the cost. I have that covered." Her smile is now conspiratorial.

"What do you mean? I don't need you to buy my dress." *Why on earth would she want to pay for this?*

"Oh, I'm not, don't worry." She reaches into the back pocket of her jeans and pulls out a credit card to show me. It's Ryan's.

"What the hell?" I stop on the sidewalk, confused. "Why would Ryan pay for my dress? That's crazy."

"Not just him. Jude is pitching in too."

"Why?" I still don't understand.

"And not only the dress, but shoes and accessories." She grabs my hand, dragging me forward to the next store. "And a massage, facial, hair, and makeup in..." she glances at her watch, "two hours, so we need to get moving."

"You're kidding, right? Why would they do this?"

"Because they realize they are Matt's family now and want him to be happy. And Matt is happy when he's with you."

Something about those words, "*Matt is happy*

when he's with you," undoes me inside. For other people to notice the change in him, and attribute it to me somehow, is so heartwarming and special. I don't know what to say or how to respond to this fantastic gesture.

"Does Matt know about all this?" I'll be more comfortable with the expense if he approves of it or at least knows.

"I don't think so." She opens the door to the next store for me, and as soon as I walk in, I see it. *The dress.* Hanging on the end of a rack facing the entrance. Sarah spots it too, and we both gasp at its perfection. All thoughts about who is paying for what goes out the window. *I have to have it.*

"That's it. That's the one." I'm afraid to move too close to it, or it will magically vanish or something.

She pulls the hanger off the rack and, looking at the tag, announces, "It's your size...."

I have never, ever, fallen in love with a piece of clothing, but this dress is different. I could give two shits about what I wear, but tonight is important to me, and that black lace fabric on that hanger is too perfect.

I tentatively take the dress and walk over to a floor-length mirror against the wall, holding it up to my chin and against me, examining it from different angles. It's a halter swing dress in black lace over satin that ties around the neck with an open back. I think it will land about mid-thigh, but I will need to try it on first.

"Will this be appropriate for wherever we're going tonight?" Everyone's been sworn to secrecy and won't give me a single hint as to where Matt is taking me tonight, and it's driving me mad. I do not like surprises.

She studies the dress in the mirror for a minute, then nods. "Yeah. I think it'll be fine."

"Be fine? I don't want to just '*be fine.*'" I'm getting exasperated now with all the secrecy. I need to know what to prepare for. "Can't you tell me where we're going already? You guys are being nuts."

"Nope." She smiles and walks away. "Go try it on, and next we need to find shoes, oh, and maybe some big hoop earrings?"

I sigh, coming to terms with the fact that I will not know where we are going tonight until I'm literally wherever we go. I cannot change this, so I need to let it be. But the control freak within me is not a happy camper...

After a day of shopping, pampering, and primping, I'm feeling very much like a fairy tale princess ready to meet her prince. The hairdresser and makeup artists didn't make me look like someone else, just a more put-together and less bruised version of myself. I snap a quick selfie to send to my mom, and she responds with her usual snark.

> MOMMY DEAREST: Who is this and what have you done with my daughter?

> MOMMY DEAREST: Just kidding. You're always beautiful. Have fun tonight!

Not long after, I receive a text from Matt.

> MATT: Hey. Sorry. Running super late, and car won't start. Been sitting too long. Can you come to my place and we'll leave from here?

> ME: Sure no problem. Address?

He sends me the address, and after double-checking my makeup, I head to the hotel lobby to order a car to take me to Matt and Jude's place. The excitement building within me for this date has my hands shaking with nervous energy. I've never been this riled up over a date before, and I kind of like it. The anticipation of seeing Matt in a suit gets me twisted up inside. I can't wait to lay eyes on him all dressed up.

They aren't kidding about LA traffic being horrible. I should have brought a snack; it takes 45 minutes to get to his place. The Spanish-style duplex is modest, but I can see a balcony on the second floor. Bright pink bougainvillea climbs the stucco walls and arch over the driveway making an impressive entrance. I find the stairway to the second floor and climb up to the entryway.

Before I can knock, the door swings open, and Matt appears, still shrugging into his suit jacket, tie crooked, and a bit out of breath, as though he ran to answer the door. But even in this scattered state, he is simply gorgeous. Matt in a suit and tie is more than I could ever imagine. The suit is black and fitted, and his crisp white shirt with a deep burgundy tie sets off his green eyes in the most intriguing way. He takes my breath away. Actually, we're both speechless as we take everything of each other in from head to toe. We must like what we see because when our eyes meet, the smiles on our faces could light up all of LA tonight.

"Can I come in?" I ask, not being snarky but unsure of the plan now. I don't know if Jude is home too and wants us gone right away or what's happening.

"Oh shit, yes. Please come in." He steps back to let me pass, and the scent of his cologne that could buckle my knees if I let it mixes with the delicious aroma of food. *What the...?* "Can I take your wrap?

I shrug the black lace off my shoulders and hand

it to him, taking in the apartment. It's a lot nicer than I thought it would be for some reason. I guess I thought two guys living together wouldn't be very décor savvy. I was very wrong. The space is warm and inviting.

"Wow." He says, taking in my dress or overall appearance; I can't tell which. "You are magnificent." His face shifts into that of an animal stalking its prey, and I squirm in the best way under his gaze. I also note that he said *'are magnificent,'* not *'look magnificent.'* And I appreciate the subtle difference.

"Thank you. You're not so bad yourself. Are you cooking, Matt Sturridge?" I turn to him, and he nods his head with a switch from predator to a sheepish grin.

"I am indeed." He takes my hand and leads me to the open kitchen, where the mouthwatering smells of food grow more potent, making my stomach growl. *Holy shit, if he can cook, he's the one.* "A little birdie told me that Chicken Marsala was a favorite dish of yours, and it happens to be one of my specialties."

"A little birdie, huh? Was that chick's name Sarah, by chance?" *Of course it was.*

"Maybe." He smacks his forehead, "Shit. I forgot. Hang on." He rushes to the refrigerator, pulls out a bouquet of flowers wrapped in craft paper, and hands it to me. "I forgot to give you these. Part of the whole fairy tale thing."

I take them and pull back the wrapping to find dark purple lilacs and light pink roses mixed with baby's breath. The fragrance instantly transfers me back home to my parents' house and their lilac and rose bushes. My eyes are misty as I hug them to me. "My favorite."

"Are they? Good. I didn't ask about those. I guessed from your perfume." He looks so proud of himself, I want to pinch his cheeks.

"They're perfect." I bounce on tip-toe to kiss his cheek, he's so damned tall, and he blushes the cutest fucking shade of pink I've ever seen on a guy. It's hard not to grab that tie and pull him to the bedroom, but I don't know which one is his, which could be awkward if I guessed wrong. "Is Jude here? Or did he go out?"

"No, he went up to Ojai for the night. So we have the place to ourselves." His sly smile shines with a hopeful glean as he wiggles his eyebrows at me.

"Oh?" Is all I can say as a blush spreads over *my* face as I think of how we can fill time this evening.

He steps up to me and puts his arms around me. I can sense his heat at this close proximity, and when his hands touch my bare back, we both melt into each other, our mouths crashing together. Our tongues seek the other to connect languidly and deeply before coming up for air.

"Jesus, Samantha. I don't know how I'm going to make it through dinner," he groans into my ear, his

340

teeth nipping at my earlobe. A ripple of desire flows through me, and as his lips travel down my neck, I can't stop a shudder from releasing at his touch.

"Then let's hurry up and eat." I recapture his mouth, giving him a kiss so full of promise that it's difficult to break away. But somehow, we do.

We eat dinner on the balcony while watching the amazing sunset, and the food is delicious. I am pleasantly surprised at how good of a cook he is. He shows me so many new and interesting sides of himself every other day that I don't think I could ever be bored with him.

Our discussion during dinner ranges from religion and philosophy to bad reality television. We agree on a lot, but not everything, making for lively conversation. I learn of his love of animals and regret at not being able to keep a pet due to all the traveling he has to do for the band. Take another row of bricks out of the wall between Matt and myself. This man is quickly becoming irresistible.

After clearing the dishes, we carry our wine to the sitting area, but he takes my glass from me and sets it on the coffee table before I can sit down. He holds his hand out to me in invitation. I raise a skeptical eyebrow, not sure what it means.

"May I have this dance?"

"You dance?" I swear I will jump him if he keeps this up.

"Well... I hug in a circle." *Oh my god. This man.*

"I would be honored to hug in a circle with you." And our dance is just as sweet as I pictured it would be when he said it. His arms around my waist and mine around his neck. His head rests on mine as I lean against his firm chest, listening to his racing heartbeat that eventually slows and synchronizes with mine the longer we dance.

Up until now, I hadn't paid attention to the music playing on the stereo system, but it's beautiful Spanish guitar songs that fit the mood remarkably well. Apart from when he was tending to my injuries after our accident, I haven't seen a lot of the gentle side of Matt. I have to admit that I like it a lot, maybe even more than his physical and aggressive side, like when he plays his drums. He's typically full of kinetic energy that radiates off of him. This softer, more relaxed Matt is endearing.

Not stopping our circle, he presses his lips to my forehead, cheek, chin, tracing a line down my throat and lazily across my collarbone to my shoulder. Every inch of his journey pulses from where his lips touch my skin down to my core, causing me to lean my hips into him, and he's deliciously hard against me.

I start to move his suit jacket off his shoulders,

but he takes over, shrugging it off, so I move to untie his tie. I'm desperate to touch his bare skin. Our lips are crushing against each other again, and my skin feels like it's on fire, and only he can cool me. Tie thrown to the floor somewhere, I start unbuttoning his shirt, and his arms are around me again, but he's unbuttoning his cuffs, as eager as I am to get it off of him.

When the buttons are undone, I spread my fingers across his glorious chest, dragging them down along his abs, every taut muscle beneath my hands tense with want or need or both. I start to unbuckle his belt when his hands stop me, his lips leaving mine longing for his as he leans back to gaze down at me. *No...don't stop.*

"Are you sure you want to do this, Samantha?" His breath is ragged, just as mine is.

I meet his eyes and find the passion and yearning in them. Something in his stare makes me feel so wanted, I can't put a word to it. It makes me feel more beautiful than I ever felt before. No man's ever done that to me.

"I am."

He doesn't need to hear anything else and leans down to effortlessly scoop me up and carry me to his bedroom. He sits me gently on the bed, kneeling before me. Carefully, he removes my shoes and lifts my foot, bringing it to his lips to kiss a line from my inner ankle leisurely up to my knee, his eyes fixed on mine, watching me react. I struggle to maintain eye contact, but it's too hot to turn away from him or close my eyes. Watching his mouth move and drag along my skin so sensually is mesmerizing, and I couldn't look away if I wanted to.

As his kisses begin to run up my inner thigh, his hands start to move under the hem of my skirt, his touch barely skimming my skin, sending shivers through me. His fingers deftly find the edge of my panties, and he shimmies the skimpy lace fabric down and off. My breath catches when his hand returns up my skirt, his thumb rubbing exquisite circles around my clit, sending swells of shockwaves throughout my body.

Looping his arms under my legs, he slides me forward to the edge of the bed, forcing me to fall back onto the pillow-soft comforter. I keep my fingers curled in his silky hair as his mouth takes over the attention on my sex, his tongue expertly licking and pressing against me, swirling and sweeping me closer to the edge of my orgasm. His mouth possesses me, lingering and teasing, then greedy and urgent, and when I peak, my back arches off the bed, my entire body trembling with the rolling waves of fiery bliss. My hands pull at his hair as he continues to stroke me, extending my orgasm beyond imagination until I'm weightless.

He releases me and pulls himself up to tent over me on the bed. I drape my hands around his neck and draw him down into a scorching kiss, our breath hot and unsteady. He lowers his weight onto me as his fingers run through my hair. His erection bears down on me, and I wrap my legs around his waist and, being careful of my cast, roll him over to straddle him.

"My turn," I say, my voice full of pleasure and desire as I tug his shirt back over his shoulders, exposing his solid and perfect chest.

forty-three

SOMEBODY

MATT

When Samantha licks her lips and says, "*My turn,*" I can hardly contain myself. I have never wanted anyone as much as I want her at this moment. It takes everything in me to let her have her way instead of taking control as I'm used to. I think I'm going to enjoy her asserting power, though.

She struggles a little with my belt buckle due to her cast, and I help as much as she'll let me. My shirt is off, my pants are off, and my boxers aren't far behind, I'm sure, yet she's still in her dress. *This doesn't seem fair.* As she leans over to kiss me, I reach around and untie the bow fastening the dress around her neck, the satin strips glide apart effortlessly under my fingers, and the front falls forward, making it easy to slip the entire thing over her head.

She traces wet kisses across my chest and down

my torso, and the room's cool air gives my skin goosebumps in her wake. When her lips reach my erection, her tongue brushes the tip delicately as her warm mouth takes me in.

"*Fuuuuuck*, Samantha," I groan, air skidding in through my clenched teeth as I fight for control. I'm in big trouble if I'm this close after that slight touch.

This only encourages her to lick feather-light strokes along my length before ravaging me again, this time taking me in her mouth as far as she can. It's too good. It's too fucking good. I try to lift her head to allow me to catch my breath, but she's persistent, and all I can do is flex and tremble beneath her, preparing for the oncoming spike of pleasure.

She stops right before the wave crests, glancing up at me with a wicked grin, running her tongue along her lips. I throw my head back and let the breath out I've been holding for forever as I fight to withhold my orgasm.

"Where are your condoms? Here?" She's reaching over to open the drawer of the nightstand. I don't have any brains to answer her at the moment, but she finds the box without my response anyway and pulls out a foil packet. The sight of her sheathing me with a condom is almost enough to shove me over the edge. But the real test is when she crawls up my body and lowers herself onto me, taking me inside her completely. We're a perfect fit, hitting all the right spots for both of us. As she starts rocking at a slow pace, her rotating hips start the intense building of unmistakable pressure.

I reach up and knead her smooth breasts, rolling her nipples between my fingers until she's practically purring. She speeds up her rhythm, surging against the intense waves until they crash into both of us. We cling to each other as we erupt together, ecstasy resounding in our racing pulses. Our breaths are ragged and unsteady as she nuzzles her head into my neck, still enveloping me as her spasms continue to twitch around me.

I wipe the hair clinging to her skin away from her face, which is flush from exertion, and I hope as much pleasure as I felt.

"You are... incredible." I can't think of adjectives strong enough to express how amazing she is. The heavenly fire burning through me is all-encompassing and is so much more than what just happened. I need to find a way to convey this. "And not only the mind-blowing sex we just had either. I mean everything about you."

She pushes up and hovers over me, shoving her hair behind an ear so she can study me, trying to gauge if I'm being honest. She raises an eyebrow, "You know how in sports, you're the most vulnerable after you score? The same is true of sex."

"What?" I can't help but laugh. That came out of

freaking nowhere. "I'm not following the analogy. Explain."

She reluctantly eases off of me and falls to my side. "Go do your manly after sex thing and come back. I'll explain."

I do as she commands, and when I return, she's already wearing my shirt from earlier with the sleeves rolled up, leaning against the headboard with her wineglass in hand. She is quick because I was not gone *that* long.

I throw on a pair of boxers, fully aware that she's not taken her eyes off me since I walked back into the room but loving every second. I like feeling wanted by her.

"Okay. Manly after sex job complete. Explain yourself, woman." I slide in next to her against the headboard and sip from her wine before kissing her thoroughly.

When we finally break away from each other, she continues as if never interrupted, "I was saying, there is this thing in sports that when you score, you get this false sense of security, and something happens in your brain where you almost think you're invincible, but that is when you're at your weakest, and the other team is most likely to score against you. This is mostly true in sports like hockey or soccer, where scoring chances are fewer."

"Okay. And sex is like that, how?" I'm still not understanding the connection.

She places her wineglass on the nightstand and curls into my chest as I put an arm around her. "When people have sex, the same endorphins are released, and you have that same false sense of security...."

"Whoa. Hold up. Wrong. Do not pass Go. Do not collect $200." I lean back and lift her chin so she can read the truth of my words on my face. "There is nothing false about anything that happened in this house tonight. Absolutely nothing. Is that how you feel? That this was fake somehow?"

She stares at me long and hard, reading me closely as she always does with those crystal blue eyes. I can only hope she sees my sincerity. This was the furthest thing from false.

"No. I guess I don't feel that way. It was a blip of insecurity." She reaches up and rubs my bottom lip with her thumb. Her touch is exhilarating. "I know I come across all bold and confident, but I'm a ball of uncertainty deep down."

I pull her closer to me, wrapping both arms around her tightly. "Well, you can be certain that this is real. I promise you that."

"Wow. Reality and promises in one night. I'm a lucky girl," she giggles.

"Nowhere near as lucky as I am."

The week in LA flies by, with Samantha and I spending every free moment together. The same is true of the rest of the summer tour. The three months leading up to the last show on Labor Day in upstate New York fly by just as fast, if not faster. We're at an amphitheater on a lake where the sunset is magnificent as we sit by the bus filming our final group documentary interview. Jude is waxing philosophical about all of our success.

"I mean, seriously. Not just this summer, but this whole year has been insane. Ryan and Sarah got together while producing the album. That was a wild ride. And then Matt's whole *thing* at the beginning of the summer, and he lands a girlfriend too." He winks at me before I can say anything, shutting me up. "And me, well, let's say I do not want for girlfriends, if you know what I mean. That remains a constant that will never change."

"Do you think Indigo King has made it?" Samantha asks. "By whatever your definition is?"

"No." Ryan shakes his head, and Jude and I do the same. "There's always more. Always something else to achieve. Another set of ears to win over to our side of the stage."

"Will you ever make it then?"

"I mean, there are the Rolling Stones, the Beatles, hell, even Incendiary Ink levels of making it. It would be nice," I say, looking at the guys for affirmation. "But that's the goal. Whether we make it or not is yet to be seen. Do we want it? Absolutely. Will we bust our asses to get there? Again, absolutely. But, we're just getting started." I flash her a knowing smile, sure that she understands that I'm also talking about us.

We wrap the interview a few questions later, and our small group celebrates to mark the end of the tour, which Samantha also films. Our interview's somber and serious tone carries over into the celebration, not putting a damper on anything but marking the significance of what we've accomplished this past year.

We still have a small headlining European leg ahead of us in a month. At least we do get some time off in between. I've been trying to convince Samantha to come with us to Europe, but she's concerned that if she doesn't finish editing the documentary before we leave, she'll never finish if she goes. So, that decision is still up in the air and probably means I won't see much of her in the next month outside of one particular event.

She and Sarah's friend Jenny is getting married in two weeks, and Ryan and I will be going along with our respective dates. I guess the 'wedding of the century' that had been planned for years had to be moved because of Sarah's tour schedule or something, which was very upsetting to the bride. I'm not sure of all the details, but I'm glad I only need to show up and hug Samantha in a circle for a bit. I don't think I've ever been to a wedding, come to think of it. *Nope. Not a one.* Marriage was never on my mind, let alone within my circle of friends, but I've been thinking about it a lot lately, and apparently, so has Ryan. He was planning to propose to Sarah at Jenny's wedding, but Samantha told him that it would be rude to steal the spotlight from the bride and groom, which is understandable, and would be a low-key dick move. His plan is to propose in London after getting approval from her brother Benji, which is noble of him.

I, on the other hand, don't know what the fuck I'm doing. About one month into my relationship with Samantha, I knew I wanted to spend my life with her, but she's so damned independent. I don't know if she wants to be tied down like that, though I don't think of it that way. She might. With her parent's relationship so perfect, it might be daunting for her to try to meet or beat that. It is a concern for me.

I met her parents through video chats they've had and have to admit their love is kind of intimidating; it's so perfect. But, it also gives me hope that love like that does exist in the world. The love I never thought would come my way or be in my life. My entire childhood was loveless, and I never thought I was worthy of it. But she lets me know every day how worthy I truly am. And I do my best to make her feel exactly the same way.

To allow myself to be loved has been the single most important thing I've ever done. Or probably will ever do. I still have moments of fear, doubt, and self-hatred for my past, but I'm learning to deal with it and move past it. And all because of Samantha.

epilogue

HEAVY METAL DRUMMER

SAMANTHA

I finish the documentary in time to deliver it to Blackmore Records a week after Jenny's wedding, which means I can travel with Matt to Europe as I hoped I would be able to.

We had such a great time on the wedding weekend. He met my parents in person, and they love him almost as much as I do. My mother tried her hardest to embarrass me in front of him with questions about our future plans, etc., but he took it all in stride and surprised me with some of his answers. I knew I had fallen ass over tea kettle for him a while ago, but to hear he has done the same and tell my parents about it was entirely something else.

At different points of our visit, each parent pulled me aside and told me, "he's the one." Now that's a sign if I ever needed one. I have an idea of what to do about it, but I still need to feel things out before acting.

And when Ryan proposes to Sarah in London, my idea goes right out the window. I am so happy for her and Ryan, though, don't get me wrong. I don't want to steal their thunder by proposing to Matt like I wanted to. And the proposal was so romantic. Just beforehand, Ryan told me what he was going to do and asked if I would record it, and of course, I agreed.

That night, during their show at a fabulous venue called The Wheelhouse, which is actually a round building, Ryan and Sarah were going to sing their single *'Almost,'* but instead of playing that song, he sang another one that included his proposal to her. She, of course, said yes, and the crowd went bonkers. It was so beautiful. I had a hard time filming since I was crying so hard. I'm glad I was there not only to witness it along with a thousand other people but to capture it for posterity for them.

So, my idea of proposing to Matt will have to wait until we're back home. We haven't really talked about that yet; what we'll do after the European shows are done. He'll go back to LA, and I'll go back to Ohio. Maybe I'll look into apartments in LA and for jobs. Where else for a music history/filmmaker to live but LA, right? It would make sense. Not like Matt would ever ask me to move in with him, *would he?* He's always so concerned about giving me my 'space' and 'independence' when all I want to do is spend time with him. I appreciate the sentiment, and I'm not going against any of my independent ideals by wanting to spend time with him. I think loving someone that much is a good thing.

The final shows on the tour are in Paris, and wow, this city during the autumn is beyond gorgeous. With the trees changing colors, and all the Parisians in their best autumn coats and scarves, it's like we're in a movie. After taking French in high school, and a little in college, I can navigate the city and restaurants pretty well for all of us. I have always wanted to visit Paris, and Matt indulges the tourist in me by accompanying me to all the usual spots; the Louvre Museum, Notre Dame, the Moulin Rouge, and the Eiffel Tower. We take a bus tour to the different locations, and I am beside myself with joy by the end of the day.

We decide to walk back along the Seine to our hotel when nighttime hits. There is a sidewalk along the river that is well lit, and now and then, we'll pass another couple with the same idea of an evening stroll. For October, the night is warm, and we come upon a row of large alcoves along the river, each well-lit by street lamps and full of dancers. But the dancers are dancing to the different music playing in each nook. One plays salsa music, another a polka, and another swing music. The final one has 1950s doo-wop music playing, and I can't help but stop and stare at its splendor.

We stand there for a minute, watching the different couples move to their own music, which isn't overlapping. Each alcove contains its own music somehow. I'm in awe of the engineering, let alone the wonder of it. Matt, too, seems to be mesmerized by it but is watching me watch the dancers, not the dancers himself, which is strange. And making me self-conscious, even though he does this a lot.

"Come with me," he smiles, pulling me by the hand into one of the alcoves. I do not know what he is doing because he cannot dance to save his life, but I catch him nodding at someone. I discover Ryan and Sarah with their guitars and someone else, Jude, turning off the music player. *What the hell?* "Dance with me." His voice is husky and low in my ear, and he pulls me into his arms, 'hugging me in a circle' as he calls it, as Ryan and Sarah sing the song *'So Close'* that they've changed some of the lyrics to. The other dancers, in on this weird hijacking, start dancing in pairs as well.

My heart swells as we turn slowly; the smell of his cologne mixing with the water of the Seine makes me lightheaded. The song's words, which mean a lot to both of us, really strike home and only increase my love for this man. I don't know if I can wait until we're home for me to tell him that. I pull him into a kiss as the song ends, unable to stop a few tears of joy from escaping. "I love you. That was perfect," I whisper against his mouth. He's smiling a mile wide.

"I'm not done," he says as he lets go of me and steps back, then gets on one knee, and Jude runs over and hands him a small velvet box. *Oh my god. Oh my god. Oh my god.*

"You totally are stealing my move, Matt Sturridge." I'm trying to make light, or I will be balling my eyes out.

"Sorry, but I call dibs on the proposing, seeing as I'm the one on my knee in the middle of Paris with a ring?" He grins, and his eyes dance. I'm sure he can tell I'm freaking out; it's written all over my face.

"Okay, okay, you win. Go ahead." *What the fuck is that? "go ahead?" Really?* I hope nobody is recording this. I glance around nervously, and *everyone* is holding up phones recording this. *Fuck.*

"Samantha Fisher," he starts, and his voice shakes slightly. *God, I love this man.* "Since the day I met you, I knew that you would change my life. I didn't know how or why, just that meeting you was the biggest thing to ever happen to me. I fought it. I fought you. I fought my demons and my past. And the whole time, you were right there with me. Whether it was to put me in my place, which was *often* warranted." The crowd laughs at that. "Or to help put me back together after tearing myself apart, you were there. I want you to be there from now on, and I want to be there for you. Forever. I love you with every fiber of my being, Samantha. Will you marry me?"

His eyes are getting misty, making me cry even harder, causing my glasses to steam up a little. This is crazy. Beyond crazy. We have been through so much together, but we've come out the other side of it stronger.

"You'd better say yes!" My mother's voice yells. *My mother's voice. What the hell?* I turn toward the sound and find my mother and father holding up their phones, recording this along with everyone else. *They knew about this? When did they get here?*

I look back at Matt; so much expectation and hope in his eyes and so much love for me. I can't deny it. Hell, I was going to ask him. He just beat me to it. "Yes. Yes, I will marry you, Matt Sturridge."

He jumps up and wraps me in his arms, picking me up and twirling me around. The smile on his face is so huge it could light up this City of Lights. The kiss he lands on me could make my toes curl if they weren't solidly in my boots. *Holy hell.* Then he slides the ring on my finger, and I gasp. "Mom! This is your engagement ring! Are you sure?"

My parents join the others encircling us with congratulations. The music restarts in all the alcoves now that the show is over, and the dancers have resumed their proverbial cutting of rugs.

"I'm sure," my mother says, pulling me into a vice-like hug while my father shakes Matt's hand. "Didn't I tell you he was the one? Such a gentleman. He asked your father and me both for permission to ask you back when you were in town for Jenny's wedding. And he arranged for us to come out to be here for this. It was fun planning this surprise for you. You're usually so tuned into everyone around you, I didn't think we'd pull it off."

"Yeah, well, you sure did. I didn't see that coming at all. Well done." I still can't believe it happened. I'm engaged. To Matt Sturridge. In Paris. *Is this my life?*

I glance over at Matt, still talking to my father, and take him in. This man who started off by scaring me in a dark parking lot will now be my husband and the father of my very far in the future children. And he's going to be excellent at all of it. Because he doesn't quit. He doesn't give up on the things that are important to him. He never gave up on me. We each came *so close* to throwing this all away. Now, we're so close to each other, we'll never let the other quit. Not when it can be this good.

-THE END-

EPILOGUE

. . .

afterword

Sibling abuse is a real issue, with real psychological and physical consequences. It is even more common than parent-child abuse. According to the New York Times, "Nationwide, sibling violence is by far the most common form of family violence, occurring four to five times as frequently as spousal or parental child abuse." If you or someone you love are having difficulty dealing with an abusive situation, know that you are not alone, and there are resources available that can help you.

National Child Abuse Hotline at 1-800-422-4453

National Domestic Violence Hotline 1-800-799-SAFE (7233)

https://hope4siblings.com/

so close playlist

Spotify:
https://open.spotify.com/playlist/32voGtOxSX7ybe-KjfLkEfJ

1. CVRCHES, *Get Out*
2. Jimmy Eat World, *Bleed American*
3. *Pixies, Where Is My Mind?*
4. Chevelle, *The Red*
5. *Wilco, How To Fight Loneliness*
6. OneRepublic, *Run*
7. Foo Fighters, *In The Clear*
8. You Me at Six, *Room to Breathe*
9. *The National, Mistaken For Strangers*
10. *Queens of the Stone Age, The Lost Art Of Keeping A Secret*
11. Tristan Prettyman, *Who We Are*
12. Bruno Major, *Easily*

13. mehro, *perfume*
14. The Velvet Underground, Nico, *I'll Be Your Mirror*
15. Jann Arden, *Insensitive*
16. *Linkin Park, One Step Closer*
17. Alana Davis, *32 Flavors*
18. Apocalyptica, Brent Smith, *Not Strong Enough*
19. *Joseph Vincent, Someone You Loved*
20. *Morrisey, The More You Ignore Me, The Closer I Get*
21. Foo Fighters, *My Hero*
22. Fleetwood Mac, *Peacekeeper*
23. Suzanne Vega, *Night Vision*
24. *Pearl Jam, Rearviewmirror*
25. Grant Lee Buffalo, *Honey Don't Think*
26. Three Days Grace, *Me Against You*
27. *The Fray, Look After You*
28. *Red, Damage*
29. Kygo, Ella Henderson, *Here For You*
30. *Arcade Fire, My Body Is A Cage*
31. *Sia, Breathe Me*
32. Rob Thomas, *Pieces*
33. HELLYEAH, *Hush*
34. Better Than Ezra, *Breathless*
35. *Sick Puppies, You're Going Down*
36. *Darren Korb, Out of Tartarus*
37. Civil Twilight, *River Child*
38. Sick Puppies, *Killing Time*

39. Andrew McMahon In the Wilderness, *So Close*
40. Boyce Avenue, Jennel Garcia, *Demons*
41. Nothing But Thieves, *Impossible*
42. *Joanna Wang, The Best Mistake I've Ever Made*
43. Depeche Mode, *Somebody*
44. *Epilogue. Wilco, Heavy Metal Drummer*

also by amy booker

Near Miss Series

Almost

So Close

Barely

Near Miss Rock Star Collection

Drive Me Wild Series

Ms. Fortune

Ms. Chief

Ms. Lead

Ms. Take

The Mischief Motors Collection

Upcoming Rhapsody Series (2023)

Coda

Reprise

Overture

Waltz

Sustain

All books are stand-alone, but set in the same

universe, so you can pick them up wherever and whenever!

Sign up for my VIP mailing list here! You'll be the first to learn about new releases, sales, available preorders, and freebies. Note: Be sure to add admin@amybookerauthor.com to your contacts before signing up to ensure the emails go straight into your inbox.

Books are available in audiobook and paperback. Please go to my website for links or to buy direct!

contact amy

My website: http://www.amybookerauthor.com

Facebook: www.facebook.com/amybookerauthor
Instagram: www.instagram.com/
amy_booker_author/
TikTok: www.TikTok.com/@amybookerauthor
Email: amybookerauthor@gmail.com

Add my books to your Goodreads

Join my ARC/ALC teams

Join my Facebook Group